PRAISE FOR TIM POWERS:

"Powers orchestrates reality and fantasy so nothing is not allowed a moment's doubt."
  The New Yorker

"One of the field's truly distinct voices."
  Locus

"Powers writes action and adventure that Indiana Jones could only dream of. And, just when it threatens to get out of hand, there's a dash of humor and irony that keeps you reading for the joy of it."
  The Washington Post

"Tim Powers is a brilliant writer."
  William Gibson, author of *Neuromancer* and *Pattern Recognition*

"Philip K. Dick felt that one day Tim Powers would be one of our greatest fantasy writers. Phil was right."
  Roger Zelazny, author of *Nine Princes in Amber* and *Lord of Light*

"Powers has already proved that he is a master of what he terms 'doing card tricks in the dark,' referring to the incredible amount of historical, biographical, and practical research that goes into his works."
  Harvard Review

"Powers plots like a demon."
  The Village Voice Literary Supplement

"Whether writing about zombie pirates of the Caribbean (*On Stranger Tides*), female vampires preying on Romantic poets (*The Stress of Her Regard*), or the escapades of a time traveler in 19th-century England (*The Anubis Gates*), Powers always goes the distance, never taking easy shortcuts that tempt authors with lesser imaginations."
  San Francisco Chronicle

STRANGE ITINERARIES

Strange Itineraries

Tim Powers

CONTRA COSTA COUNTY LIBRARY

TACHYON PUBLICATIONS

SAN FRANCISCO

Tachyon Publications
1459 18th Street #139
San Francisco, CA 94107
(415) 285-5615
www.tachyonpublications.com

Series Editor: Jacob Weisman

ISBN: 1-892391-23-6

Printed in the United States of America
by Edwards Brothers, Inc.

First Edition: 2005

9 8 7 6 5 4 3 2

CONTENTS

In Which Corner of the Compass is Ago?

Paul Di Filippo

Tim Powers is haunted.

Tim Powers is haunting.

These two statements are not mutually exclusive, even though they conjure up the paradoxical image of a ghost pursued by other ghosts.

And why shouldn't bogeymen have spooks that frighten *them?* If the study of ecology has taught us anything, it's that every species has its predators. The chain of bigger bugs biting littler bugs goes on ad infinitum. It seems only right and fair and just that the uneasy spirits that haunt mankind should in turn be continually looking over their spectral shoulders for higher- or lower-level ghouls. In fact, if I'm not taking excessive pride in my own ingenuity, I would call this conceit a very Powers-like notion.

But wait – perhaps I am in fact merely recalling such a preexisting trope from one of Powers's many fine novels. After enjoying his writing for over twenty-five years now, ever since *The Drawing of the Dark* in 1979, I have tended to regard the world from time to time through a Powers-ish lens. Could my mind and his have become astrally conflated somehow, overlapping at curious junctions, as in one of Powers's own eerie fabulist tales?

You'll pardon my temporary mental confusion and the above digression, I hope. It's just that a concentrated dose of Powers – as I've just experienced while enjoying this seminal collection of his rare short stories, and as you are about to experience – has a way of un-hinging the consensus reality.

Back to our theme of haunting and being haunted.

For Powers, who is surely the closest living successor to the mas-terful ghost-monger, M. R. James, the world is populated by spec-tral remnants of emotion. Ambition, frustration, lust, nostalgia, shame, regret, love – these emotions, born in the crucible of the human heart and mind, acquire a life outside their originators, be-coming tangible influences in the daily existence of Powers's pro-tagonists. His ghosts are not so much scary strangers to those they visit, as they are familiar revenants from the past, snippets of the victim's own personality.

As such, these haunts have a way of distorting the flow of time. Past and present blend into a formless forever in most Powers sto-ries – at least until the protagonist manages to resolve his plight. Here we detect an echo from another famous modern Gothicist, William Faulkner, who proclaimed that the past is never dead, nor even truly past.

So: Powers's tales, and his characters, are literally haunted.

And as a result of Powers's immense talents, these haunted stories become in themselves haunting: unforgettable, tenacious, insistent phantoms perched on the shoulders of his lucky – but definitely not untouched – readers. Fiction as near-tangible specters.

Now, my focus on Powers as a dealer in afterlife imagery, while accurate and essential to an appreciation of his oeuvre, I believe, conceals nearly as much as it reveals.

For instance, I have not yet spoken of other major themes in his work, such as the doppelgänger motif. In story after story, charac-ters often come face to face with themselves, with revelatory conse-quences. Just consider, as a prime example, "Itinerary," which man-ages to be the best ouroboros-style narrative since Heinlein's "'All

You Zombies.'" Or "Fifty Cents" (co-written, along with two other selections, with Powers's kindred spirit, James Blaylock), wherein an ostensibly simple craphounding trip across the American desert develops into a mystical journey worthy of David Lynch.

Mention of the setting of "Fifty Cents" brings me to another important aspect of Powers's writing, and that's his concern with the specifically American landscape and with forging modern myths.

Powers's characters and the settings they move through and the objects they come in contact with are relentlessly modern and quotidian and quintessentially of these United States, yet still tinged with magic. No supermen or high wizards need apply for leading roles in his books. (The Zelazny-style clan of "The Way Down the Hill" are an exception to this observation.) His leading men and women are average joes fallen into exceptional vortices of circumstance. And he's able to imbue such "innocent," commonplace objects as a chain letter or a garden gnome or a deck of cards – or a simple tomato plant even – with the same mana that lesser writers find in such overblown tokens as magic swords and dragons. By highlighting the overlooked mystery of the everyday locales and appurtenances of our North American lifestyle, he freshens our vision and appreciation of the life we all share in common.

This concern with both representative heroes and with modern mythologies calls to mind two older writers who serve, I think, as models for Powers. The first, Philip K. Dick, is an acknowledged influence, having been a personal friend to Powers. In a story like "Where They Are Hid," with its remarkable imagery of characters following scripted routines even when reality warps around them, we can see the pure Phildickian stream of surreality and metareality. Likewise, "Night Moves," with its threat of a life sentence in an entropic bubble universe, and an evil female psychopomp, could have come from the pen of the primo 1960s-era Dick.

The other author I place in the honorable lineage leading to Powers is perhaps less obvious. But it seems to me that Fritz Leiber could be seen as one of Powers's literary godfathers. Having practically invented Urban Fantasy (arguably more so than even Ray Bradbury), and having in his later years found California a congenial locus for both his physical body and his body of work (as does Powers), Leiber shares more than surface similarities to the younger writer.

Both Dick and Leiber also possessed a sardonic sense of humor frequently ignored or misconstrued by readers and critics. The same is true of Powers. Perhaps above all, in the end, Powers is a comic writer. Tragedy he does not deny. But he affirms the superior resiliency and salving effect of humor, even unto the pratfall. If you don't find yourself laughing at least a few times in every Powers story, you're missing something. Certainly the most humorous piece in this collection is "The Better Boy," whose protagonist experiences one indignity after another, without ever quite losing his essential nobility – a nobility we can all aspire to in its attainability. But even in the midst of such a chiller as "We Traverse Afar," whose narrator is sorely afflicted, we get a suburban Jesus-impersonator rummaging through his sackcloth for spare change. Now, if that doesn't crack you up, then you're one of Powers's undead, who are generally distinguished from the living by precisely that lack of a sense of humor.

I've had the pleasure of meeting Tim Powers face to face on one or two occasions. Our conversation, regretably, has been short and inconsequential, due to the press of circumstances. But even from those brief exchanges, I walked away with the impression of a fellow whose ready smile and chipper mien contrasted with sad eyes and certain inner preoccupations, a man wryly appreciative of life's entertaining enigmas, fully intent on sharing what wisdom he had gleaned in his life, while also a shade despairing of ever finding any satisfying answers this side of death.

Or beyond.

STRANGE ITINERARIES

Itinerary

THE DAY before the Santa Ana place blew up, the telephone rang at about noon. I had just walked the three blocks back from Togo's with a tuna-fish sandwich, and when I was still out in the yard I heard the phone ringing through the open window; I ran up the porch steps, trying to fumble my keys out of my pocket without dropping the Togo's bag, and I was panting when I snatched up the receiver in the living room. "Hello?"

I thought I could hear a hissing at the other end, but no voice. It was October, with the hot Santa Ana winds shaking the dry pods off of the carob trees, and the receiver was already slick with my sweat. I used to sweat a lot in those days, what with the beer and the stress and all. "Hello?" I said again, impatiently. "Am I talking to a short circuit?" Sometimes my number used to get automatic phone calls from an old abandoned oil tank in San Pedro, and I thought I had rushed in just to get another of those.

It was a whisper that finally answered me, very hoarse; but I could tell it was a man: "Gunther! Jesus, boy – this is – Doug Olney, from Neff High School! You remember me, don't you?"

"Doug? Olney?" I wondered if he had had throat cancer. It had been nearly twenty years since I'd spoken to him. "Sure I remember! Where are you? Are you in town – "

"No time to talk. I don't want to – change any of your plans." He seemed to be upset. "Listen, a woman's gonna call your number in

3

a minute; she's gonna ask for me. You don't know her. Say I just left a minute ago, okay?"

"Who is she – " I began, but he had already hung up.

As soon as I lowered the receiver into the cradle, the phone rang again. I took a deep breath and then picked it up again. "Hello?"

It was a woman, sure enough, and she said, "Is Doug Olney there?" I remember thinking that she sounded like my sister, who's married, in a common-law and probably unconsummated sense, to an Iranian who lives at de Gaulle Airport in France; though I hadn't heard from my sister since Carter was president.

I took a deep breath. "He just left," I said helplessly.

"I bet." A shivering sigh came over the line. "But I can't do any more." Again I was holding a dead phone.

We grew up in a big old Victorian house on Lafayette Avenue in Buffalo. The third floor had no interior partitions or walls, since it was originally designed to be a ballroom; by the time we were living there the days of balls were long gone, and that whole floor was jammed to capacity with antique furniture, wall to wall, floor to twelve-foot ceiling, back to front. My sister and I were little kids then, and we could crawl all through that vast lightless volume, up one canted couch and across the underside of an inverted table, squeezing past rolled carpets and worming between Regency chair legs. Of course there was no light at all unless we crowded into a space near one of the dust-filmed windows; and climbing back down to the floor, and then tracing the molding and the direction of the floor planks to the door, was a challenge. When we were finally able to stand up straight again out in the hall, we'd be covered with sour dust and not eager to explore in there again soon.

· The nightmare I always had as a child was of having crept and wriggled to the very center of that room all by myself in the middle of the night, pausing roughly halfway between the floor and ceiling in pitch darkness on some sloped cabinet or sleigh bed – and then hearing a cautious scuffle from some remote cubic yard out there, in that three-dimensional maze of Cabriole legs and cartouches that you had to touch to learn the shapes of. And in the dream I knew it was some lonely boy who had hidden away up there with all the furniture years and years ago, and that he wanted to play, to show me whatever old shoe buckles or pocket watches or fountain pens he had found in drawers and coat pockets. I always pictured him skeletal and pale, though of course he'd be careful never to get near enough to the windows to be seen, and I knew he'd speak in a whisper.

I always woke up from that dream while it was still dark outside my window, and so tense that I'd simply lie without moving a muscle until I could see the morning light through my eyelids.

I was in the yard of the Santa Ana house early the next morning, sipping at a can of Coors beer and blinking tears out of my eyes as I tried to focus on the tomato vines through the sun glare on the white garden wall, when I heard a pattering like rain among the leaves. I sat down abruptly in the damp grass to push the low leaves aside.

It was bits of glass falling out of the sky. I touched one shard, and it was as hot as a serving plate. A cracking and thumping started up behind me then, and I fell over backward trying to stand up in a hurry. Red clay roof tiles were shattering violently on the grass and tearing the jasmine branches. The air was sharp with the acid smell of burned, broken stone, and then a hard punch of scorchingly hot air lifted me off my feet and rolled me over the top of the picnic table. I was lying facedown and breathless in the grass when the bass-note boom deafened me and stretched my hair out straight, so that it stood up from my scalp for days; I still have trouble combing it down flat, not that I try frequently.

The yard looked like a battlefield. All the rose bushes were broken off flush with the ground, and the ceramic duck that we'd had forever was broken into a hundred pieces. I was dimly glad that the duck had been able to tour California once in his otherwise uneventful life.

The eastern end of the house, where the kitchen had been, was broken wide open, with tar-paper strips standing up along the roof edge like my hair, and beams and plaster chunks lay scattered out across the grass. Everything inside the kitchen was gone, the table and the refrigerator and the pictures on the wall. Propane is heavier than air, and it had filled the kitchen from the floor upward, until it had reached the pilot light on the stove.

The explosion had cracked my ribs and burned my eyebrows off and scorched my throat, and I think I got sick from radon or asbestos that had been in the walls. I took a daylong ride on a bus out here to San Bernardino to recuperate at my uncle's place, the same rambling old ranch-style house where we lived happily for a year right after we moved from New York, before my mother found the Santa Ana house and began making payments on it.

The ceramic duck might have been the first thing my mother bought for the house. He generally just sat in the yard, but shortly after my sister and I turned seven he was stolen. We didn't get very excited about that, but we were awestruck when the duck mysteriously showed up on the lawn again, six months later – because propped up against him in the dewy grass was a photo album full of pictures of the ceramic duck in various locations around the state: the duck in front of the flower bank at the entrance to Disneyland, the duck on a cable-car seat in San Francisco, the duck sitting between the palm prints of Clark Gable; along with a couple of more mundane shots, like one of the duck just leaning against an avocado tree in somebody's yard out behind a weather-beaten old house. I think all the stories you hear about world-travelling lawn gnomes these days started with the humbler travels of our duck, back in '59. Or vice versa, I suppose.

My uncle's place hasn't changed at all since my sister and I explored every hollow and gully of the weedy acre and climbed the sycamores along the back fence so many years ago – our carved initials are still visible on the trunk of one of them, I discover, still only a yard above the dirt, though my sister isn't interested in seeing them now. There's a surprising lot of our toys, too, old wooden Lincoln Logs and Nike missile launchers; I've gathered them from among the weeds and put them near the back of the garage where my uncle supposedly keeps his beer, but she doesn't want to see them either.

Always in San Bernardino you see women on the noonday sidewalks wearing shorts and halter tops, and from behind they look young and shapely with their long brown legs and blonde hair; but when the car you're in has driven past them, and you hike around in the passenger seat to look back, their faces are weary, and shockingly old. And at night along Base Line, under the occasional clusters of sodium-vapor lights, you can see that the bar parking lots are jammed with cars, but you can generally also see four or five horses tied up to a post outside the bar door. My uncle says this is a semi-desert climate, right below the Cajon Pass and Barstow in the high desert, and so we get a lot of patches of mirage.

I'll let my sister drive me as far as the Stater Brothers market on Highland, though that doesn't cheer her up, probably because I mostly shoplift the fruits and cheese and crackers that are all I can keep down anymore. She flew back from France after I hurt myself, and when she can borrow an old car from a friend she drives out to visit me. She keeps trying to trick me into coming back to live in Santa Ana again, or anywhere besides my uncle's house – she wants to drive me to a hospital, actually – but I don't dare. I've told her not to tell anyone where I am, and I've taken a false name, not that anyone asks me.

Her family, I have to admit, has given her a lot of grief. Her husband was born in a part of Iran that was under British jurisdiction, and when he tried to go back there after going to school in England the Iranians said he was an enemy of the Shah; they took his passport and gave him some papers that permitted him to leave but never come back, and he got as far as Charles de Gaulle Airport, but France wouldn't let him in without a passport and Customs wouldn't let him get on another plane. He's lived on the Boutique Level of Terminal One now for decades, sleeping on a plastic couch and watching TV, and Lufthansa flight attendants give him travel kits so that he can shave and brush his teeth. My sister met him there during a layover on a European tour my mother bought for her right after high school, and now she's got a job and an apartment in Roissy so she can be near him. I keep telling her she's going to lose her job, staying away like this, but she says she has no choice, because nobody else can get through to me the way she still can. I'm *backward,* she says.

My uncle makes himself scarce when she drives up the dirt track out front in one beat old borrowed car or another; so does everybody. When I hobbled off the bus at his warped chain-link front gate, all scorched and blinking and hoarse and dizzy from the radon, he was waiting for me out in the front yard with his usual straw hat pulled down over his gray hair; all you really see is the bushy mustache. The house is empty now, just echoing rooms with one old black Bakelite telephone on the kitchen floor and a lot of wires sticking out of the walls where there used to be lights, but he told me I could sleep in my old room, and I've carried in some newspapers to make a nest in the corner there. I'm thinking about moving the nest into the closet.

"Don't bother anybody you might see here," my uncle told me on that first day. "Just leave 'em alone. They probably live here." And I have seen a very old man in the kitchen, always crying quietly over the sink, and wearing one of those senior-citizen jumpsuits that zip up from the ankle to the neck; I've just nodded to him and discreetly shuffled past across the dusty linoleum. What could we have to say to each other that the other wouldn't already know? And a couple of times I've seen two kids out at the far end of the back-yard. Let them play, I figure. My uncle is generally walking around in circles behind the garage trying to find his beer. There's a patch of mirage out there – if you step into the weeds by the edge of the driveway, walking away from the house, you find with no shift at all that you've just stepped *onto* the driveway, *facing* the house.

"It's been that way forever," he told me one day when he was taking a break from it, sitting on the hood of his wrecked old truck. "But one night a few winters ago I stepped out there and *wasn't* facing the house; and I was standing on one of your mom's long-ago rosebushes. The flowers were open, like they thought it was day, and the leaves were warm. Time doesn't pass in mirages, everybody knows that – so I hopped right in the truck and bought two cases of Budweiser out of the cooler at Top Cat, and stashed 'em there right by the rosebush. The next morning it was the two-for-one-step mirage again, but whenever it slacks off, I know where there's a lot of cold beer."

I nodded a number of times, and so did he, and it was right after this conversation with him that I started keeping all our old toys back there.

Yesterday my sister came rocking up the dirt driveway in a shiny green Edsel, and when she braked it in a cloud of dust and clanked the door open I could see that she'd been crying at some point on the drive up. It's a long drive, and it takes a lot out of her.

My voice is gone because of the explosion having scorched my throat, so I stepped closer to her to be heard. "Come in the house and have ... some water," I rasped – awkwardly, because she's doing all this for my sake. We don't have any glasses, but she could drink it out of the faucet. "Or crackers," I added.

"I can't stand to see the inside of the house," she said, crossly. "We had good times in this house, *when we were all living* in it." She squinted out past the dogwood tree at the infinity of brown hillocks that is the backyard. "Let's talk out there."

"You're testy," I noted as I followed her up the dirt driveway, past the house. She was wearing a blue sundress that clung to her sweaty back.

"Why do you suppose that is, Gunther?"

I glanced around quickly, but there wasn't even a bird in the empty blue sky. "Doug," I reminded her huskily, trying to project my frail voice. The name had been suggested by the phone call I'd got on the day before the explosion, and certainly Doug Olney himself would never hear about the deception, wherever he might be. "Always, you promised."

We were walking out past the end of the driveway among the burr-weeds now, and I saw her shoulders shrug wearily. "Why do you suppose that is – Mr. Olney?" she called back to me.

I lengthened my stride to step up beside her. The soles of my feet must be tough, because the burrs never stick in my skin. "I bet it's expensive to rent a classic Edsel," I hazarded.

"Yes, it is." Her voice was flat and harsh. "Especially in the summer, with all the Mexican weddings. It's a '57, but it must have a new engine or something in it – I could hardly see the signs on the old Route 66 today. Just 'Foothill Boulevard' all the way. I may not be able to come out here again, get through to you, not even your own *twin*, who *lived* here, *with* you! Not even in a car from those days. And Hakim needs me too." She turned to face me and stamped her foot. "He could figure some way to get out of that airport if he really wanted to! And look at you! Damn it – Doug – how long do you think a comatose body can *live,* even in a hospital like Western Medical, with its soul off hiding *incognito* somewhere?"

"Well, *soul …* "

"This is certainly unsanctified ground. Is it a crossroads? Have you got *rue* growing out here with the weeds?" She was crying again. *"Propane leak.* Why were you found out in the yard, out by the duck? You changed your mind, didn't you? You were trying to walk away from it. Good! Keep *on* walking away from it, don't stop here in the, in the … terminal, the nowhere in-between. Walk right now to that silly old car back there, and let me drive you to Western Medical while I still can, while you can still make the trip. You can *wake up.*"

I smiled at her and shook my head. I know now that I was never scared of the boy in the dark ballroom. I was tense with fear of each fresh unknown dawn, which the boy had found a way to hide from, but which always did come to me mercilessly shining right through my closed eyelids. I opened my mouth to croak some reassurance to her, but she was looking past me with an empty expression.

"Jesus," she said then, reverently, in a voice almost as hoarse as mine, "this is where that other picture was taken. The photo of the duck by the avocado tree. In the photo album, remember?" She pointed back toward the house. "There's no tree here now, but the angle of the house, the windows – look, it's the very same view, we just didn't recognize it then because we remembered this house freshly painted, not all faded and peeled like it is now, and like it was in the picture, and because in the picture there was a big distracting avocado tree in the foreground!"

I stood beside her and squinted through watering eyes against the sun glare. She might have been right – if you imagined a tree to the right, with the poor duck leaning against the trunk, this view was at least very like the one in that old photo album.

"The person with the camera was standing right here," she said softly.

Or *will* be standing, I thought.

"Could you drive me to Stater Brothers?" I said.

Several times I've gone out and looked since she drove away, and I'm still not sure she was right. The trouble is, I don't remember the photograph all that clearly. It might have been this house. All I can do is wait.

I don't imagine that I'll be going to Stater Brothers again soon, if ever. The trip was upsetting, with so many curdles and fractures of mirage in the harsh daylight that you'd think San Bernardino was populated by nothing but walking skeletons and one-hoss shays. I did get an avocado, along with my crackers and processed cheese-food slices, and my sister left off a box of our dad's old clothes because I've been wearing the scorched pants and shirt still, and she said it broke her heart to see me walking around all killed. I haven't looked in the box, but it stands to reason that there's one of those jumpsuits in it.

I know now that she's going back, at last, to poor stalled Hakim at the airport in Roissy. I called her from the phone in the kitchen here.

"I'm on my way to the hospital," I told her. "You can go back to France."

"You're – Gunth – I mean, *Doug,* where are you calling from?"

"I'm back in Santa Ana. I just want to change my clothes, try to comb my hair, before I get on a bus to the hospital."

"Santa Ana? What's the number there, I'll call you right back."

That panicked me. Helplessly I gave her the only phone number I could think of, my old Santa Ana number. "But I didn't mean to take up any more of your time," I babbled, "I just wanted to – "

"That's our old number," she said. "How can you be at our old number?"

"It – stayed with the house." If I could still sweat, I'd have been sweating. "These people who live here now don't mind me hanging around." The lie was getting ahead of me. "They like me; they made me a sandwich."

"I bet. Stay by the phone."

She hung up, and I knew it was a race then to see which of us would be able to dial the old number most rapidly. She must have been hampered by a rotary-dial phone too, because I got ringing out of the earpiece; and after it had rung four times I concluded that the number must be back in service again, because I would have got the recording by then if it had not been. My lips were silently mouthing, *Please, please,* and I was aching with anxious hope that whoever answered the line would agree to go along with what I'd tell them to say.

Then the phone at the other end was lifted, and the voice said, breathlessly, "Hello?"

Of course I recognized him, and the breath clogged in my numb throat.

"Hello?" came the voice again. "Am I talking to a short circuit?"

Yes, I thought.

That oil tank in San Pedro hadn't been in use for years, but it had once been equipped with an automatic-dial switch to call the company's main office when its fuel was depleted; a stray power surge had apparently turned it on again, and the emergency number it called was by that time ours. Probably the oil tank hadn't had any fuel in it at all anymore, and only occasionally noticed. Certainly there had been nothing we could do about it.

"Gunther!" It hurt my teeth to say the name. "Jesus, boy – this is – Doug Olney, from Neff High School! You remember me, don't you?"

"Doug?" said the half-drunk, middle-aged man at the other end of the line, befuddledly wondering if I had throat cancer. "Olney? Sure I remember! Where are you? Are you in town – "

"No time to talk," I said, trying not to choke. What if Doug Olney, the real one, *had* been in town, in Santa Ana? Would this unhappy loser have suggested that the two of them get together for lunch? "I don't want to – " Stop you, I thought; save you, for damn sure. " – change any of your plans." My eyes were watering, even in the dim kitchen. "Listen, a woman's gonna call your number in a minute; she's gonna ask for me. You don't know her," I assured him; I didn't want him to be at all thinking he might. "Say I just left a minute ago, okay?"

"Who is she – "

I just hung up. You'll find out, I thought.

My uncle's beer appeared in the yard today, two cases of it, still cold from the cooler at Top Cat. The roses are still fresh, and I looked at the clip-cuts on some stems and tried to comprehend that my mother had cut the flowers only a few hours earlier, by the rosebush's time; the smears in the white dust on the rose hips were probably from her fingers. Sitting in the dirt driveway in the noonday sun, my uncle and I got all weepy and sentimental, and drank can after can of the Budweiser in toasts to missing loved ones, though probably nobody was in the house, and the two children were by then long gone from the backyard.

I've planted the golf-ball-sized seed from the avocado, right where the tree was in the picture – if it was in fact a picture of this house. Eventually it will be a tree, and maybe one day the duck will be there, leaning on the trunk, on his way back from Disneyland and Grauman's Chinese Theatre to the house where my sister and I are still seven years old. I plan to tag along, if he'll have me.

The Way Down the Hill

Then I was frightened at myself, for the cold mood
That envies all men running hotly, out of breath,
Nowhere, and who prefer, still drunk with their own blood,
Hell to extinction, horror and disease to death.
— GEORGE DILLON, FROM THE FRENCH
OF CHARLES BAUDELAIRE

I HADN'T BEEN to the place since 1961, but I still instinctively down-shifted as I leaned around the curve, so that the bike was moving slowly enough to take the sharp turn off the paved road when it appeared. The old man's driveway was just a long path of rutted gravel curling up the hillside, and several times I had to correct with my feet when the bald back tire lost traction, but it was a clear and breezy afternoon, with the trees and the tan California hillside making each other look good, and I was whistling cheerfully as I crested the hill and parked my old Honda beside a couple of lethal-looking Harley-Davidsons.

I was late. The yard spread out in front of the old man's Victorian-style house was a mosaic of vans, Volkswagens, big ostentatious sedans, sports cars and plain anonymous autos. There were even, I noticed as I stuffed my gloves into my helmet and strode up to the front steps, a couple of skateboards leaning on the porch rails. I grinned and wondered who the kids would be.

The heavy door was pulled open before I could touch the knob, and Archie was handing me a foaming Carlsberg he'd doubtless fetched for someone else. Somehow I can always recognize Archie.

"Come in, sibling!" he cried jovially. "We certainly can't expect Rafe yet, so you must be Saul or Amelia." He studied my face as I stepped inside. "Too old to be Amelia. Saul?"

"Right," I said, unknotting my scarf. "How's the old man, Arch?"

"Never better. He was asking just a few minutes ago if you'd showed up yet. Where the hell have you been, anyway, for … how many years?"

"Twenty – missed the last three meetings. Oh, I've been wandering around. Checked out Europe one more time and took a couple of courses back east before the old boredom effect drifted me back here. Living in Santa Ana now." I grinned at him a little warily. "I imagine I've got a lot of catching up to do."

"Yeah. Did you know Alice is gone?"

I tossed my helmet onto a coat-buried chair, but kept my leather jacket because all my supplies were in it. "No," I said quietly. I'd always liked Alice.

"She is. Incognito underground, maybe – but more likely … " He shrugged.

I nodded and took a long sip of the beer, grateful for his reticence. Why say it, after all? People do let go sometimes. Some say it's hard to do, as difficult as holding your breath till you faint – others say it's as easy as not catching a silver dollar tossed to you. Guesses.

Archie ducked away to get another beer, and I walked across the entry hall into the crowded living room. The rich, leathery smell of Latakia tobacco told me that old Bill was there, and I soon identified him by the long, blackened meerschaum pipe he somehow found again every time. The little girl puffing at it gave me a raised eyebrow.

"Howdy, Bill," I said. "It's Saul."

"Saul, laddie!" piped the little girl's voice. "Excuse the nonrecognition. You were a gawky youth when I saw you last. Been doing anything worthwhile?"

I didn't even bother to give the standard negative reply. "I'll talk to you later," I said. "Got to find something for this beer to chase."

Bill chuckled merrily. "They laid in a dozen bottles of Laphroaig Scotch in case you came." He waved his pipe toward the dining room that traditionally served as the bar. "You know your way down the hill."

It was a long-standing gag between us, deriving from one night when a girlfriend and I had been visiting a prominent author whose house sat on top of one of the Hollywood hills; the girlfriend had begun stretching and yawning on the couch and remarking how tired she was, and the prominent author obligingly told her she could spend the night right there. Turning briefly toward me, he inquired, "You know your way down the hill, don't you?" Bill and I now used the phrase to indicate any significant descent. I smiled as I turned toward the bar.

I stiffened, though, and my smile unkinked itself, when I saw a certain auburn-haired girl sipping a grasshopper at a corner table.

I could feel my face heat up even before I was sure I recognized her. It hadn't been long ago, a warm August evening at the Orange Street Fair, with the blue and rose sky fading behind the strings of light bulbs that swayed overhead. I'd been slouched in a chair in the middle of Glassell Street, momentarily left in a littered clearing by an ebb in the crowd. The breeze was from the south, carrying frying smells from the Chinese section on Chapman, and I was meditatively sipping Coors from a plastic cup when she dragged up another chair and straddled it.

I don't remember how the conversation started, but I know that through a dozen more cups of beer we discussed Scriabin and Stevenson and David Bowie and A. E. Housman and Mexican beers. And later she perched sidesaddle, because one of the passenger foot-pegs fell off long ago, on the back of my motorcycle as I cranked us through the quiet streets to my apartment.

She went out for a newspaper and ice cream the next afternoon, and never came back. I'd been wryly treasuring the memory, in a two-ships-that-pass-in-the-night way, until now.

Restraining my anger, I crossed to her table and sat down. The girl's face looked up and smiled, obviously recognizing me.

"Hello, Saul."

"Goddamn it," I gritted. "All right, who are you?"

"Marcus. Are you upset? Why? Oh, I know! I still owe you for that newspaper." Marcus started digging in his purse.

"Less of the simpering. You knew it was me?"

"Well, sure," he said. "What's wrong. I broke an *unwritten law* or something? Listen, you haven't been around for a while. Customs change, ever notice? What's wrong with members of the clan having relations with each other?"

"Christ. Lots of things," I said hoarsely. Could the old man have sanctioned this? "It makes me sick." I could remember going bar-hopping with Marcus in the 1860s when he was a bearded giant, both of us drunkenly prowling the streets of Paris, hooting at women and trading implausible and profane reminiscences.

"Don't run off." Marc caught me by the arm as I was getting up. "There are a few things I've got to tell you before the ceremony at six. Sit down. Laphroaig still your drink? I'll get a bottle – "

"Don't bother. I want to go talk to the old man. Save whatever you've got to say until the meeting."

"It's old Hain I want to talk about. You've got to hear this sooner or later, so – "

"So I'll hear it later," I said, and strode out of the bar to find Sam Hain, our patriarch. I'd been there only about five minutes, but I was already wishing I hadn't come. If this was the current trend, I thought, I can't blame Alice for disappearing.

Back in the high-ceilinged living room I caught the eye of a little boy who was pouring himself a glassful of Boodle's. "Where's our host?" I asked.

"Library. Amelia?"

"Saul. Robin?" Robin was always fond of good gin.

"Right. Talk to you later, yes?" He wandered off toward the group around the piano.

From the corner of my eye I saw Marcus – who'd put on a bit of weight since that night, I noted with vindictive satisfaction – hurry out of the bar. I braced myself, but he just crossed to the entry and thumped away up the stairs. Doubtless in a snit, I thought.

I pictured old Marc sniffling and dabbing at his mascara'd eyes with a perfumed hankie, and shook my head. It always upset me to consider how thoroughly even the keenest-edged minds are at the mercy of hormones and such biological baggage. We are all indeed windowless gonads, as Leibnitz nearly said.

Old Sam Hain was asleep in his usual leather chair when I pushed open the library door, so I sipped my beer and let my eyes rove over the shelves for a minute or two. As always, I envied him his library. The quarto *Plays of Wharfinger, Ashbless' Odes,* Blaylock's *The Wild Man of Tango-Raza*, all were treasures I'd admired for decades – though, at least in a cursory glance, I didn't notice any new items.

I absently reached for the cigar humidor, but my fingers struck polished tabletop where it should have been. Suddenly I noticed an absence that had been subconsciously nagging at me ever since I'd arrived – the house, and the library particularly, was not steeped in the aroma of Caribbean cigars anymore.

Behind me the old man grunted and raised his head. "Saul?"

"Yes sir." It never failed to please me, the way he could always recognize me after a long separation. I sat down across the table from him. "What's become of the cigars?"

"Ahh," he waved his hand, "they began to disagree with me." He squinted speculatively at me. "You've been away twenty years, son. Have you, too, begun to disagree with me?"

Embarrassed and a little puzzled, I shifted in my chair. "Of course not, sir. You know I just wander off for a while sometimes – I missed four or five in a row at the end of the last century, remember? Means nothing. It's just to indulge my solitary streak once in a while."

Hain nodded and pressed his fingertips together. "Such impulses should be resisted – I think you know that. We are a clan, and our potentially great power is... vitiated if we persist in operating as individuals."

I glanced at him sharply. This seemed to be an about-face from his usual opinions – more the kind of thing I'd have expected from Marcus or Rafe.

"Ho. It sounds as if you're saying we should go back to the way we were in the days of the Medici – or as Balzac portrayed us in *The Thirteen*." I spoke banteringly, certain he'd explain whatever he'd actually meant.

"I've been doing some deep thinking for a number of years, Saul," he said slowly, "and it seems to me that we've been living in a fantasy daydream since I took over in 1861 and made such drastic changes in traditional clan policy. They were well-intentioned changes, certainly – and in a decent world they'd be practical. But we're not living in a decent world, ever notice? No, I no longer think our isolation and meek, live-and-let-live ways are realistic. Ah, don't frown, Saul. I know you've enjoyed this last hundred and twenty years more than any other period... but surely you can see you've – we've all – been ignoring certain facts? What do you think would happen if the ephemerals ever learned of our existence?"

"It wouldn't matter," I cried, unhappily aware that I was taking the side he'd always taken in this perennial question. "They'd kill some of us, I suppose, but we've all had violent deaths before. I prefer quick deaths to slow ones anyway. Why can't we just leave them alone? *We're* the parasites, after all."

"You're talking rot," he snapped. "Do you really think killing us is the worst they could do? What about perpetual maintenance on an artificial life-support system, with no means of suicide? What about administering mind-destroying drugs, so you spend the rest of your incarnations drooling and cutting out paper dolls in one half-wit asylum after another? And even if you could get to your suicide kit or jump in the way of a car before they seized you … do you think it's still absolutely impossible for them to track a soul to its next host?"

"I don't know," I muttered after a pause. In spite of my convictions his words had shaken me, touching as they did our very deepest fears. Maybe he's right, I thought miserably. We *are* parasites – all the liquor and food and music and poetry we enjoy is produced by the toiling ephemerals – but surely even parasites have to defend themselves?

"Saul," he said kindly, "I'm sorry to rub your nose in it this way, but you see we have to face it. Go have a drink and mix with the siblings; this will all be discussed after dinner. By the way, have you talked to Marcus?"

"Briefly."

"Talk to him at more length, then. He's got something important to tell you before the meeting."

"Can you tell me?"

"Let him. Relax, it's good news. Now if you'll excuse me, I'll finish my nap. It seems to be ripening to a real Alexandrian feast out there, and if it's going to last on into tomorrow I'd best catch some shut-eye."

"Right, sir."

I closed the door as I left, and went back to the bar, slumping into the same chair I'd had before. Archie was tending bar now, and I called my order to him, and when it arrived I tossed back a stiff gulp of the nearly warm Scotch and chased it with a long draft of icy Coors.

Being a member of the clan, I was used to seeing cherished things come and go – "This too will pass" was one of our basic tenets – but the old man had, in only a hundred and twenty years, become a rock against the waves of change, an immortal father, a symbol of values that outlast individual lifetimes. But now *he* had changed.

One corner of my mind was just keening. Even *this*, it wailed, even *this* will pass?

I remembered the meeting at which he'd first appeared, on a chilly night in 1806 at Rafe's Boston mansion. Sam was then a boy of about ten, and though he knew everyone and greeted the mature ones by name, he never did say who he'd been before. This upset a lot of us, but he was cordially firm on that point; and we couldn't deduce it by a process of elimination, either – a number of siblings had suicided in the early 1790s, after the tantalizingly hopeful French Revolution had degenerated into the Terror, and several apparently let go, never to come back. There was, of course, a lot of speculation about which one he was … though a few whispered that he wasn't any one of our lost siblings, but a new being who'd somehow infiltrated us.

The crowd in the bar slacked off. Most of the clan had carried their drinks out into the backyard, where the barbecue pit was already flinging clouds of aromatic smoke across the lawn, and the dedicated drinkers who remained were now working more slowly, so Archie came out from behind the bar and sat down at my table.

"Have a drink, Archimago," I said.

"Got one." He waved a tequila sour I hadn't noticed.

I took a long sip of the Laphroaig. "Are we all present and accounted for?"

"Nearly. The count's at forty these days now that Alice is gone – and there are thirty-eight of us here. Not a bad turnout."

"Who's missing?"

"Amelia and Rafe. Amelia's currently a man, about forty years old. Maybe she killed herself. And of course Rafe just died two months ago, so we can't expect to see him for another decade."

"How'd he go this time?" I didn't care, really. Marcus and Rafe were fast friends, but though in some incarnations I liked Marcus, I could never stand Rafe.

"Shot himself through the roof of the mouth in his apartment on Lombard Street in San Francisco. Nobody was surprised, he was nearly fifty." Archimago chuckled. "They say he managed to pull the trigger twice."

I shrugged. "If a thing's worth doing, it's worth doing thoroughly," I allowed.

Archie looked across the room and got to his feet. "Ah, I see Vogel is out of akvavit. Excuse me."

Most of us choose to die at about fifty, to ride the best years out of a body and then divorce ourselves from it by means of pills or a bullet or whatever strikes our fancy, so that our unencumbered soul can – though we rarely talk about it – dart through the void to the as yet unfirmly rooted soul of some unborn child, which we hungrily thrust out into the darkness, taking its embryonic body for ourselves. It sounds horrible baldly stated, and there's a mournful ballad called "The Legion of Lost Children," which none of us ever even hums, though we all know it, but it's hard to the point of impossibility to stare into the final, lightless abyss, and feel yourself falling, picking up speed … and not grab the nearest handhold.

Sam Hain, though, seemed to be an exception to this. He was born in mid-1796 and never died once after that, somehow maintaining his now one-hundred-and-eighty-five-year-old body on red wine, sashimi, tobacco and sheer will power. His physical age made him stand out among us even more than the obscurity of his origin did, and being patient, kindly and wise as well, he was elected Master at our 1861 meeting.

Up until then the Master post had meant little, and carried no duties except to provide a house and bountiful food and liquor for the five yearly meetings. I was Master myself for several decades in the early part of the sixteenth century, and some of the clan never did find out – or even ask – who the host of the meetings was. Sam Hain, though, made changes: for one thing, he arbitrarily changed the date of the meetings from the thirty-first of October to November first; he began to cut back on the several vast, clan-owned corporations that provide us all with allowances; and he encouraged us to get more out of a body, to carry it, as he certainly had, into old age before unseating some unborn child and taking its fresh one. I believe it was Sam, in fact, who first referred to us all as "hermit crabs with the power of eviction."

I looked up from my drink and saw Marcus enter the bar and signal Archie. The alcohol had given me some detachment toward the whole business, and I admitted to myself that Marc had certainly drawn a good body this time – tall and slender, with cascades of lustrous coppery hair. I could no longer be attracted to it, but I could certainly see why I'd been so entranced at the street fair.

"Hello, Marc," I said levelly. "Sam says you've got some good news for me."

"That's right, Saul." He sat down just as Archie brought him his creamy, pale green drink, and he took a sip before going on. "You're going to be a father."

For several moments I stared at him blankly. I finally choked, "That night…?"

He nodded, grinning, and fished from his purse a slip of folded paper. "Tested out positive."

"Goddamn you," I said softly. "Was it for this that you picked me up in the first place?"

He shrugged. "Does it matter? I should think your main concern at this point is the welfare of the child."

Though sick and cold inside, I nodded, for I saw the teeth of the trap at last – if one of us dies while in physical contract with a pregnant woman, it is her fetus that that one will take. And though we of the clan can generally have children, the hermit-crab reincarnation ability doesn't breed true – our children are all ephemerals.

"A hostage to fortune," I said. "You're holding my unborn child for ransom, right? Why? What do I have that you want?"

"You catch on fast," Marc said approvingly. "Okay, listen – if you cooperate with me and a couple of others, I'll allow your child to be born, and you can take it away or put it up for adoption or whatever. We'll even triple your allowance, and you don't use more than half of it now." He had another sip of his disgusting drink. "Of course, if you *don't* cooperate, one of the clan is likely to die while holding my hand, and... well, the Legion would have one more squalling member."

I didn't flinch at the reference to the strictly tabooed song, for I knew he'd hoped to shock me with it. "Cooperate? In what?"

He spread his hands. "Something I don't think you'd object to anyway. The, uh," he patted abdomen, "hostage is just insurance. Would you like a fresh drink? I thought so. Arch! Another boiler-maker here. Well, Saul, you've heard the good news – take it easy! – and now I'm afraid I've got some bad." He just sat and watched me until I'd had a sip of the new drink.

"Sam Hain is dead," he said, very quietly. "He blew his head off, in this very house, late in 1963. Please don't interrupt! Rafe and I found his body only a few hours afterward, and came to a decision you might disapprove of – the next meeting wasn't for three years, so we had one of the secret, advanced branches of our DIRE Corporation construct a simulacrum."

I opened my mouth to call him a liar, but closed it again. I realized I was certain it was true. "What does smoke do, clog the thing's circuits or something?"

He nodded. "It's rough on the delicate machinery, so we had him give up the cigars, as you noticed. It was me speaking to you through the simulacrum, from the controls upstairs."

"I saw you run out of the bar." Marc started to speak, but I interrupted him. "Wait a minute! You said '63? That can't be – he'd be...

eighteen now, and he'd be here today. If this is – "

Marc took my hand. "He *would* be eighteen, Saul. If he came back... but he didn't. He let go. We were pretty sure he would, or we wouldn't have gone to the trouble of having the sim built."

I jerked my hand away. I didn't doubt him – Sam Hain was just the sort who'd choose to drop away into the last oblivion rather than cheat an unborn child of life – but I wanted no intimacy with Marc.

"All right, so you've got this robot to take his place. Why involve me in – "

I broke off my sentence when a dark-haired man with a deeply lined face lurched into the bar; his tie was loose, his jacket looked slept in, and he'd clearly been doing some preliminary drinking elsewhere. "Who's doling out the spirits here?' he called.

Archimago waved to him. "Right here, Amelia. We didn't think you were going to show. What'll you have?"

"Ethanol." Amelia wove with drunkard dignity across the room and ceremoniously collapsed into the third chair at our table. "Okay if I join you? Who are you anyway?"

I overrode Marc's brushing-off excuses, wanting some time to consider what he'd been saying. "Sure, keep your seat, Amelia. I'm Saul, and this is Marcus."

"Yeah," Amelia said, "I know. I visited Marc last year at his apartment in Frisco. Still living there, Marc? Nice little place, on that twisty street and all. 'Member that night we drove to – "

"You're late," Marcus said coldly, "and drunk. Why is that?"

Amelia's eyes dulled, and though her expression grew, if anything, more blank, I thought she was going to cry. "I had a stop to make this morning, a visit, before coming here."

Marc rolled his eyes toward the ceiling. "This *morning*? Where, in New York?"

Archie brought a glass of some kind of whiskey, and Amelia seized it eagerly. "In Costa Mesa," she breathed, after taking a liberal sip. "Fairview State Mental Hospital."

"I hope they didn't say they were too full to take you," Marc said sweetly.

"Shut up, Marc," I said. "Who were you visiting?"

"My... fiancé, from my last life," Amelia said, "when I was a woman."

The incongruity of a woman talking out of a man's body rarely bothered me, but it did now.

"He's seventy-two years old," she went on. "White hair, no teeth... a face like a desert tortoise."

"What's he doing in the hatch?" Marc inquired.

His sarcasm was lost on the inward-peering Amelia. "We were engaged," he said, "but we got into a fight one evening. This was in 1939. I'd gone out to dinner with a guy I'd met at a party, and Len said I shouldn't have. I was drunk, of course, and I laughed and told him... the truth, that I'd slept around long before I met him, and would be doing it long after he was dead."

"Can this romance be saved?" said Marc, looking tremendously bored.

"Anyway, he belted me. First time... only time... he ever did. God I was mad. I can't now, as a man, *imagine* being that mad. So you know what I did? I went into the kitchen and got a big knife out of the drawer and, while he stood there muttering apologies, I shoved the blade up to the handle into my stomach. And I pulled it out and laughed at him some more and called him every filthy name I knew, for three whole goddamned hours, as I lay there on the floor and bled to death. He never moved. Well, he sat down."

Even Marc was looking a little horrified. "I don't wonder the poor bastard's in Fairview now," he said. "And you *visited* him?"

"Yeah. I forget why. I think I wanted to apologize, though I was a thirty-year-old woman when he last saw me... I told them I was a relative, and quoted enough family history to get in." She took another big sip of the whiskey. "He was in a little bed, and his dried-up body didn't raise the blankets any more than a couple of brooms would. I was looking respectable, freshly shaved, dressed like you see, smiling… and yet he *knew* me, he recognized me!" Amelia gulped her whole drink. "He started yelling and crying and, in his birdy old voice, begging me to *forgive* him." She grinned, her man's face wrinkling. "Can you beat that? Forgive him."

"Absolutely fascinating," pronounced Marcus, slapping the table. "Now why don't you go find somebody else to tell it to, hmm? Saul and I have to talk."

"I want to talk to the old man," said Amelia weakly as she got to her feet and tottered away.

"Oh, God," Marc moaned, exasperated.

"Hadn't you better dash upstairs again?" I suggested. "With no one at the sim's controls she'll think it's a corpse."

"No," he said, staring after Amelia, "it's equipped to run independently, too. Speaks vague platitudes and agrees with nearly everything that's said to it. Oh, well, she's too lushed to notice anything. Okay, now, listen, Saul, you started to ask why we dragged you in on this – I'll tell you, and then you can call me a son of a bitch, and then do what I ask, and then, if you want, take the hostage when it shows up and disappear and never come back. As I say, you and the kid will be financially provided for.

"Through the simulacrum, Rafe and I have been gradually changing clan policy, restoring things to the way they were before Hain took over in 1861. DIRE is going to resume the genetic and conditioning researches Hain made them stop in the 1950s, and, oh, we've bought and cultivated acres of farmland near Ankara for… certain lucrative enterprises he would never have permitted, and – anyway, you see? As a matter of fact, we hope soon to be able to maintain a farm of healthy perpetually pregnant ephemerals, so that we can have our deaths performed under controlled conditions and be sure the fetus we move on to is a healthy, well-cared-for one. Honestly, wouldn't it be nice not to find yourself born in slums anymore? Not to have to pretend to be a child for a dreary decade until you can leave whatever poor family you elbowed your way into? And we can begin taking hormone injections quite young, to bring us more quickly to a mature – "

Suddenly I was sorry I'd had so much to drink. "That's filthy," I said. "All of it. More abominable than ... than I can say."

He pursed his painted lips. "I'm sorry you can't approve, Saul. We'd hoped your long absence was a sign of dissatisfaction with the way things were. But with our ... hostage to fortune, as you put it, we don't need your approval. Just your cooperation. Some siblings have commented on the changes in the old man, and we can't afford to have them even suspect that what they see is a phony. If they knew he was gone it would be impossible to get them to work together, or even allow ... Anyway, if they all see you, Sam's traditional favorite, drinking with the old man and reminiscing and laughing and agreeing with everything that comes out of his mouth, why, it'll be established in their minds, safely below the conscious level, that this is certainly the genuine Sam Hain they've unquestioningly obeyed for more than a century."

"You want me to kiss him?"

Marc frowned, puzzled. "That won't be necessary. Just friendly, like you've always been. And of course, if you don't, then I'll go hold Amelia's hand in one of mine and," he patted his purse, "blow her head off with the other. And then it'll be her I give birth to in six months. Maybe she'd even be able to visit that poor son of a bitch at Fairview again, as a baby this time."

"I know, I know," I told him impatiently. "I comprehended the threat the first time. Shut up and let me think."

I've had a number of children, over the centuries, and they're all as dead-and-gone as Marc was threatening to make this one. It never bothered me much, even when, in a few cases, I'd actually seen them die – they'd had their little lives, and their irreversible deaths. And of course the ... eviction of unborn babies from their bodies, though not a concept I was really at ease with, was anything but a new one to me. Still... I didn't want a child of mine to get just alive enough to die and then be pushed away to sink into the dark. "They give birth astride a grave," Beckett said, "the light gleams an instant, then it's night once more." That's how it is for the ephemerals, certainly. But let them have that instant's gleam of light!

"All right," I said dully. "If Sam's gone, I don't care what becomes of you all anyway. I'll take the kid and go incognito underground."

"The wisest choice," approved Marcus with a grin that brought out smile lines in his cheeks. What, I wondered, would this girl have been like today, if Marc hadn't taken over her embryonic body years ago? Perhaps we'd still have met at the street fair, and talked about Stevenson.

It took me a few seconds to stand up, and I heard my chair clatter over behind me, but I felt coldly sober. "Trot upstairs and get in the driver's seat," I said. "I'd like to get home by midnight."

"Archimago will run the sim," Marc said, giving a thumbs-up to Archie, who nodded and strode out of the bar without looking at me.

"I'm going to take a walk out back," I said. "Clear the fumes out of my head... and give your wind-up man time to join the others ahead of me. You don't want this to look rehearsed."

"I suppose not. Okay, but don't wander off or anything."

"You're holding the stake," I reminded him.

Scattered between the house and the backdrop of trees silhouetted against the darkening sky, my siblings were beginning to deal with dinner. The fire-pit blazed fiercely, seeming to lack only a bound martyr for some real nostalgia, and the crowd, as if to supply it, was dragging up a whole side of beef wired to a revolving black iron frame. They'd got into the cellar, and I picked my way through a litter of half-empty Latour and Mouton bottles on my way to the unlighted, vine-roofed patio on the west side of the house.

After dark we of the clan generally prefer noisy, bright-lit groups to solitude, and I wasn't surprised to find the deep-shadowed patio empty. I fished a cigarette from my left jacket pocket and struck a match on the side of the bench I was sitting on, and drew a lungful and then let the smoke hiss out and flit away on the cool, eucalyptus-scented breeze.

I stared at the dark bulk of the old house and wondered where its master was buried. Though it was like Sam to have let go, I blamed him for having killed himself. Surely he must have known we'd slide back into our old, ruthless ways once he was gone, like domesticated dogs thrown back out into the wilderness.

A dim green glow defined a window in the third story, near where several heavy cables were moored to the shingles. Doubtless the room, I thought, where Archie is hunched over whatever sort of controls a simulacrum requires. I picked a loose chip from one of the flagstones and cocked my arm to pitch it at the window – then sadly decided the move would be a mistake, and let it fall back to the pavement instead.

I was aware that it would be quite a while before I'd know whether Marc had kept his end of the bargain. I shook my head and flicked away the cigarette. Marc and his crew were maneuvering me around – from the seduction three months ago to the curt orders of tonight – like a scarecrow, no more independent than their mechanical Sam Hain. Predictable is what you are, I told myself bitterly, and as helplessly useful as one of those keys for opening sardine cans.

Before I knew what I was doing I found myself standing on the seat of the concrete bench and gripping one of the horizontal beams that the vine trellises were nailed to. By God, I thought, I'll at least give Archie a scare, make him tangle the puppet strings a little. I chinned myself up and, driving my legs through the brittlely snapping trellis, jackknifed forward and wound up sitting on the beam, brushing dust, splinters and bits of ivy from my hair.

I stood up on the beam cautiously. It dipped here and there, but took my weight without coming unmoored, and in a moment I had flapped and tottered my way to the house wall, and steadied myself by grabbing a drainpipe that, overhead, snaked right past the window I wanted to get to. Not wanting to lose my drunken impetus, I immediately swarmed up it in my best rock-climbing style, leaving most of the skin of my palms on the rough seams of the pipe.

I reached the level of the dim green window and braced a foot on one of the pipe's brackets; then I leaned sideways, gripped the windowsill and made a fearsome wide-eyed, open-mouthed face while scrabbling at the glass with the nails of my free hand.

There was no response – just an uninterrupted, muted hum of machinery. I banged the pane with my forehead and made barking sounds. Still nothing.

I was beginning to get irritable. I dug in my right jacket pocket and pulled out the compact but heavy pistol I always kept there, and knocked in the glass. There were a few glass splinters in the frame when I was done, but I knew my leather jacket would protect me from them.

I brought my other hand quickly to the sill, heaved, and dove into the room, landing on my fingertips and somersaulting across a linoleum floor.

"I'll take over the controls, Arch," I gasped, springing to my feet. "How do you make the thing do a jig? Or – "

I stopped babbling. The room was empty except for a long plastic case on the floor, about three feet deep and connected by tubes to a bank of dimly illuminated dials on one wall.

I sagged. My only concern at this point was to get out of there without having to answer any questions as to why I had thought it worth my while to break into what was doubtless the room housing the building's air-conditioning unit. I hurried toward the metal door in the far wall, but jerked to a halt when I peripherally glimpsed a face under the curved plastic surface of that suddenly-recognizable-as-coffin-sized case.

Sweat sprang out on my temples – I was afraid I'd recognized the face, and I didn't want to look again and confirm it. You didn't see anything, my mind assured me. Go rejoin the party.

I think I'd have taken its advice if its tone hadn't been so like Marc's. I knelt in front of the case and stared into it. As I had thought, the sleeping face inside was Sam Hain's, clearly recognizable in spite of the fact that the head had been shaved of its curly white hair and a couple of green plastic tubes had been poked into the nostrils and taped down beside the jaw.

There didn't seem to be any way to open the case, but I didn't need to – I was certain this was the real Sam Hain, maintained, imprisoned, in dim, lobotomized half-life in this narrow room. So much for Marc's story of a suicide and refusal to be reborn! Marc and his friends had gone to a lot of trouble to make sure Sam was out of the picture without being freed from his old body.

I was still holding the little gun with which I'd broken the window, and I set it down on the plastic case long enough to whip off my jacket; then I picked it up and wrapped it and my hand tightly in the folds of leather. It was a little two-shot pistol I'd had made in 1900 for use on myself if I should ever want to leave a body quickly – its two bullets were .50 caliber hollow-points, pretty sure to do a thorough job at close range – and I didn't grudge Sam one of them.

I braced my wrist with my free hand and pressed the leather-padded muzzle against the section of plastic over Sam's head. "The cage door's open, Sam," I whispered. "Take off." I squeezed the trigger.

There was a jarring thump, but the layers of leather absorbed most of the noise. I untangled the gun and put on the jacket, slapping it to dispel clinging smoke. One glance at the exploded ruin under the holed case was enough to tell me I'd freed Sam, so I tucked the gun back into my jacket pocket and turned to the window.

Getting out wasn't as easy as getting in had been, and I had a gashed finger, a wrenched ankle and a long tear in the left leg of my pants by the time I stood wheezing on the flagstones of the still-empty patio. I combed my hair, straightened my now-perforated jacket, and walked around the corner, through the fire-lit mob in the backyard, to the living room.

It was a superficially warm and hearty scene that greeted me as I let the screen door bang shut at my back; yellow lamplight made the smoke-misty air glow around the knot of well-groomed people clustered around the piano, and the smiling, white-haired figure with his hand on the pianist's shoulder fairly radiated benign fatherly wisdom. A stranger would have needed second sight to know that several of the company, particularly Amelia, were dangerously drunk, and that perhaps a third of them were currently a physical gender that was at odds with their instinctive one, and that their beaming patriarch was, under his plastic skin, a mass of laboring machinery.

Marcus, perched on the arm of the couch, raised his thin eyebrows at my rumpled, dusty appearance, then gave me a little nod and glanced toward the simulacrum. I obediently crossed the room and stood beside the thing.

"Well, Saul!" the machinery said. "It's good to see you, lad. Say, have you thought about what we were discussing earlier in the library?"

"Yes, Sam," I said with as warm a smile as I could muster, "and I can see it all makes perfect sense. We really do need to establish a position of power, so we can defend ourselves against the ephemerals…if that should ever become necessary."

I wanted to gag or laugh. I hope, I mentally told the embryo in Marcus, you may some day appreciate what I'm doing right now to buy you a life.

"I'm glad," nodded the simulacrum. "Some truths are hard to face…but you never were one to flinch, Saul." It smiled at the company. "Well, siblings, another song or two and then we'll get down to the meeting, hmm? Saul and Marcus and I have a few proposals to air."

Mirabile resumed banging away at the piano, and we went through a couple of refrains each of "Nichevo" and "Ich Bin Von Kopf Bis Fus" as a bottle of Hennessy made the circuit and helped the music to lend the evening an air of pleasantly wistful melancholy. I took a glass of cognac, and winced to see Marc working on still another grasshopper.

"Here, Mirabile," muttered Amelia, edging the pianist off the bench. "I learned to play, last life." After finding a comfortable position, she poised her unsteady hands over the keys, and then set to.

And despite all her hard drinking she played beautifully, wringing real heartbreak out of "St. James Infirmary," which we all sang so enthusiastically that we set the glasses to rattling in the cupboard.

We were all singing the last lines when it became clear that Amelia was playing and singing a different song, and our voices faltered away as the new chords moaned out of the piano and Amelia's lyrics countered ours.

She was handling her man's voice as well as she handled the piano, and some of us didn't immediately realize what song it was that she was rendering.

"...*Throw on another log*," she sang, " – *but draw*
    the curtains shut!
For across the icy fields our yellow light
Spills, and has raised a sobbing in the night.

"*Sing louder, friends! Drown out that windy,*
    wavering song
Of childish voices, and step up the beat,
For a rainy pattering, like tiny feet,
Draws nearer every moment. For so very long
They've wandered, wailing in a mournful chorus,
Searching through all of hell and heaven for us."

I don't know whether it was the vapors of the cognac that caused it, or the mood of gentle despair that hung about us like the tobacco smoke, but a couple of voices actually joined her in the nearly whispered refrain:

"And at the close of some unhappy Autumn day,
From their cold, unlighted region,
Treading soft, will come the Legion
Of Lost Children and they'll suck our souls away."

Then a number of things happened simultaneously. Marc's little fist, as he lunged from the couch arm, cracked into Amelia's jaw and sent her and the heavy bench crashing over on the hardwood floor; Mirabile slammed the cover down over the keys, producing one final rumbling chord; the simulacrum just stood and gaped stupidly, and the rest of the company, pale and unmoving, registered varying mixtures of anger, embarrassment and fear.

Marc straightened, shot a look toward the sim, and then glanced furtively at me – and snatched his eyes away immediately when mine met them.

"Get her out of here," he rasped to Mirabile. "Don't be gentle."

"To hell with the songs," said the Sam Hain replica expressionlessly. "It's time for the meeting." I reached into my right jacket pocket. "Just a minute," I said. They all looked up, and I could see a dew of sweat on Marc's forehead – he was wary, even a little scared, and I believed I knew why. "I'll be back in a moment," I finished lamely, and walked into the kitchen.

Just outside the window over the sink was a thermometer, and I cut the screen with a butter knife to reach it. It unsnapped easily from the clamp that held it to the wall, and I pulled the glass tube off and slipped it into my pants pocket. To explain my exit I took a can of beer from the refrigerator and tore the tab off as I strolled back into the living room.

"Sorry to hold everybody up," I said. "We rummies need our crutch."

"Sit down, Saul," said Bill quietly. His pipe lay across his bony knees, and his little-girl fingers were busy stuffing it with black tobacco. "Marc went out back to drag everybody in."

I didn't sit down – for one thing, I found myself vaguely disturbed to see discolored teeth and red, wrinkle-bordered eyes in what should have been the face of an eight-year-old girl – but crossed to Marc's place instead. His creamy green drink was still cold, so I fished the thermometer tube from my pocket and, leaning over to hide the action, snapped it in half and shook the glittering drops of mercury into the drink.

Oddly, I felt only a tired depression as I moved away, and not the sorrow I'd have expected – but perhaps the empathy circuits in all of us were fused and blown out centuries ago, and we don't notice it because we so seldom care to call upon those circuits. The knowledge that my child had been killed two months ago, at any rate, grieved me only a little more than would news of the cancellation of some concert I'd been looking forward to.

For I'd figured it out, of course; the pieces were all there, and it had been Marc's involuntary, worried glance, after that song, that put them all together for me. Rafe, Marc's closest friend in the clan, had shot himself two months ago in an apartment on Lombard Street; and Marc, Amelia had said, was also living in an apartment on that street – the same one, I was certain. Obviously they'd been living together, in accord with Marc's new clan ethics. I wondered with a shudder whether Rafe had been jealous when Marc came down for the street fair.

Probably Marc *had* intended to keep my unborn child as a hostage ... but then Rafe must have got sick or injured or something, and decided to ditch his middle-aged body ... and was Marc going to let his old buddy take his chances with whatever fetus randomness might provide, when there was a healthy one so ready to hand?

And so Marc had taken Rafe's hand – and the gun too, I think, judging from the report that Rafe shot himself twice – and held on until the ruined body was quite still and he could be sure his friend's soul was safely lodged in the month-old fetus that had been my child's.

Standing there by the piano that night, I was certain of all this. At my leisure, since, I have occasionally had sick moments of doubt, and have had to fetch the Laphroaig bottle to dull my ears to any "sobbing in the night."

Marc led in those who'd been out back, many of them still gnawing bones and complaining about being taken from their dinner.

"Shut up now, damn it," Marc told them. "The meeting's going to be a short one this time, you'll be back to your food in ten minutes. Saul and Sam have just got a few ideas to propose."

He nodded to the simulacrum, which stood up, smiled and cleared its throat convincingly. "Siblings," it said, "we all – "

I palmed my little gun and stood up. "Excuse me, Sam," I said, "I'd like to begin, if you don't mind."

"Sit down, Saul," Marc said through clenched teeth.

"No," I said, pointing the gun at him, "you sit down. Don't let your damned drink get warm. I want to open the meeting."

The rest of the clan began showing some interest, hoping for some diverting violence. Marc pursed his lips, then shrugged and sat down, not relishing the idea of losing his current body while it was still so young and usefully good-looking. I smiled inwardly to see him snatch up his glass and down the remainder of his drink at one gulp, and apparently not even notice, under the thick crème de menthe and cream, whatever taste mercury has.

For all I knew, the mercury might just pass through him, as inertly harmless in that form as a wad of bubble gum, but I hoped not – I wanted to throw acid on the wiring of his mind, sand in the clockwork of his psyche, so that, though he might be reborn again and again until the sun goes out, every incarnation would be lived in a different home for the retarded. I hoped – still hope – the mercury could do the job, and with any luck get Rafe too.

"Siblings," I said, "I haven't been around for the last three meetings, but I gather there have been new trends afoot, fostered mainly by him," I jabbed the gun toward Marc, "and *him*," toward the simulacrum. "Quiet, don't interrupt me. For more than a century Sam Hain tried to civilize us, and now these two are eroding his efforts, throwing us back to the cruel, greedy old days of pretending to be gods to the ephemerals… when actually we're a sort of immortal tapeworm in humanity's guts. What's that, Bill? No, I'm not drunk – sit down, Marc, or I swear I'll blow that beautiful face out through the back of your head – no, I'm not drunk, Bill, why? Oh, you're saying if these two are wrecking Sam Hain's teaching, then who do I think the guy with the white beard is? I'll show you."

I raised my arm and pulled the trigger, and the barrel clouted my cheek as the gun slammed back in recoil. My ears were ringing from the unmuffled report and the gunpowder smoke had my eyes watering, and I couldn't see the simulacrum at all.

Then I saw it. It was on its hands and knees in the middle of the rug, and all of its head from the nose upward had been taken out as if by a giant ice-cream scoop. Bits of wire and tubing and color-coded plastic were scattered across the floor, and two little jets of red liquid – artificial blood meant to lend verisimilitude in case of a cut in the cheek – fountained out onto the rug from opposite sides of the head.

The eyes, three-quarters exposed now, clicked rapidly up and down and back and forth in frantic unsynchronized scanning, and the mouth opened: "I'm hurt," the thing quacked, as the automatic damage circuits overrode anything Archie might be trying to do. "I'm hurt. I'm hurt. I'm hurt. I'm – "

I gave it a hard kick in the throat that shattered its voice mechanism and knocked it to the floor. "The real Sam Hain is upstairs," I said quietly, prodding my bruised cheek. "He was being maintained unconscious on a life-support system – and probably would have been forever if I hadn't shot him fifteen minutes ago." Marc stood up. "Give my regards to Rafe when he's born, in six months," I said. After a moment Marc sat down again. I faced the crowd. "Leave the clan," I told them, tossing my gun away. "Take all your money out of DIRE stocks. Stop coming to these horrible meetings and supporting the maniac ravings of people like Marcus and Rafe. Go incognito underground – any of you can afford to live well anywhere, even without your allowances."

No one said anything, so I strode around them to the entry hall and found my helmet. "And when you die this time," I called back as I opened the door, "take the death you've had coming for so long! Let go! The Legion has members enough."

I left the door slightly ajar and trudged down the dark path toward my bike. It started up at the first kick, and the cool night air was so restoring that I snapped my helmet to the sissy bar and let the wind's fingers brush my hair back as the bike and I coursed down the curling road toward the winking lights of Whittier. The headwind found the bullet holes in my jacket and cooled my damp shirt, and by the time I stopped at the traffic signal on Whittier Boulevard my anger had dissipated like smoke from an open-windowed room.

And so I've decided to let go, this time. It occurs to me that we've all been like children repeating eighth grade over and over again, and finally coming to believe that there's nothing beyond it. And when a century goes by and I haven't shown up, they'll say, What could have made him do it? Not realizing the real question is, What stopped preventing him?

Pat Moore

"Is it okay if you're one of the ten people I send the letter to," said the voice on the telephone, "or is that redundant? I don't want to screw this up. 'Ear repair' sounds horrible."

Moore exhaled smoke and put out his Marlboro in the half inch of cold coffee in his cup. "No, Rick, don't send it to me. In fact, you're screwed — it says you have to have ten friends."

He picked up the copy he had got in the mail yesterday, spread the single sheet out flat on the kitchen table and weighted two corners with the dusty salt and pepper shakers. It had clearly been photocopied from a photocopy, and originally composed on a typewriter.

> This has been sent to you for good luck. The original is
> in San Fransisco. You must send it on to ten friend's, who,
> you think need good luck, within 24 hrs of recieving it.

"I could use some luck," Rick went on. "Can you loan me a couple of thousand? My wife's in the hospital and we've got no insurance."

Moore paused for a moment before going on with the old joke; then, "Sure," he said, "so we won't see you at the lowball game tomorrow?"

"Oh, I've got money for *that*." Rick might have caught Moore's hesitation, for he went on quickly without waiting for a dutiful laugh: "Mark 'n' Howard mentioned the chain letter this morning on the radio. You're famous."

> The luck is now sent to you – you will recieve Good Luck within three days of recieving this, provided you send it on. Do not send money, since luck has no price.

On a Wednesday dawn five months ago now, Moore had poured a tumbler of Popov Vodka at this table, after sitting most of the night in the emergency room at – what had been the name of the hospital in San Mateo? Not St. Lazarus, for sure – and then he had carefully lit a Virginia Slims from the orphaned pack on the counter and laid the smoldering cigarette in an ashtray beside the glass. When the untouched cigarette had burned down to the filter and gone out, he had carried the full glass and the ashtray to the back door and set them in the trash can, and then washed his hands in the kitchen sink, wondering if the little ritual had been a sufficient goodbye. Later he had thrown out the bottle of vodka and the pack of Virginia Slims too.

> A young man in Florida got the letter, it was very faded, and he resovled to type it again, but he forgot. He had many troubles, including expensive ear repair. But then he typed ten copy's and mailed them, and he got a better job.

"Where you playing today?" Rick asked.

"The Garden City in San Jose, probably," Moore said, "the six-and-twelve-dollar Hold 'Em. I was just about to leave when you called."

"For sure? I could meet you there. I was going to play at the Bay on Bering, but if we were going to meet there you'd have to shave – "

"And find a clean shirt, I know. But I'll see you at Larry's game tomorrow, and we shouldn't play at the same table anyway. Go to the Bay."

"Naw, I wanted to ask you about something. So you'll be at the Garden City. You take the 280, right?"

> Pat Moore put off mailing the letter and died, but later found it again and passed it on, and received threescore and ten.

"Right."

"If that crapped-out Dodge of yours can get up to freeway speed."

"It'll still be cranking along when your Saturn is a planter somewhere."

"Great, so I'll see you there," Rick said. "Hey," he added with forced joviality, "you're famous!"

> Do not ignore this letter
> ST LAZARUS

"Type up ten copies with your name in it, you can be famous too," Moore said, standing up and crumpling the letter. "Send one to Mark 'n' Howard. See you."

He hung up the phone and fetched his car keys from the cluttered table by the front door. The chilly sea breeze outside was a reproach after the musty staleness of the apartment, and he was glad he'd brought his denim jacket.

He combed his hair in the rearview mirror while the Dodge's old slant-six engine idled in the carport, and he wondered if he would see the day when his brown hair might turn gray. He was still thirty years short of threescore and ten, and he wasn't envying the Pat Moore in the chain letter.

The first half hour of the drive down the 280 was quiet, with a Gershwin CD playing the *Concerto in F* and the pines and green meadows of the Fish and Game Refuge wheeling past on his left under the gray sky, while the pastel houses of Hillsborough and Redwood City marched across the eastern hills. The car smelled familiarly of Marlboros and Doublemint gum and engine exhaust.

Just over those hills, on the 101 overlooking the bay, Trish had driven her Ford Granada over an unrailed embankment at midnight, after a St. Patrick's Day party at Bay Meadows. Moore was objectively sure he would drive on the 101 some day, but not yet.

Traffic was light on the 280 this morning, and in his rearview mirror he saw the little white car surging from side to side in the lanes as it passed other vehicles. Like most modern cars, it looked to Moore like an oversized computer mouse. He clicked up his turn signal lever and drifted over the lane-divider bumps into the right lane.

The white car – he could see the blue Chevy cross on its hood now – swooped up in the lane Moore had just left, but instead of rocketing on past him, it slowed, pacing Moore's old Dodge at sixty miles an hour.

Moore glanced to his left, wondering if he knew the driver of the Chevy – but it was a lean-faced stranger in sunglasses, looking straight at him. In the moment before Moore recognized the thing as a shotgun viewed muzzle-on, he thought the man was holding up a microphone; but instantly another person in the white car had blocked the driver – Moore glimpsed only a purple shirt and long dark hair – and then with squealing tires the car veered sharply away to the left.

Moore gripped the hard green plastic of his steering wheel and looked straight ahead; he was braced for the sound of the Chevy hitting the center-divider fence, and so he didn't jump when he heard the crash – even though the seat rocked under him and someone was now sitting in the car with him, on the passenger side against the door. For one unthinking moment he assumed someone had been thrown from the Chevrolet and had landed in his car.

He focused on the lane ahead and on holding the Dodge Dart steady between the white lines. Nobody could have come through the roof, or the windows; or the doors. Must have been hiding in the back seat all this time, he thought, and only now jumped over into the front. What timing. He was panting shallowly, and his ribs tingled, and he made himself take a deep breath and let it out.

He looked to his right. A dark-haired woman in a purple dress was grinning at him. Her hair hung in a neat pageboy cut, and she wasn't panting.

"I'm your guardian angel," she said. "And guess what my name is."

Moore carefully lifted his foot from the accelerator – he didn't trust himself with the brake yet – and steered the Dodge onto the dirt shoulder. When the car had slowed to the point where he could hear gravel popping under the tires, he pressed the brake; the abrupt stop rocked him forward, though the woman beside him didn't shift on the old green upholstery.

"And guess what my name is," she said again.

The sweat rolling down his chest under his shirt was a sharp tang in his nostrils. "Hmm," he said, to test his voice; then he said, "You can get out of the car now."

In the front pocket of his jeans was a roll of hundred-dollar bills, but his left hand was only inches away from the .38 revolver tucked into the open seam at the side of the seat. But both the woman's hands were visible on her lap, and empty.

She didn't move.

The engine was still running, shaking the car, and he could smell the hot exhaust fumes seeping up through the floor. He sighed, then reluctantly reached forward and switched off the ignition.

"I shouldn't be talking to you," the woman said in the sudden silence. *"She* told me not to. But I just now saved your life. So don't tell me to get out of the car."

It had been a purple shirt or something, and dark hair. But this was obviously not the person he'd glimpsed in the Chevy. A team, twins?

"What's your name?" he asked absently. A van whipped past on the left, and the car rocked on its shock absorbers.

"Pat Moore, same as yours," she said with evident satisfaction. He noticed that every time he glanced at her she looked away from something else to meet his eyes, as if whenever he wasn't watching her she was studying the interior of the car, or his shirt, or the freeway lanes.

"Did you – get threescore and ten?" he asked. Something more like a nervous tic than a smile was twitching his lips. "When you sent out the letter?"

"That wasn't me, that was *her.* And she hasn't got it yet. And she won't, either, if her students kill all the available Pat Moores. You're in trouble every which way, but I like you."

"Listen, when did you get into my car?"

"About ten seconds ago. What if he had backup, another car following him? You should get moving again."

Moore called up the instant's glimpse he had got of the thing in front of the driver's hand – the ring had definitely been the muzzle of a shotgun, twelve-gauge, probably a pistol-grip. And he seized on her remark about a backup car because the thought was manageable and complete. He clanked the gearshift into park, and the Dodge started at the first twist of the key, and he levered it into drive and gunned along the shoulder in a cloud of dust until he had got up enough speed to swing into the right lane between two yellow Stater Brothers trucks.

He concentrated on working his way over to the fast lane, and then when he had got there, his engine roaring, he just watched the rearview mirror and the oncoming exit signs until he found a chance to make a sharp right across all the lanes and straight into the exit lane that swept toward the southbound 85. A couple of cars behind him honked.

He was going too fast for the curving interchange lane, his tires chirruping on the pavement, and he wrestled with the wheel and stroked the brake.

"Who's getting off behind us?" he asked sharply.

"I can't see," she said.

He darted a glance at the rearview mirror, and was pleased to see only a slow-moving old station wagon, far back.

"A station wagon," she said, though she still hadn't turned around. Maybe she had looked in the passenger-side door mirror.

He had got the car back under control by the time he merged with the southbound lanes, and then he braked, for the 85 was ending ahead at a traffic signal by the grounds of some college.

"Is your neck hurt?" he asked. "Can't twist your head around?"

"It's not that. I can't see anything you don't see."

He tried to frame an answer to that, or a question about it, and finally just said, "I bet we could find a bar fairly readily. Around here."

"I can't drink, I don't have any ID."

"You can have a Virgin Mary," he said absently, catching a green light and turning right just short of the college. "Celery stick to stir it with." Raindrops began spotting the dust on the windshield.

"I'm not so good at touching things," she said. "I'm not actually a living person."

"Okay, see, that means what? You're a *dead* person, a ghost?"

"Yes."

Already disoriented, Moore flexed his mind to see if anything in his experience or philosophies might let him believe this, and there was nothing that did. This woman, probably a neighbor, simply knew who he was, and she had hidden in the back of his car back at the apartment parking lot. She was probably insane. It would be a mistake to get further involved with her.

"Here's a place," he said, swinging the car into a strip-mall parking lot to the right. "Pirate's Cove. We can see how well you handle peanuts or something, before you try a drink."

He parked behind the row of stores, and the back door of the Pirate's Cove led them down a hallway stacked with boxes before they stepped through an arch into the dim bar. There were no other customers in the place at this early hour, and the room smelled more like bleach than beer; the teenaged-looking bartender barely gave them a glance and a nod as Moore led the woman across the worn carpet and the parqueted square to a table under a football poster. There were four low stools instead of chairs.

The woman couldn't remember any movies she'd ever seen, and claimed not to have heard about the war in Iraq, so when Moore walked to the bar and came back with a glass of Budweiser and a bowl of popcorn, he sat down and just stared at her. She was easier to see in the dim light from the jukebox and the neon bar-signs than she had been out in the gray daylight. He would guess that she was about thirty – though her face had no wrinkles at all, as if she had never laughed or frowned.

"You want to try the popcorn?" he asked as he unsnapped the front of his denim jacket.

"Look at it so I know where it is."

He glanced down at the bowl, and then back at her. As always, her eyes fixed on his as soon as he was looking at her. Either her pupils were fully dilated, or else her irises were black.

But he glanced down again when something thumped the table and a puff of hot salty air flicked his hair, and some popcorn kernels spun away through the air.

The popcorn remaining in the bowl had been flattened into little white jigsaw-puzzle pieces. The orange plastic bowl was cracked.

Her hands were still in her lap, and she was still looking at him. "I guess not, thanks."

Slowly he lifted his glass of beer and took a sip. That was a powerful raise, he thought, forcing himself not to show any astonishment – though you should have suspected a strong hand. Play carefully here.

He glanced toward the bar; but the bartender, if he had looked toward their table at all, had returned his attention to his newspaper.

"Tom Cruise," the woman said.

Moore looked back at her and after a moment raised his eyebrows.

She said, "That was a movie, wasn't it?"

"In a way." *Play carefully here.* "What did you – is something wrong with your vision?"

"I don't have any vision. No retinas. I have to use yours. I'm a ghost."

"Ah. I've never met a ghost before." He remembered a line from a Robert Frost poem: *The dead are holding something back.*

"Well, not that you could see. You can only see me because… I'm like the stamp you get on the back of your hand at Disneyland; you can't see me unless there's a black light shining on me. *She*'s the black light."

"You're in her field of influence, like."

"Sure. There's probably dozens of Pat Moore ghosts in the outfield, and *she*'s the whole infield. I'm the shortstop."

"Why doesn't… *she* want you to talk to me?" He never drank on days he intended to play, but he lifted his glass again.

"She doesn't want me to tell you what's going to happen." She smiled, and the smile stayed on her smooth face like the expression on a porcelain doll. "If it was up to me, I'd tell you."

He swallowed a mouthful of beer. "But."

She nodded, and at last let her smile relax. "It's not up to me. She'd kill me if I told you."

He opened his mouth to point out a logic problem with that, then sighed and said instead, "Would she know?" She just blinked at him, so he went on, "Would she know it, if you told me?"

"*Oh* yeah."

"How would she know?"

"You'd be doing things. You wouldn't be sitting here drinking a beer, for sure."

"What would I be doing?"

"I think you'd be driving to San Francisco. If I told you – if you asked – " For an instant she was gone, and then he could see her again; but she seemed two-dimensional now, like a projection on a screen – he had the feeling that if he moved to the side he would just see this image of her get narrower, not see the other side of her.

"What's in San Francisco?" he asked quickly.

"Well if you asked me about Maxwell's Demon-n-n-n – "

She was perfectly motionless, and the drone of the last consonant slowly deepened in pitch to silence. Then the popcorn in the cracked bowl rattled in the same instant that she silently disappeared like the picture on a switched-off television set, leaving Moore alone at the table, his face suddenly chilly in the bar's air conditioning. For a moment "air conditioning" seemed to remind him of something, but he forgot it when he looked down at the popcorn – the bowl was full of brown BBs – unpopped dried corn. As he watched, each kernel slowly opened in white curls and blobs until all the popcorn was as fresh-looking and uncrushed as it had been when he had carried it to the table. There hadn't been a sound, though he caught a strong whiff of gasoline. The bowl wasn't cracked anymore.

He stood up and kicked his stool aside as he backed away from the table. She was definitely gone.

The bartender was looking at him now, but Moore hurried past him and back through the hallway to the stormy gray daylight.

What if she had backup? he thought as he fumbled the keys out of his pocket; and, *She doesn't want me to tell you what's going to happen.*

He only realized that he'd been sprinting when he scuffed to a halt on the wet asphalt beside the old white Dodge, and he was panting as he unlocked the door and yanked it open. Rain on the pavement was a steady textured hiss. He climbed in and pulled the door closed, and rammed the key into the ignition –

– when the drumming of rain on the car roof abruptly went silent, and a voice spoke in his head: *Relax. I'm you. You're me.*

And then his mouth opened and the words were coming out of his mouth: "We're Pat Moore, there's nothing to be afraid of." His voice belonged to someone else in this muffled silence.

His eyes were watering with the useless effort to breathe more quickly.

He knew this wasn't the same Pat Moore he had been in the bar with. This was the *her* she had spoken of. A moment later the thoughts had been wiped away, leaving nothing but an insistent pressure of *all-is-well.*

Though nothing grabbed him, he found that his head was turning to the right, and with dimming vision he saw that his right hand was moving toward his face.

But *all-is-well* had for some time been a feeling that was alien to him, and he managed to resist it long enough to make his infiltrated mind form a thought – *she's crowding me out.*

And he managed to think, too, *Alive or dead, stay whole.* He reached down to the open seam in the seat before he could lose his left arm too, and he snatched up the revolver and stabbed the barrel into his open mouth. A moment later he felt the click through the steel against his teeth when he cocked the hammer back. His belly coiled icily, as if he were standing on the coping of a very high wall and looking up.

The intrusion in his mind paused, and he sensed confusion, so he threw at it the thought, *One more step and I blow my head off.* He added, *Go ahead and call this bet, please. I've been meaning to drive the 101 for a while now.*

His throat was working to form words that he could only guess at, and then he was in control of his own breathing again, panting and huffing spit into the gun barrel. Beyond the hammer of the gun he could see the rapid distortions of rain hitting the windshield, but he still couldn't hear anything from outside the car.

The voice in his head was muted now: *I mean to help you.*

He let himself pull the gun away from his mouth, though he kept it pointed at his face, and he spoke into the wet barrel as if it were a microphone. "I don't want help," he said hoarsely.

I'm Pat Moore, and I want help.

"You want to... take over, possess me."

I want to protect you. A man tried to kill you.

"That's your pals," he said, remembering what the ghost woman had told him in the car. "Your students, trying to kill all the Pat Moores – to keep you from taking one over, I bet. Don't joggle me now." Staring down the rifled barrel, he cautiously hooked his thumb over the hammer and then pulled the trigger and eased the hammer down. "I can still do it with one pull of the trigger," he told her as he lifted his thumb away. "So you – what, you put off mailing the letter, and died?"

The letter is just my chain mail. The only important thing about it is my name in it, and the likelihood that people will reproduce it and pass it on. Bombers evade radar by throwing clouds of tinfoil. The chain mail is my name, scattered everywhere so that any blow directed at me is dissipated.

"So you're a ghost too."

A prepared ghost. I know how to get outside of time.

"Fine, get outside of time. What do you need me for?"

You're alive, and your name is mine, which is to say your identity is mine. I've used too much of my energy saving you, holding you. And you're the most compatible of them all – you're a Pat Moore identity squared, by marriage.

"Squared by – " He closed his eyes, and nearly lowered the gun. "Everybody called her Trish," he whispered. "Only her mother called her Pat." He couldn't feel the seat under him, and he was afraid that if he let go of the gun it would fall to the car's roof.

Her mother called her Pat.

"You can't have me." He was holding his voice steady with an effort. "I'm driving away now."

You're Pat Moore's only hope.

"You need an exorcist, not a poker player." He could move his right arm again, and he started the engine and then switched on the windshield wipers.

Abruptly the drumming of the rain came back on, sounding loud after the long silence. She was gone.

His hands were shaking as he tucked the gun back into its pocket, but he was confident that he could get back onto the 280, even with his worn-out windshield wipers blurring everything, and he had no intention of getting on the 101 anytime soon; he had been almost entirely bluffing when he told her, *I've been meaning to drive the 101 for a while now.* But like an alcoholic who tries one drink after long abstinence, he was remembering the taste of the gun barrel in his mouth: That was easier than I thought it would be, he thought.

He fumbled a pack of Marlboros out of his jacket pocket and shook one out.

As soon as he had got onto the northbound 85 he became aware that the purple dress and the dark hair were blocking the passenger-side window again, and he didn't jump at all. He had wondered which way to turn on the 280, and now he steered the car into the lane that would take him back north, toward San Francisco. The grooved interchange lane gleamed with fresh rain, and he kept his speed down to forty.

"One big U-turn," he said finally, speaking around his lit cigarette. He glanced at her; she looked three-dimensional again, and she was smiling at him as cheerfully as ever.

"I'm your guardian angel," she said.

"Right, I remember. And your name's Pat Moore, same as mine. Same as everybody's, lately." He realized that he was optimistic, which surprised him; it was something like the happy confidence he had felt in dreams in which he had discovered that he could fly, and leave behind all earthbound reproaches. "I met *her*, you know. She's dead too, and she needs a living body, and so she tried to possess me."

"Yes," said Pat Moore. "That's what's going to happen. I couldn't tell you before."

He frowned. "I scared her off, by threatening to shoot myself." Reluctantly he asked, "Will she try again, do you think?"

"Sure. When you're asleep, probably, since this didn't work. She can wait a few hours; a few days, even, in a pinch. It was just because I talked to you that she switched me off and tried to do it right away, while you were still awake. *Jumped the gun*," she added, with the first laugh he had heard from her – it sounded as if she were trying to chant in a language she didn't understand.

"Ah," he said softly. "That raises the ante." He took a deep breath and let it out. "When did you ... die?"

"I don't know. Some time besides now. Could you put out the cigarette? The smoke messes up my reception, I'm still partly seeing that bar, and partly a hilltop in a park somewhere."

He rolled the window down an inch and flicked the cigarette out. "Is this how you looked, when you were alive?"

She touched her hair as he glanced at her. "I don't know."

"When you were alive – did you know about movies, and current news? I mean, you don't seem to know about them now."

"I suppose I did. Don't most people?"

He was gripping the wheel hard now. "Did your mother call you Pat?"

"I suppose she did. It's my name."

"Did your... friends, call you Trish?"

"I suppose they did."

I suppose, I suppose! He forced himself not to shout at her. She's dead, he reminded himself, she's probably doing the best she can.

But again he thought of the Frost line: *The dead are holding something back.*

They had passed under two gray concrete bridges, and now he switched on his left turn signal to merge with the northbound 280. The pavement ahead of him glittered with reflected red brake lights.

"See, my wife's name was Patricia Moore," he said, trying to sound reasonable. "She died in a car crash five months ago. Well, a single-car accident. Drove off a freeway embankment. She was drunk." He remembered that the popcorn in the Pirate's Cove had momentarily smelled like spilled gasoline.

"I've been drunk."

"So has everybody. But – you might be her."

"Who?"

"My wife. Trish."

"I might be your wife."

"Tell me about Maxwell's Demon."

"I would have been married to you, you mean. We'd *really* have been Pat Moore then. Like mirrors reflecting each other."

"That's why *she* wants me, right. So what's Maxwell's Demon?"

"It's... she's dead, so she's like a smoke ring somebody puffed out in the air, if they were smoking. Maxwell's Demon keeps her from disappearing like a smoke ring would, it keeps her ..."

"Distinct," Moore said when she didn't go on. "Even though she's got no right to be distinct anymore."

"And me. Through her."

"Can I kill him? Or make him stop sustaining her?" And you, he thought; it would stop him sustaining you. Did I stop sustaining you before? Well, obviously.

Earthbound reproaches.

"It's not a *him*, really. It looks like a sprinkler you'd screw onto a hose to water your yard, if it would spin. It's in her house, hooked up to the air conditioning."

"A sprinkler." He was nodding repeatedly, and he made himself stop. "Okay. Can you show me where her house is? I'm going to have to sleep sometime."

"She'd kill me."

"Pat – Trish – " Instantly he despised himself for calling her by that name. " – you're already dead."

"She can get outside of time. Ghosts aren't really in time anyway, I'm wrecking the popcorn in that bar in the future as much as in the past, it's all just cards in a circle on a table, none in front. None of it's really now or not-now. She could make me not ever – she could take my thread out of the carpet – you'd never have met me, even like this."

"Make you never have existed."

"Right. Never was any *me* at all."

"She wouldn't dare – Pat." Just from self-respect he couldn't bring himself to call her Trish again. "Think about it. If you never existed, then I wouldn't have married you, and so I wouldn't be the Pat Moore squared that she needs."

"If you *did* marry me. *Me*, I mean. I can't remember. Do you think you did?"

She'll take me there, if I say yes, he thought. She'll believe me if I say it. And what's to become of me, if she doesn't? That woman very nearly crowded me right out of the world five minutes ago, and I was wide awake.

The memory nauseated him.

What becomes of a soul that's pushed out of its body, he thought, as *she* means to do to me? Would there be *anything* left of *me,* even a half-wit ghost like poor Pat here?

Against his will came the thought, You always did lie to her.

"I don't know," he said finally. "The odds are against it."

There's always the 101, he told himself, and somehow the thought wasn't entirely bleak. Six chambers of it, hollow-point .38s. Fly away.

"It's possible, though, isn't it?"

He exhaled, and nodded. "It's possible, yes."

"I think I owe it to you. Some Pat Moore does. We left you alone."

"It was my fault." In a rush he added, "I was even glad you didn't leave a note." It's true, he thought. I was grateful.

"I'm glad she didn't leave a note," this Pat Moore said.

He needed to change the subject. *"You're* a ghost," he said. "Can't you make *her* never have existed?"

"No. I can't get far from real places or I'd blur away, out of focus, but she can go way up high, where you can look down on the whole carpet, and – twist out strands of it; bend somebody at right angles to *everything,* which means you're gone without a trace. And anyway, she and her students are all blocked against that kind of attack, they've got ConfigSafe."

He laughed at the analogy. "You know about computers?"

"No," she said emptily. "Did I?"

He sighed. "No, not a lot." He thought of the revolver in the seat, and then thought of something better. "You mentioned a park. You used to like Buena Vista Park. Let's stop there on the way."

Moore drove clockwise around the tall, darkly wooded hill that was the park, while the peaked roofs and cylindrical towers of the old Victorian houses were teeth on a saw passing across the gray sky on his left. He found a parking space on the eastern curve of Buena Vista Avenue, and he got out of the car quickly to keep the

Pat Moore ghost from having to open the door on her side; he remembered what she had done to the bowl of popcorn.

But she was already standing on the splashing pavement in the rain, without having opened the door. In the ashy daylight her purple dress seemed to have lost all its color, and her face was indistinct and pale; he peered at her, and he was sure the heavy raindrops were falling right through her.

He could imagine her simply dissolving on the hike up to the meadow. "Would you rather wait in the car?" he said. "I won't be long."

"Do you have a pair of binoculars?" she asked. Her voice too was frail out here in the cold.

"Yes, in the glove compartment." Cold rain was soaking his hair and leaking down inside his jacket collar, and he wanted to get moving. "Can you … *hold* them?"

"I can't hold anything. But if you take out the lens in the middle you can catch me in it, and carry me."

He stepped past her to open the passenger-side door, and bent over to pop open the glove compartment, and then he knelt on the seat and dragged out his old leather-sleeved binoculars and turned them this way and that in the wobbly gray light that filtered through the windshield.

"How do I get the lens out?" he called over his shoulder.

"A screwdriver, I guess," came her voice, barely audible above the thrashing of the rain. "See the tiny screw by the eyepiece?"

"Oh. Right." He used the small blade from his pocketknife on the screw in the back of the left barrel, and then had to do the same with a similar screw on the forward end of it. The eyepiece stayed where it was, but the big forward lens fell out, exposing a metal cross on the inside; it was held down with a screw that he managed to rotate with the blade-tip – and then a triangular block of polished glass fell out into his palm.

"That's it, that's the lens," she called from outside the car.

Moore's cell phone buzzed as he was stepping backward to the pavement, and he fumbled it out of his jacket pocket and flipped it open. "Moore here," he said. He pushed the car door closed and leaned over the phone to keep the rain off it.

"Hey Pat," came Rick's voice, "I'm sitting here in your Garden City club in San Jose, and I could be at the Bay. Where are you, man?"

The Pat Moore ghost was moving her head, and Moore looked up at her. With evident effort she was making her head swivel back and forth in a clear *no* gesture.

The warning chilled Moore. Into the phone he said, "I'm – not far, I'm at a bar off the 85. Place called the Pirate's Cove."

"Well, don't chug your beer on my account. But come over here when you can."

"You bet. I'll be out of here in five minutes." He closed the phone and dropped it back into his pocket.

"They made him call again," said the ghost. "They lost track of your car after I killed the guy with the shotgun." She smiled, and her teeth seemed to be gone. "That was good, saying you were at that bar. They can tell truth from lies, and that's only twenty minutes from being true."

Guardian angel, he thought. "You killed him?"

"I think so." Her image faded, then solidified again. "Yes."

"Ah. Well – good." With his free hand he pushed the wet hair back from his forehead. "So what do I do with this?" he asked, holding up the lens.

"Hold it by the frosted sides, with the long edge of the triangle pointed at me; then look at me through the two other edges."

The glass thing was a blocky right-triangle, frosted on the sides but polished smooth and clear on the thick edges; obediently he held it up to his eye and peered through the two slanted faces of clear glass.

He could see her clearly through the lens – possibly more clearly than when he looked at her directly – but this was a mirror image: the dark slope of the park appeared to be to the left of her.

"Now roll it over a quarter turn, like from noon to three," she said.

He rotated the lens ninety degrees – but her image in it rotated a full 180 degrees, so that instead of seeing her horizontal he saw her upside down.

He jumped then, for her voice was right in his ear. "Close your eyes and put the lens in your pocket."

He did as she said, and when he opened his eyes again she was gone – the wet pavement stretched empty to the curbstones and green lawns of the old houses.

"You've got me in your pocket," her voice said in his ear. "When you want me, look through the lens again and turn it back the other way."

It occurred to him that he believed her. "Okay," he said, and sprinted across the street to the narrow stone stairs that led up into the park.

His leather shoes tapped the ascending steps, and then splashed in the mud as he took the uphill path to the left. The city was gone now, hidden behind the dense overhanging boughs of pine and eucalyptus, and the rain echoed under the canopy of green leaves. The cold air was musky with the smells of mulch and pine and wet loam.

Up at the level playground lawn the swingsets were of course empty, and in fact he seemed to be the only living soul in the park today. Through gaps between the trees he could see San Francisco spread out below him on all sides, as still as a photograph under the heavy clouds.

He splashed through the gutters that were made of fragments of old marble headstones – keeping his head down, he glimpsed an incised cross filled with mud in the face of one stone, and the lone phrase "in loving memory" on another – and then he had come to the meadow with the big old oak trees he remembered.

He looked around, but there was still nobody to be seen in the cathedral space, and he hurried to the side and crouched to step in under the shaggy foliage and catch his breath.

"It's beautiful," said the voice in his ear.

"Yes," he said, and he took the lens out of his pocket. He held it up and squinted through the right-angle panels, and there was the image of her, upside down. He rotated it counterclockwise ninety degrees and the image was upright, and when he moved the lens away from his eye she was standing out in the clearing.

"Look at the city some more," she said, and her voice now seemed to come from several yards away. "So I can see it again."

One last time, he thought. Maybe for both of us; it's nice that we can do it together.

"Sure." He stepped out from under the oak tree and walked back out into the rain to the middle of the clearing and looked around.

A line of trees to the north was the panhandle of Golden Gate Park, and past that he could see the stepped levels of Alta Vista Park; more distantly to the left he could just make out the green band that was the hills of the Presidio, though the two big piers of the Golden Gate Bridge were lost behind miles of rain; he turned to look southwest, where the Twin Peaks and the TV tower on Mount Sutro were vivid above the misty streets; and then far away to the east the white spike of the Transamerica Pyramid stood up from the skyline at the very edge of visibility.

"It's beautiful," she said again. "Did you come here to look at it?"

"No," he said, and he lowered his gaze to the dark mulch under the trees. Cypress, eucalyptus, pine, oak – even from out here he could see that mushrooms were clustered in patches and rings on the carpet of wet black leaves, and he walked back to the trees and then shuffled in a crouch into the aromatic dimness under the boughs.

After a couple of minutes, "Here's one," he said, stooping to pick a mushroom. Its tan cap was about two inches across, covered with a patch of white veil. He unsnapped his denim jacket and tucked the mushroom carefully into his shirt pocket.

"What is it?" asked Pat Moore.

"I don't know," he said. "My wife was never able to tell, so she never picked it. It's either *Amanita lanei,* which is edible, or it's *Amanita phalloides,* which is fatally poisonous. You'd need a real expert to know which this is."

"What are you going to do with it?"

"I think I'm going to sandbag her. You want to hop back into the lens for the hike down the hill?"

He had parked the old Dodge at an alarming slant on Jones Street on the south slope of Russian Hill, and then the two of them had walked steeply uphill past close-set gates and balconies under tall sidewalk trees that grew straight up from the slanted pavements. Headlights of cars descending Jones Street reflected in white glitter on the wet trunks and curbstones, and in the wakes of the cars the tire tracks blurred away slowly in the continuing rain.

"How are we going to get into her house?" he asked quietly.

"It'll be unlocked," said the ghost. "She's expecting you now."

He shivered. "Is she. Well I hope I'm playing a better hand than she guesses."

"Down here," said Pat, pointing at a brick-paved alley that led away to the right between the Victorian-gingerbread porches of two narrow houses.

They were in a little alley now, overhung with rosebushes and rosemary, with white-painted fences on either side. Columns of fog billowed in the breeze, and then he noticed that they were human forms – female torsos twisting transparently in the air, blank-faced children running in slow motion, hunched figures swaying heads that changed shape like water balloons.

"The outfielders," said the Pat Moore ghost.

Now Moore could hear their voices: *Goddamn car – I got yer unconditional right here – excuse me, you got a problem? – He was never there for me – So I told him, you want it you come over here and take it – Bless me Father, I have died –*

The acid smell of wet stone was lost in the scents of tobacco and jasmine perfume and liquor and old, old sweat.

Moore bit his lip and tried to focus on the solid pavement and the fences. "Where the hell's her place?" he asked tightly.

"This gate," she said. "Maybe you'd better – "

He nodded and stepped past her; the gate latch had no padlock, and he flipped up the catch. The hinges squeaked as he swung the gate inward over flagstones and low-cut grass.

He looked up at the house the path led to. It was a one-story 1920s bungalow, painted white or gray, with green wicker chairs on the narrow porch. Lights were on behind stained-glass panels in the two windows and the porch door.

"It's unlocked," said the ghost.

He turned back toward her. "Stand over by the roses there," he told her, "away from the … the outfielders. I want to take you in in my pocket, okay?"

"Okay."

She drifted to the roses, and he fished the lens out of his pocket and found her image through the right-angle faces, then twisted the lens and put it back into his pocket.

He walked slowly up the path, treading on the grass rather than on the flagstones, and stepped up to the porch.

"It's not locked, Patrick," came a woman's loud voice from inside.

He turned the glass knob and walked several paces into a high-ceilinged kitchen with a black-and-white-tiled floor; a blonde woman in jeans and a sweatshirt sat at a formica table by the big old refrigerator. From the next room, beyond an arch in the white-painted plaster, a steady whistling hiss provided an irritating background noise, as if a teakettle were boiling.

The woman at the table was much more clearly visible than his guardian angel had been, almost aggressively three-dimensional – her breasts under the sweatshirt were prominent and pointed, her nose and chin stood out perceptibly too far from her high cheekbones, and her lips were so full that they looked distinctly swollen.

A bottle of Wild Turkey bourbon stood beside three Flintstones glasses on the table, and she took it in one hand and twisted out the cork with the other. "Have a drink," she said, speaking loudly, perhaps in order to be heard over the hiss in the next room.

"I don't think I will, thanks," he said. "You're good with your hands." His jacket was dripping rainwater on the tiles, but he didn't take it off.

"I'm the solidest ghost you'll ever see."

Abruptly she stood up, knocking her chair against the refrigerator, and then she rushed past him, her Reeboks beating on the floor; and her body seemed to rotate as she went by him, as if she were swerving away from him; though her course to the door was straight. She reached out one lumpy hand and slammed the door.

She faced him again and held out her right hand. "I'm Pat Moore," she said, "and I want help."

He flexed his fingers, then cautiously held out his own hand. "I'm Pat Moore too," he said.

Her palm touched his, and though it was moving very slowly his own hand was slapped away when they touched.

"I want us to become partners," she said. Her thick lips moved in ostentatious synchronization with her words.

"Okay," he said.

Her outlines blurred for just an instant; then she said, in the same booming tone, "I want us to become one person. You'll be immortal, and – "

"Let's do it," he said.

She blinked her black eyes. "You're – agreeing to it," she said. "You're accepting it, now?"

"Yes." He cleared his throat. "That's correct."

He looked away from her and noticed a figure sitting at the table – a transparent old man in an overcoat, hardly more visible than a puff of smoke.

"Is he Maxwell's Demon?" Moore asked.

The woman smiled, baring huge teeth. "No, that's… a soliton. A poor little soliton who's lost its way. I'll show you Maxwell's Demon."

She lunged and clattered into the next room, and Moore followed her, trying simultaneously not to slip on the floor and to keep an eye on her and on the misty old man.

Moore stepped into a parlor, and the hissing noise was louder in here. Carved dark wood tables and chairs and a modern exercise bicycle had been pushed against a curtained bay window in the far wall, and a vast carpet had been rolled back from the dusty hardwood floor and humped against the chair legs. In the high corners of the room and along the fluted top of the window frame, things like translucent cheerleaders' pompoms grimaced and waved tentacles or locks of hair in the agitated air. Moore warily took a step away from them.

"Look over here," said the alarming woman.

In the near wall an air-conditioning panel had been taken apart, and a red rubber hose hung from its machinery and was connected into the side of a length of steel pipe that lay on a TV table. Nozzles on either end of the pipe were making the loud whistling sound.

Moore looked more closely at it. It was apparently two sections of pipe, one about eight inches long and the other about four, connected together by a blocky fitting where the hose was attached, and a stove stopcock stood half-open near the end of the longer pipe.

"Feel the air," the woman said.

Moore cupped a hand near the end of the longer pipe, and then yanked it back – the air blasting out of it felt hot enough to light a cigar. More cautiously he waved his fingers over the nozzle at the end of the short pipe; and then he rolled his hand in the air-jet, for it was icy cold.

"It's not supernatural," she boomed, "even though the air conditioner's pumping room-temperature air. A spiral washer in the connector housing sends air spinning up the long pipe; the hot molecules spin out to the sides of the little whirlwind in there, and it's them that the stopcock lets out. The cold molecules fall into a smaller whirlwind inside the big one, and they move the opposite way and come out at the end of the short pipe. Room-temperature air is a mix of hot and cold molecules, and this device separates them out."

"Okay," said Moore. He spoke levelly, but he was wishing he had brought his gun along from the car. It occurred to him that it was a rifled pipe that things usually come spinning out of, but which he had been ready to dive into. He wondered if the gills under the cap of the mushroom in his pocket were curved in a spiral.

"But this is counter-entropy," she said, smiling again. "A Scottish physicist named Maxwell p-postulay-postul – guessed that a Demon would be needed to sort the hot molecules from the cold ones. If the Demon is present, the effect occurs, and vice versa – if you can make the effect occur you've summoned the Demon. Get the effect, and the cause has no choice but to be present." She thumped her chest, though her peculiar breasts didn't move at all. "And once the Demon is present, he – he – "

She paused, so Moore said, "Maintains distinctions that wouldn't ordinarily stay distinct." His heart was pounding, but he was pleased with how steady his voice was.

Something like an invisible hand struck him solidly in the chest, and he stepped back.

"You don't touch it," she said. Again there was an invisible thump against his chest. "Back to the kitchen."

The soliton old man, hardly visible in the bright overhead light, was still nodding in one of the chairs at the table.

The blonde woman was slapping the wall, and then a white-painted cabinet, but when Moore looked toward her she grabbed the knob on one of the cabinet drawers and yanked it open.

"You need to come over here," she said, "and look in the drawer."

After the things he'd seen in the high corners of the parlor, Moore was cautious; he leaned over and peered into the drawer – but it contained only a stack of typing paper, a felt tip laundry-marking pen, and half a dozen yo-yos.

As he watched, she reached past him and snatched out a sheet of paper and the laundry marker; and it occurred to him that she hadn't been able to see the contents of the drawer until he was looking at them.

I don't have any vision, his guardian angel had said. *No retinas. I have to use yours.*

The woman had stepped away from the cabinet now. "I was prepared, see," she said, loudly enough to be heard out on Jones Street, "for my stupid students killing me. I knew they might. We were all working to learn how to transcend time, but I got there first, and they were afraid of what I would do. So *boom-boom-boom* for Mistress Moore. But I had already set up the Demon, and I had xeroxed my chain mail and put it in addressed envelopes. Bales of them, the stamps cost me a fortune. I came back strong. And I'm going to merge with you now and get a real body again. You accepted the proposal – you said 'Yes, that's correct' – you didn't put out another bet this time to chase me away."

The cap flew off the laundry marker, and then she slapped the paper down on the table next to the Wild Turkey bottle. "Watch me!" she said, and when he looked at the piece of paper, she began vigorously writing on it. Soon she had written PAT in big sprawling letters and was embarked on MOORE.

She straightened up when it was finished. "Now," she said, her black eyes glittering with hunger, "you cut your hand and write with your blood, tracing over the letters. Our name is us, and we'll merge. Smooth as silk through a goose."

Moore slowly dug the pocketknife out of his pants pocket. "This is new," he said. "You didn't do this name-in-blood business when you tried to take me in the car."

She waved one big hand dismissively. "I thought I could sneak up on you. You resisted me, though – you'd probably have tried to resist me even in your sleep. But since you're accepting the inevitable now, we can do a proper contract, in ink and blood. Cut, cut!"

"Okay," he said, and unfolded the short blade and cut a nick in his right forefinger. "*You've* made a new bet now, though, and it's to me." Blood was dripping from the cut, and he dragged his finger over the *P* in her crude signature.

He had to pause halfway through and probe again with the blade-tip to get more freely flowing blood; and as he was painfully tracing the *R* in MOORE, he began to feel another will helping to push his finger along, and he heard a faint drone like a radio carrier-wave starting up in his head. Somewhere he was crouched on his toes on a narrow, outward-tilting ledge with no handholds anywhere, with vast volumes of emptiness below him – and his toes were sliding –

So he added quickly, "And I raise back at you."

By touch alone, looking up at the high ceiling, he pulled the mushroom out of his shirt pocket and popped it into his mouth and bit down on it. Check-and-raise, he thought. Sandbagged. Then he lowered his eyes, and in an instant her gaze was locked onto his.

"What happened?" she demanded, and Moore could hear the three syllables of it chug in his own throat. "What did you do?"

"*Amanita,*" said the smoky old man at the table. His voice sounded like nothing organic – more like sandpaper on metal. "It was time to eat the mushroom."

Moore had resolutely chewed the thing up, his teeth grating on bits of dirt. It had the cold-water taste of ordinary mushrooms, and as he forced himself to swallow it he forlornly hoped, in spite of all his bravura thoughts about the 101 freeway, that it might be the *lanei* rather than the deadly *phalloides*.

"He ate a mushroom?" the woman demanded of the old man. "You never told me about any mushroom! Is it a poisonous mushroom?"

"I don't know," came the rasping voice again. "It's either poisonous or not, though, I remember that much."

Moore was dizzy with the first twinges of comprehension of what he had done. "Fifty-fifty chance," he said tightly. "The Death Cap Amanita looks just like another one that's harmless, both grow locally. I picked this one today, and I don't know which it was. If it's the poison one, we won't know for about twenty-four hours, maybe longer."

The drone in Moore's head grew suddenly louder, then faded until it was imperceptible. "You're telling the truth," she said. She flung out an arm toward the back porch, and for a moment her bony forefinger was a foot long. "Go vomit it up, now!"

He twitched, like someone mistaking the green left-turn arrow for the green light. No, he told himself, clenching his fists to conceal any trembling. Fifty-fifty is better than zero. You've clocked the odds and placed your bet. Trust yourself.

"No good," he said. "The smallest particle will do the job, if it's the poisonous one. Enough's probably been absorbed already. That's why I chose it." This was a bluff, or a guess, anyway, but this time she didn't scan his mind.

He was tense, but a grin was twitching at his lips. He nodded toward the old man and asked her, "Who *is* the lost sultan, anyway?"

"Soliton," she snapped. "He's you, you – dumb-brain." She stamped one foot, shaking the house. "How can I take you now? And I can't wait twenty-four hours just to see if I *can* take you!"

"Me? How is he me?"

"My name's Pat Moore," said the gray silhouette at the table.

"Ghosts are solitons," she said impatiently, "waves that keep moving all-in-a-piece after the living push has stopped. Forward or backward doesn't matter to them."

"I'm from the *future*," said the soliton, perhaps grinning.

Moore stared at the indistinct thing, and he had to repress an urge to run over there and tear it apart, try to set fire to it, stuff it in a drawer. And he realized that the sudden chill on his forehead wasn't from fright, as he had at first assumed, but from profound embarrassment at the thing's presence here.

"I've blown it all on you," the blonde woman said, perhaps to herself even though her voice boomed in the tall kitchen. "I don't have the ... sounds like 'courses' ... I don't have the energy reserves to go after another living Pat Moore *now*. You were perfect, Pat Moore squared – why did you have to be a die-hard suicide fan?"

Moore actually laughed at that – and she glared at him in the same instant that he was punched backward off his feet by the hardest invisible blow yet.

He sat down hard and slid, and his back collided with the stove; and then, though he could still see the walls and the old man's smoky legs under the table across the room and the glittering rippled glass of the windows, he was somewhere else. He could feel the square tiles under his palms, but in this other place he had no body.

In the now-remote kitchen, the blonde woman said, "Drape him," and the soliton got up and drifted across the floor toward Moore, shrinking as it came so that its face was on a level with Moore's.

Its face was indistinct – pouches under the empty eyes, drink-wrinkles spilling diagonally across the cheekbones, petulant lines around the mouth – and Moore did not try to recognize himself in it.

The force that had knocked Moore down was holding him pressed against the floor and the stove, unable to crawl away, and all he could do was hold his breath as the soliton ghost swept over him like a spiderweb.

You've got a girl in your pocket, came the thing's raspy old voice in his ear.

Get away from me, Moore thought, nearly gagging.

Who get away from who?

"I can get another living Pat Moore," the blonde woman was saying, "if I never wasted any effort on you in the first place, if there was never a *you* for me to notice." He heard her take a deep breath. "I can do this."

Her knee touched his cheek, slamming his head against the oven door. She was leaning over the top of the stove, banging blindly at the burners and the knobs, and then Moore heard the triple click of one of the knobs turning, and the faint thump of the flame coming on. He peered up and saw that she was holding the sheet of paper with the ink and blood on it, and then he could smell the paper burning.

Moore became aware that there was still the faintest drone in his head only a moment before it ceased.

"Up," she said, and the ghost was a net surrounding Moore, lifting him up off the floor and through the intangible roof and far away from the rainy shadowed hills of San Francisco.

He was aware that his body was still in the house, still slumped against the stove in the kitchen, but his soul, indistinguishable now from his ghost, was in some vast region where *in front* and *behind* had no meaning, where the once-apparent dichotomy between *here* and *there* was a discarded optical illusion, where comprehension was total but didn't depend on light or sight or perspective, and where even *ago* and *to come* were just compass points; everything was in stasis, for motion had been left far behind with sequential time.

He knew that the long braids or vapor trails that he encompassed and which surrounded him were lifelines, stretching from births in that direction to deaths in the other – some linked to others for varying intervals, some curving alone through the non-sky – but they were more like long electrical arcs than anything substantial; they were stretched across time and space, but at the same time they were coils too infinitesimally small to be perceived, if his perception had been by means of sight; and they were electrons in standing waves surrounding an unimaginable nucleus, which also surrounded them – the universe, apprehended here in its full volume of past and future, was one enormous and eternal atom.

But he could feel the tiles of the kitchen floor beneath his fingertips. He dragged one hand up his hip to the side-pocket of his jacket, and his fingers slipped inside and touched the triangular lens.

No, said the soliton ghost, a separate thing again.

Moore was still huddled on the floor, still touching the lens – but now he and his ghost were sitting on the other side of the room at the kitchen table too, and the ghost was holding a deck of cards in one hand and spinning cards out with the other. The ghost stopped when two cards lay in front of each of them. The Wild Turkey bottle was gone, and the glow from the ceiling lamp was a dimmer yellow than it had been.

"Hold 'Em," the ghost rasped. "Your whole lifeline is the buy-in, and I'm going to take it away from you. You've got a tall stack there, birth to now, but I won't go all-in on you right away. I bet our first seven years – Fudgsicles, our dad flying kites in the spring sunsets, the star decals in constellations on our bedroom ceiling, our mom reading the Narnia books out loud to us. Push 'em out." The air in the kitchen was summery with the pink candy smell of Bazooka gum.

Hold 'Em, thought Moore. I'll raise.

Trish killed herself, he projected at his ghost, *rather than live with us anymore. Drove her Granada over the embankment off the 101. The police said she was doing ninety, with no touch of the brake.* Again he smelled spilled gasoline –

– and so, apparently did his opponent; the pouchy-faced old ghost flickered, but came back into focus. "I make it more," said the ghost, "the next seven. Bicycles, the Albert Payson Terhune books, hiking with Joe and Ken in the oil fields, the Valentine from Teresa Thompson. Push 'em out, or forfeit."

Neither of them had looked at their cards, and Moore hoped the game wouldn't proceed to the eventual arbitrary showdown – he hoped that the frail ghost wouldn't be able to keep sustaining raises.

I can't hold anything, his guardian angel had said.

It hurt Moore, but he projected another raise at the ghost: *When we admitted we had deleted her poetry files deliberately, she said, "You're not a nice man." She was drunk, and we laughed at her when she said it, but one day after she was gone we remembered it, and then we had to pull over to the side of the road because we couldn't see through the tears to drive.*

The ghost was just a smoky sketch of a midget or a monkey now, and Moore doubted it had enough substance even to deal cards. In a faint birdlike voice it said, "The next seven. College, and our old motorcycle, and – "

And Trish at twenty, Moore finished, grinding his teeth and thinking about the mushroom dissolving in his stomach. *We talked her into taking her first drink. Pink gin, Tanqueray with Angostura bitters. And we were pleased when she said, "Where has this been all my life?"*

"All my life," whispered the ghost, and then it flicked away like a reflection in a dropped mirror.

The blonde woman was sitting there instead. "What did you have?" she boomed, nodding toward his cards.

"The winning hand," said Moore. He touched his two face-down cards. "The pot's mine – the raises got too high for him." The cards blurred away like fragments left over from a dream.

Then he hunched forward and gripped the edge of the table, for the timeless vertiginous gulf, the infinite atom of the lifelines, was a sudden pressure from outside the world, and this artificial scene had momentarily lost its depth of field.

"I can twist your thread out, even without his help," she told him. She frowned, and a vein stood out on her curved forehead, and the kitchen table resumed its cubic dimensions and the light brightened. "Even dead, I'm more potent than you are."

She whirled her massive right arm up from below the table and clanked down her elbow, with her forearm upright; her hand was open.

Put me behind her, Pat, said the Pat Moore ghost's remembered voice in his ear.

He made himself feel the floor tiles under his hand and the stove at his back, and then he pulled the triangular lens out of his pocket; when he held it up to his eye he was able to see himself and the blonde woman at the table across the room, and the Pat Moore ghost was visible upside down behind the woman. He rotated the glass a quarter turn, and she was now upright.

He moved the lens away and blinked, and then he was gripping the edge of the table and looking across it at the blonde woman, and at her hand only a foot away from his face. The fingerprints were like comb-tracks in clay. Peripherally he could see the slim Pat Moore ghost, still in the purple dress, standing behind her.

"Arm-wrestling?" he said, raising his eyebrows. He didn't want to let go of the table, or even move – this localized perspective seemed very frail.

The woman only glared at him out of her irisless eyes. At last he leaned back in the chair and unclamped the fingers of his right hand from the table-edge; and then he shrugged and raised his right arm and set his elbow beside hers. With her free hand she picked up his pocketknife and hefted it. "When this thing hits the floor, we start." She clasped his hand, and his fingers were numbed as if from a hard impact.

Her free hand jerked, and the knife was glittering in a fantastic parabola through the air, and though he was braced all the way through his torso from his firmly planted feet, when the knife clanged against the tiles the massive power of her arm hit his palm like a falling tree.

Sweat sprang out on his forehead, and his arm was steadily bending backward – and the whole world was rotating too, narrowing, tilting away from him to spill him, all the bets he and his ghost had made, into zero.

In the car the Pat Moore ghost had told him, *She can bend somebody at right angles to* everything, *which means you're gone without a trace.*

We're not sitting at the kitchen table, he told himself; we're still dispersed in that vaster comprehension of the universe.

And if she rotates me ninety degrees, he was suddenly certain, I'm gone.

And then the frail Pat Moore ghost leaned in from behind the woman, and clasped her diaphanous hand around Moore's; and together they were Pat Moore squared, their lifelines linked still by their marriage, and he could feel her strong pulse in supporting counterpoint to his own.

His forearm moved like a counterclockwise second hand in front of his squinting eyes as the opposing pressure steadily weakened. The woman's face seemed in his straining sight to be a rubber mask with a frantic animal trapped inside it, and when only inches separated the back of her hand from the formica tabletop, the resistance faded to nothing, and his hand was left poised empty in the air.

The world rocked back to solidity with such abruptness that he would have fallen down if he hadn't been sitting on the floor against the stove.

Over the sudden pressure release ringing in his ears, he heard a scurrying across the tiles on the other side of the room, and a thumping on the hardwood planks in the parlor.

The Pat Moore ghost still stood across the room, beside the table; and the Wild Turkey bottle was on the table, and he was sure it had been there all along.

He reached out slowly and picked up his pocketknife. It was so cold that it stung his hand.

"Cut it," said the ghost of his wife.

"I can't cut it," he said. Barring hallucinations, his body had hardly moved for the past five or ten minutes, but he was panting. "You'll die."

"I'm dead already, Pat. This – " She waved a hand from her shoulder to her knee " – isn't any good. I should be gone." She smiled. "I think that was the *lanei* mushroom."

He knew she was guessing. "I'll know tomorrow."

He got to his feet, still holding the knife. The blade, he saw, was still folded out.

"Forgive me," he said awkwardly. "For everything."

She smiled, and it was almost a familiar smile. "I forgave you in midair. And you forgive me too."

"If you ever did anything wrong, yes."

"Oh, I did. I don't think you noticed. Cut it."

He walked back across the room to the arch that led into the parlor, and he paused when he was beside her.

"I won't come in with you," she said, "if you don't mind."

"No," he said. "I love you, Pat."

"Loved. I loved you too. That counts. Go."

He nodded and turned away from her.

Maxwell's Demon was still hissing on the TV table by the disassembled air conditioner, and he walked to it one step at a time, not looking at the forms that twisted and whispered urgently in the high corners of the room. One seemed to be perceptibly more solid than the rest, but all of them flinched away from him.

He had to blink tears out of his eyes to see the air-hose clearly, and when he did, he noticed a plain on-off toggle switch hanging from wires that were still connected to the air-conditioning unit. He cut the hose and switched off the air conditioner, and the silence that fell then seemed to spill out of the house and across San Francisco and into the sky.

He was alone in the house.

He tried to remember the expanded, timeless perspective he had participated in, but his memory had already simplified it to a three-dimensional picture, with himself floating like a bubble in one particular place.

Which of the … jet trails or arcs or coils was mine? he wondered now. How long is it?

I'll be better able to guess tomorrow, he thought. At least I know it's there, forever – and even though I didn't see which one it was, I know it's linked to another.

Fifty Cents

James P. Blaylock & Tim Powers

ENCHILADAS, Lyle thought. Sonora style, like you get out here away from the coast.

He listened to the engine of the old blue Fairlane as he sped east down Interstate 10, into the glare of the desert. The engine was shaking perceptibly, missing a stroke — probably a fouled spark plug. But he had spare spark plugs, and tools. He even had a spare starter-motor, alternator and water pump, just in case, in the trunk. The thing about old cars was that you could pretty much keep them going forever if you didn't outright kill them. That was ironic when you thought about it – newer cars were as fragile as hothouse flowers.

He had rebuilt the Fairlane's engine a few years back, and had some transmission work done, and there were a couple of weeks when a bad coil had given him fits, but the car had never been towed while he owned it, and it had never left him stranded. With any luck it would be the last vehicle he would ever need. A car wasn't infinitely fixable, of course, but who cared about the infinite? Time and chance happened to cars just as much as they happened to people, but if you were well-prepared you could get past most of the obstacles, until the last one.

He had filled up the tank in Cabazon, and he wouldn't be surprised if he got all the way out into Arizona today; there were lots of thrift stores and used bookstores in Arizona.

He'd know the book when he saw it. *The Golden Treasury of Songs and Lyrics*, selected by Francis T. Palgrave. Not today, probably, but one day. When it came to finding old books you usually stumbled on them by chance, like so many things out here.

He could see Mount San Gorgonio now in the rearview mirror, becoming more distant with every mile, and within a few minutes he would leave it behind over the horizon and start the long haul into some real desert, out through Coachella and Desert Center and on into Blythe. There was a Mexican restaurant in Quartzsite, he recalled, just twenty minutes into Arizona, that served good enchiladas, and if he held it to sixty miles an hour, which was plenty fast enough for him, he would pull in around noon; and he hadn't checked the Quartzsite thrift-stores in months. Then he might very well angle on up Parker way for a look, and back home again along Highway 62. He would cross the river twice that way.

The air was clear out in the desert, almost like no air at all, and the sky was a deep cloudless blue. He rolled the window down and let the warm air blow through the car, sluicing out the old smells of map-paper and gun-oil with the timeless scents of hot stone and creosote. He wondered whether you could still buy the old burlap water bags that you strapped to the front bumper. There was something about that water, which always tasted a little like burlap and maybe a little like exhaust, that was better than just about anything.

A big tumbleweed came blowing along the right shoulder of the highway now, and a gust of wind sent it rollicking across in front of the Fairlane. It bounced once before clipping his front fender and rolling straight across the hood, showering the windshield with broken twigs. For a moment he couldn't see a damned thing, but the highway was empty ahead of him anyway, and he held the car in the lane, and within half a second the windshield was clear again. And then he could.

He saw a roadside phone booth up ahead on the left, still a couple of hundred feet away, and there was a man standing beside it, though there was no car. Put up a phone booth anywhere on earth, Lyle thought, and somebody will need to make a call there.

He checked his rearview mirror and then pressed the brake, eased across the oncoming lane and pulled off onto the shoulder, rolling to a stop just on the far side of the booth.

The man looked like a desert prospector of some kind – grizzled white hair and beard, stained khaki pants and a T-shirt, red suspenders. His pant legs were rolled up, and he had on a pair of work boots that had seen some hard times. He was a big man, tall and heavy, obviously well fed. The wind blew his white hair like streamers of old newspaper caught in a fence.

"Need a lift?" Lyle called through the open window. He switched off the engine, and the desert was dead quiet except for the whisper of wind.

The man peered around the phone booth at him indecisively, clearly puzzled, although it didn't seem to be Lyle's question that had him snowed. His whole face showed a deep confusion, like a man who had just waked up in unfamiliar surroundings and hadn't remembered yet where he was or why he was there.

Nut case, Lyle thought, but all the more reason to give him a lift.

"Nope," the man said abruptly. "You got a couple of quarters for the phone? Mine don't work." He had a voice like a shovel in a gravel pit, but it was airy and a little high, as if there was just a shade of helium in the mix.

"Probably bent," Lyle said, leaning away to open the glove box. He took out a little leather coin purse and unsnapped it, digging out a couple of quarters and then clicking it shut, tossing it back in and closing the glove box. For a moment he considered digging under the driver's seat too, but decided that quarters would do.

"Name's Lyle," he called to the man as he levered open the door and stepped out onto the packed shoulder sand. "George Lyle." He trudged up to the booth, holding out the two coins on the palm of his hand.

The man stared back at him, as if names in general meant nothing to him. He didn't take the quarters. On the other side of the highway a little wind devil spun up out of the desert, whirling toward them across the broad pavement, and as it swept over them Lyle could hear sand grains ping against the metal phone-booth hood.

"You got one of them cellulite phones?" the man asked, oblivious to it. The wind devil whirled away past them and out of existence.

"No, sorry," Lyle said, repressing a smile. "I don't know much about that kind of thing." He waved his open hand. "Try these two quarters on for size, Bub."

The man took the coins awkwardly, as if he had arthritis. His fingers were cold, Lyle noticed. Imminent heatstroke? It wasn't a hot day, especially, not for the desert, but it was a good eighty degrees or more and the man must have walked a ways; Lyle couldn't see a broken-down car anywhere ahead, and he hadn't passed any in the last hour or so. "You feeling all right?" he asked. The man was standing there looking at the coins, as if he still wasn't quite sure about something. "I'll be happy to give you a lift. East or west, doesn't matter a damn bit. I'm just out … on a scavenger hunt."

"I got a call to make," the man said, turning around and feeding the coins into the slot. "I've got to talk to my daughter."

Lyle heard him say this clearly enough, although the man by now seemed to be talking to the wind. Slowly he pushed the buttons, hesitating between each. He started to push a button and then abandoned it for another one as if digging the number out of the deep recesses of his mind. He held the receiver tight to his ear finally and stood looking east toward where the Chuckwalla Mountains stood out against the blue like an etching. Above the mountains were five white vapor trails, as if God were fixing to write music in the sky.

Lyle heard the *boo-dee-weet* of a missed connection.

"Can't get through yet," the man muttered, hanging up the phone. He picked the quarters out of the coin-return slot and idly rattled them in his right fist like dice, and then turned away from the telephone and blinked at Lyle, as if he had forgotten that he wasn't alone. "Thanks for the kindness," he said awkwardly. "Name's Swinger Campbell."

"Glad to meet you," Lyle said, and held out his hand again, hoping the man would realize he hadn't given back the two quarters – But Campbell didn't move to shake his hand, just licked his lips and looked east again.

"I was a good hard-rock silver miner in them days."

"Well I'm happy to give you a lift. You can tell me your story in the car. That way you won't get sandblasted by this wind."

"Broke a ton of rock and drank a quart of whiskey every day. It was our way of life."

"I'll bet it was," Lyle said.

"We had a claim up in the Panamints, me and Wino Larsen and Shave-and-Lotion MacDuff." He laughed a little now. "By God we were as hard as the rocks we busted, and that's the damned truth. I'll have to owe you that fifty cents."

"I'll put it on the tab," Lyle said. Oh well, he thought, less than a dollar at least. "Whyn't you get in the car, Swinger? Take a load off. I'll run you up to Desert Center or wherever else. Hell, I've got nothing better to do than give a man a lift. We can hash it over in the car."

But Swinger Campbell had started walking away, not down the highway, but straight out into the desert, and within seconds he was in among the Joshua trees and greasewood, his form rippling in the heat haze rising from the desert sand and rock. Lyle stood for a moment watching him, undecided, but then wearily set out after him. He couldn't just let the man walk to his death, for God's sake.

The ground was fairly hard, but was rocky, and he had to pick his way. And a hundred feet from the highway there was a dry wash, where the sand was softer, and it slowed him down even more. The wind gusted around him, and he turned away, shielding his face from blowing sand, and when he straightened up again he saw that Campbell was already a surprising distance ahead, farther than seemed possible. Lyle turned to look back toward the car. He hadn't come more than a hundred feet, and already Campbell seemed to have covered three or four times that distance.

"Swinger!" Lyle shouted, cupping his hands to his mouth, but either Campbell didn't hear or he didn't care. The heat haze was obviously distorting things, because all Lyle could see now were Campbell's black boots rising and falling and the crossed red lines of his suspenders. Then he disappeared from sight altogether, hidden for a moment by a big Joshua tree. He reappeared momentarily, then disappeared again.

There was no way Lyle was going to catch him. Apparently Swinger hadn't been kidding about being as hard as the rocks he busted, because he was moving like a damned coyote. Lyle trudged back to the phone booth and the car; he could at least call the Highway Patrol and tell them to send someone out with some kind of off-road vehicle...

Of course Swinger Campbell might not be crazy, or sick either. He might have a shack a few miles out there, and this could well be the closest phone. There were plenty of shacks out in the desert, scattered across the hundreds of miles, mostly cinderblock cubes with aluminum patios hung on the side for a little shade. Now and then you'd see one with an old broken-down windmill alongside.

There was no sign of Campbell at all now, nor of any shack, either, just unending desert. Lyle opened the Fairlane's passenger-side door and fetched two more quarters out of the purse in the glove box, but when he walked back to the pay phone and lifted the receiver, he could hear nothing.

Campbell at least got sounds out of it, Lyle thought, and dutifully dropped his two quarters into the slot. He heard them clank somewhere inside the box, but still no sound came from the receiver. He might as well be holding a rock to his ear. And when he worked the coin-return lever, nothing appeared in the slot. He hung the receiver back on its hook and made himself walk away from it without getting angry.

Lyle climbed into the parked Fairlane, started up the engine, and waited as two cars sped past, going like there was no tomorrow. Then he crossed back over into the eastbound lane and pushed it up to sixty again.

Restore some random guidance to the day, he thought ten minutes later when he saw the hitchhiker. Like with the book he was after: a directed search finds nothing. He swung the wheel to the right and pulled to a stop so close that the young man in the denim jacket just had to lean forward and take hold of the door handle. Again there was no parked car in sight. A day for lost souls.

The boy appeared to be in his early twenties, and he fumbled a pack of Camel non-filters out of his shirt pocket as soon as he had sat down and pulled the door closed. "You, uh, got a light?" he said in a high, nasal voice. He seemed to be wary of Lyle – but that was only sensible, being picked up by a stranger.

"Cigarette lighter on the dash," Lyle said over his shoulder as he looked behind and accelerated back onto the pavement.

The cigarette pack wavered in the pale hands. "I, uh – guess I've quit. You want one?"

"Sure, thanks." Lyle took the pack with his right hand and tapped one out against the wheel, then put the pack down on the seat and pushed the lighter button in. A moment later it popped back out again, and he pulled the lighter out and held the tiny red coils to the end of the cigarette.

"You're welcome, Mr. Lyle."

Lyle made himself keep his eyes on the road. Probably this kid did electrical work, and had been to his store in Fontana. "All right," said Lyle around his newly lit cigarette, "you know my name – so who are you?"

The young man didn't answer for several seconds, not until Lyle finally turned to squint at him. Then he said, "I'm you. From the future."

Lyle exhaled one syllable of surprised laughter. "Oh – oh, right? The future? You don't look anything like me. What do you do, get new bodies in the future?"

The young man shifted uneasily on the seat, and the shoulders of his worn denim jacket heaved in a shrug. "Sometimes." He kept brushing his lanky brown hair back to touch his forehead, gingerly, as if he'd been stung there.

Beyond the dusty windshield the Mojave Desert spread out to either side of the highway. Lyle reflected that this was pretty much the sort of thing he hoped for, in his long receptive drives – random input, rolling dice. "Okay, if you're me, what was my favorite restaurant back when I lived in Tucson?"

"I don't remember a lot of old stuff."

"I'd think you'd remember the camarones."

"Don Juan's. It was called Don Juan's."

"No. La Perlita. Was that gonna be your next guess?"

"Yes." There was an edge of defiance in the nasal voice. "You've got a gun under your seat. It's a .38 Special, Smith and Wesson, loaded with Hydra-Shok hollow-points." He turned to look squarely at Lyle for the first time. The wind through the open window was blowing his hair around his narrow face. "You've never been to Tucson."

Lyle's heart was thumping in his suddenly cold chest, but he forced a laugh. "I sold that gun. All I carry under the seat now is a Thomas Brothers map book – see?" He leaned forward over the steering wheel to reach under the seat with his left hand, and when he sat back again he was holding the .38 pointed across his lap at his companion. His right arm was straight, holding the wheel at the top. "I'm gonna pull over, sonny, and you're going to step out of the car."

Had this kid glimpsed the gun when he'd climbed in? – but he wouldn't have been able to tell what it was loaded with. He must somehow have seen the car before, searched it while Lyle had been in some store or diner or swap-meet; and he could have learned Lyle's name then, from the registration in the glove box.

The young man giggled nervously. "You can't kill me now."

"Nobody's killing anybody. I just don't want your company."

"Sometimes you can't choose, Mr. Lyle." He shrugged, holding his hands up as if to imply that there was nothing he could do about anything. "Look, I'm sorry. This is all my fault. I won't bother you again."

Roadside gravel was popping and grinding under the car's tires now, and the brakes were squealing. Dust obscured the view behind. No buildings or signs broke up the stony landscape that stretched away to remote mountains in the south, and the road ahead was as empty as the sky. This was as desolate a spot as the place where Lyle had picked him up. The young man opened the door and leaned forward, ready to step out.

"What is your name, by the way?" Lyle said, still pointing the revolver at him as the Fairlane rocked to a halt.

The young man paused, one foot on the dirt outside. "I told you," he said, staring out at the desert. "Albert Erlich. I won't see you again. I'm sorry for all the hassle. I hope you're all right. I was… desperate, as I recall." He looked back over his shoulder at Lyle and grinned, miserably. "Well, you take the high road and I'll take the low road, right?"

"How did you know about the gun?"

Albert Erlich stepped down and closed the door. Through the open window he said, "I've seen it before." He exhaled and stepped away from the car to look back the way they'd come, his hands shoved in the pockets of his denim jacket now. "A couple of times."

Lyle considered asking him when this had been, but he knew the answer would just be more nonsense.

"Goodbye, Albert," he said instead, and when Albert had closed the door Lyle drove along the shoulder for dozen feet or so, raising dust, even though he couldn't get back into the lane until a bus had roared on past him, just because he suddenly wanted very badly to get away from Albert Erlich.

When he did gun the old car up into the clear lane in the bus's wake, he leaned forward to tuck the revolver back under the seat, and he gasped at a sudden pain in his stomach. Ulcers? The enchiladas should settle that question, for better or worse.

I'll have to make that call, he thought. *Crazy old guy, calls himself Swinger Campbell, wandering around in the desert north of the 10, near that phone booth that's a hundred miles from anywhere.* And ideally he'd find a thrift store somewhere, a used bookstore, a yard sale; the *Golden Treasury*, squat little book issued with a yellow dust jacket, and if the dust jacket was gone the binding was gray cloth with silver stamping on the spine.

Ten minutes later he saw the figure of another hitchhiker rippling in the heat-waves ahead, and without thinking he lifted his foot from the accelerator – again there was no car in sight on the shoulder – and when he had coasted to within a few hundred feet of the figure, he recognized the denim jacket and the stringy brown hair. It wasn't another hitchhiker, it was the same one. Albert Erlich again.

Lyle's foot had touched the brake pedal before he had even consciously decided to stop. The backs of his hands were chilled on the steering wheel in spite of the hard sunlight through the windshield, and his ribs tingled as if he had soda water for blood.

Nobody's even passed me, Lyle thought, since I made the kid get out of the car.

For a moment he earnestly dredged his memory for some recollection of having turned the car around; but the sun was still in the morning half of the empty sky ahead of him. You didn't turn around, he told himself. God help you, you didn't.

There were no vehicles behind him, so it didn't matter that he hit the brakes too hard because he was leaning forward again to get the revolver. For a moment after the car rocked to a halt in a cloud of dust, he couldn't see Erlich at all; then he could see the lean figure standing very close, with one hand spread and raised in a questioning gesture.

Lyle held the gun out of sight by his left thigh, and nodded; and the door was pulled open and Erlich leaned in, gripping the roof of the car as if to steady it.

"You drive like you're mad about something," he said in the remembered nasal voice. "Let me get my friend." He straightened up and turned around, and Lyle heard him yell, "Swinger! Hey, Swinger, our ride's here!" The flat voice didn't seem to carry at all in the desert air, and there were no echoes.

"Swinger Campbell," said Lyle in a careful, conversational tone.

Erlich crouched beside the open passenger-side door. "Right, that's the guy," he said, squinting out at the desert. "He's gone. He was just here a second ago. He's looking for a phone booth."

"Has to," Lyle began, but he was out of breath. He inhaled deeply, then said, "Has to call his daughter."

"Right. Oh well." Erlich climbed into the car and pulled the door closed, then fished a pack of Camels out of his jacket pocket and peeled off the wrapper and the foil.

Lyle sniffed – the young man's breath reeked of onions and salsa and enchilada sauce.

Lyle heard himself ask, "Who *are* you?" He was pleased that his voice was steady, so he ventured to go on. "Last time you said you were me, from the future."

"Did I? Last time? Actually – " Erich's voice was solemn, " – I'm your father, from the past."

"*Goddammit – *"

"Whoa, watch your driving! My name's Albert Erlich!"

"I know that, you told me that, I meant…"

"Jesus, you gonna shoot me?"

Lyle realized that he had raised the gun and pointed it across his lap. "I hope not."

"I didn't catch *your* name," said Erlich, apparently not cowed by the sight of the gun.

"You know it," said Lyle hoarsely. "Just like you know I've never been to Tucson. Just like you know this is a Smith and Wesson .38 Special, loaded with Hydra-Shok hollow-point rounds."

"Sounds like they're full of water, hydra shock," said Erlich absently, looking out at the desert sweeping past. "Well, Tucson's no big deal. So remind me?"

"Remind you of what?"

"Your name. I can't just call you Don Juan."

Lyle sighed wearily and took his foot off the gas pedal. The car had got up to eighty miles an hour. "Lyle. George Lyle."

"We were getting along so well at first, Mr. Lyle. My fault, I'm man enough to admit it."

"How did you – get here ahead of me? I dropped you off ten miles back."

"Oh." Erlich shook his head. "Just once more?"

"How did you get here so fast?"

"Here?" said Erlich, suddenly angry. "Here from…from *there?* I didn't, you – " He was scratching his forehead again. *"You* should know how I – and what did you do to that old Swinger guy? *You* get to drive *forward*, and we – "

Erlich thrashed suddenly in the seat, perhaps intending to attack Lyle; and then Lyle's wrist was twisted painfully as a brief, deafening explosion compressed the air in the car.

I shot him. Oh my God, Lyle thought, and the car slewed in the lane as he gaped at the figure of the young man beside him.

But there was a hole in the door panel; and Albert Erlich was sitting stiffly in the seat with no blood visible on him.

Lyle's hands were shaking; he dropped the pistol onto the floor, and used both hands to steer the car toward the shoulder. Gunpowder smoke burned in his nose. "I'm sorry," he was saying, though because of the ringing in his ears he could hear his own voice only in the bones of his head. "I'm sorry, I didn't mean to shoot – "

"I know, I know!" Erlich said loudly. "Just let me out, and then you can go kill *everybody*."

When the car stopped, Erlich got out without a word, and slammed the door; and as Lyle once again steered the old car onto the asphalt, panting with what he supposed was mainly relief, he could hear the young man behind him calling, out toward the desert, "Swinger? Hey, Swinger?"

Lyle was still shaking, and consciously watching the speedometer; he could imagine coasting to a stop without being aware of it, or distractedly gunning the old vehicle up to impossible speeds.

After five miles or so he saw another figure ahead to the right, out in the desert. It was an older man, standing beside an aluminum Edison relay shed some distance from the highway down a dirt track. Mercifully, it was clearly not Swinger Campbell. Lyle didn't even slow down, and anyway the figure stepped behind the shed as he drove past.

The Colorado River was as incongruous as he remembered it – water flowing in a line from north to south through the desert ahead of him, cold and blue-green under the sky – a true border, truer than any simple demarcation laid out by surveyors. The concrete bridge over it seemed to arch over the blue to a different world.

The old Ford Fairlane rumbled up the slope of the bridge, and in the moment when the car was barrelling over the crest he glanced around at the river and the land ahead. Though the landscape behind him was barren, on the far side of the river the desert was patched with irrigated fields, squares and disks of green.

But the irrigated tracts were clustered by the river, and soon he had driven through them and on into deeper desert. He was glad to see the highway sign ahead.

Quartzsite, the green sign said, *Food – Gas – Lodging,* and Lyle pulled off the interstate and turned right onto the dusty main street, where the first thing he saw was a Goodwill thrift store in a run-down strip mall.

He slowed down, assessing it. There were weedy flowerbeds with big lumps of white rock in them, meant for decoration proba-bly, and the stores all had some kind of silver film over the windows to keep out the sun. A big, ragged sheet of it was peeling off one of the thrift store windows, giving it a desolate look, but desolate or not, it might be the place.

His wife had given him Palgrave's *Golden Treasury* on his birth-day, in 1960. It had got lost somehow when he had sold the house in Adelanto in '88, after the lung cancer killed her. It was his own care-lessness that cost him the book, and he hadn't even noticed the loss until a year or so ago, but he'd been devoting his time to searching for the *Golden Treasury* ever since, dropping into thrift stores and bookstores along the highway. *Time and chance,* he thought again, and sighed heavily. Phyllis had had a hell of a nice voice when he met her, back when they were young. She knew enough show tunes to fill a shoe box, and every now and then he had tried to help out on their old piano, but he wasn't worth much in that way, and he had left the piano to the new owners when he'd sold the house.

He would check the book section in this Goodwill – and he'd call the Highway Patrol – but right now he needed several beers to calm him down, along with lunch. The beers would be medicine, to slow his alarming heartbeat, which hadn't really throttled back since the damned gun had gone off. How the hell had the gun gone off? It had been a case of nerves. He shouldn't have been holding the thing, let alone had a finger on the trigger, for God's sake. And he shouldn't have picked up Erlich the second time and set himself up for something like that.

There was the Mexican restaurant on the corner past the Goodwill, and he had turned into the parking lot, switched off the engine, and got out of the car before he looked at the sign over the door and noticed the name of the place.

Don Juan's.

He opened the door but didn't get out, and after a while he pulled his shirt out from under his belt, picked up the revolver from the floor and tucked it into his waistband, right behind his belt buckle. Then he took the last two quarters out of the coin purse in the glove box – tip money, if he needed something other than bills. When he got out of the car he smoothed his now-untucked shirt over the angularity of the gun. It didn't show.

He locked the car door and walked across the sun-softened asphalt parking lot to the restaurant. Before he went in he looked back at the car, and from this angle he could see the hole where the bullet had punched through the door. Christ, he had shot his own car. He pulled open the restaurant door, clanging a set of bells hung on the inside of it.

The restaurant was dark inside, and cool, and it smelled just as it should, like beer and salsa and corn tortillas, and a little like mildewy air circulated through a swamp cooler. A middle-aged waitress motioned him in and waved him to a booth.

"Budweiser," he said to her when he had sat down on the side facing the front door and she had laid a menu in front of him. "Make it two, please."

"Hot out there?" she asked.

He exhaled, as if he'd been holding his breath, and smiled at her. "Not bad yet. Give it a couple of hours, though." She looked a bit like his wife Phyllis. More than a little bit. She had that sparkle in her eye and the same who-gives-a-damn hair.

"Anything to eat?" she asked, glancing at the menu on the table.

There it was again on the front of the menu: Don Juan's. Probably Erlich was familiar with this place, and had pulled the name out of his hat.

He pushed the menu away. "A couple of cheese enchiladas, please," he said, "with beans and rice."

"Coming up," she said, picking up the menu and walking away toward the kitchen.

There were dividers between the booths, wooden slats and potted plants, but he could see enough of the restaurant to know that the place was mostly empty. There was someone, a man, over across the way, just the white hair on the top of his head visible from here, and he heard another man's voice saying something to someone, probably to the waitress, but he couldn't see them either. He sat back and stretched his legs out under the table. Here came his beer, right on time, God bless it. The waitress set both bottles down and poured half of one into a small glass. The bottles were sweating heavily, and right now he couldn't think of anything that looked better.

He saw that her nametag read *Donna*. "Thanks, Donna," he said, toasting her before drinking off half the beer in the glass. He set it down and sat back again, feeling considerably better. The pistol's hammer pinched the flesh on his stomach, and he wished that he hadn't brought the damned thing in with him – although if he hadn't, sure enough that goddamn Erlich would show up and steal it out of the Fairlane.

He felt another twinge of pain in his gut, deep inside, but just then Donna brought the enchiladas. Ulcer or no ulcer he was going to eat the damned things. Out of habit he tried the beans and rice first, and they were good. You could tell a lot about a Mex restaurant from their side dishes – whether they put any effort into them or not. This was first rate. The enchiladas were hot all through and bursting with cheese and onions, and the sauce didn't taste like it was out of a can. Someone knew how to cook. When they finally came to hang him, and time was at a premium, this was what he would want to eat – cheese enchiladas, rice and beans, and a cold beer.

Before he slowed down he was halfway through the food and well into his second beer. He heard Donna's voice now from over near the register, and he half stood up to wave his emptied Budweiser bottle at her. He could see the man beyond the booth divider now.

"Swinger," he said, surprised, and the man looked up. It was him all right, right down to the red suspenders. Lyle wouldn't have to call the Highway Patrol after all. Campbell had a fork full of tamale halfway to his mouth. Lyle asked impulsively, "You get through to your daughter?"

Swinger squinted back at him, and not happily. "My daughter's been dead since before the war," he said flatly. "What the hell are you talking about?" He set the fork down on his plate. "Do I know you?"

The poor bastard's brains are fried, Lyle thought in embarrassment. "Back down the highway," Lyle said, gesturing vaguely toward the west, "across the river." But Swinger obviously didn't know him from a Chinaman, or if he did, he wasn't going to admit it. First Erlich and now Swinger Campbell, Lyle thought. Fast travellers, both of them.

"My mistake," Lyle said. "Sorry to bother you." He sat back down, remembering suddenly that Erlich had known Swinger, too. Maybe they were up to some kind of incognito thing. That's just what he needed, to get mixed up in a lot of tomfoolery, or worse. To hell with both of them. Give a man fifty cents and he acts like he doesn't know you. Maybe that was the deal, Lyle thought, draining the rest of his beer: Swinger was playing stupid to keep Lyle from mentioning the fifty cents. He looked for the waitress again. He hated like hell to have an empty beer glass. She was standing by the register, looking hard at the man facing her. A young man.

And Lyle's face was suddenly cold, and his stomach knotted up again. *Christ almighty,* he thought,_it's Erlich. He peered at the young man, hoping he was wrong.

But it had to be. Same blue denim jacket and scraggly hair. Swinger Campbell's presence suddenly seemed sinister to him, and he hunched over his plate.

Wait 'em out, he told himself tensely. Give them a minute and they'd be gone, and he could drink another beer in peace. If it came down to it he would show them the gun in his waistband. It would mean plenty to Erlich, anyway. Lyle cut out a piece of enchilada, but he chewed it without tasting it now, and without thinking he picked up his empty beer glass and tilted it up to his mouth, only then remembering that it was empty.

He sighed, then lifted one of the bottles and waved it toward Donna, but when they made eye contact he saw right away that something was wrong. Her mouth was a tight line, and her face was white – she was obviously scared stiff. Lyle bent forward, watching closely, his heart starting to hammer in his chest.

He saw that Erlich had something in his fist, and it wasn't a twenty dollar bill. It was a small automatic pistol, no more than .22 or .25 caliber. Donna started to turn away, putting her hands out, and Lyle stood up, sliding out of the booth and reaching into his waistband for his own gun.

"Hey!" he shouted, drawing the revolver.

Peripherally he saw Swinger Campbell stand up, too, but the man staggered sideways out of his booth, sweeping his plate and beer glass off onto the floor and then collapsing face down on top of them.

At the clatter of china and glass Erlich had swiveled around, looking wildly back toward where Swinger was sprawled on the linoleum. The kid was clearly scared, shaking with fear. He saw Lyle and his revolver then, and he waved his own little pistol at Lyle.

"Keep away, old man!" he shouted. "It's not worth it! Nobody moves!"

But then Donna screamed, and Erlich twisted furiously back toward her, and his gun popped loudly.

Just like that she fell backward, disappearing entirely from Lyle's view, the whole thing happening in a single long moment. Lyle stood frozen in shocked surprise, as did Erlich, whose shoulders were twitching. Suddenly coming to life, Erlich reached over the counter into the open register and took out a handful of bills.

"Erlich," Lyle said, stepping toward him and raising his revolver. Erlich spun around in surprise, pointing his pistol at Lyle, and it popped again in the same instant that Lyle pulled the revolver's trigger.

The hard crack battered his eardrums, and he swung the barrel down toward the floor, for he had seen Erlich go down but didn't know if the shot had hit him or not; then past the spot of muzzle-glare in his vision Lyle saw that Erlich was sitting on the floor, slumped against the cash-register counter, with a black hole in the center of his forehead. His gun had tumbled away somewhere, but the bills were still clutched in his dead hand.

The restaurant was silent, and reeked of the burnt-metal smell of gunpowder. Lyle heard a back door slam – the cook and busboy getting the hell out, probably – as he started toward the counter to help Donna. He was strangely winded, as if he had run half a mile, and the pain in his stomach nearly doubled him over now.

Swinger Campbell lay face down on the floor – probably his heart – but one way or another he would have to wait.

Lyle stepped over Erlich's sprawled legs and grabbed the counter-edge with his left hand to steady himself, and he blinked cold sweat out of his eyes as he peered behind the counter.

Erlich's blood was spattered on the cash register and the street-side wall, but Donna was crouched behind a stool, blinking fearfully up at him; and he was relieved to see blood staining a hole torn in the shoulder of her blouse. Not a lot of blood, nothing arterial.

He let the revolver clank onto the counter and then knelt beside her and touched her arm. "It's okay," he said. "It's okay, honey."

She looked into his eyes, and nodded, taking his word for it. But then she looked down and her eyes widened.

He glanced down at himself. There was a broad red stain on his shirt, visibly expanding: Erlich had shot him in the stomach. I'll be damned, he thought, and he sat down hard on the floor, the pain moving through him now like a hot iron.

"Telephone," Donna said to him, pushing herself up with her good arm.

And then without any jolt he was back out in the sunny desert, standing, holding two quarters in the palm of his hand as if to give them to Donna, who was gone, so that she could make the call, and he whispered, "Try these on for size."

But Donna wasn't here, he was talking to no one but himself, and he closed his fist on the two coins.

Had he left his car in Quartzsite? How had he got here? He could see that he was on the California side of the river again.

Apparently he *had* crossed the river twice that day – just as he had planned. He looked back the way he had come, remembering his car in the parking lot, the torn metal where the bullet had gone through the door, and then remembering Donna, and then Phyllis and the life they'd had together. He could still taste the enchiladas and the beer, and it occurred to him that he hadn't ever got the third Budweiser. But then he hadn't paid for it either, not in that way, and he hadn't left Donna a tip, which was worse.

He was standing in the sand beside an aluminum shed with a big, faded Edison decal on the padlocked door. The black line of Interstate 10 lay a hundred feet to the north, and a blue car was approaching from the east, still far enough away to be lapped in watery mirage; Lyle took a step forward, then heard the uneven drone of the car's engine, clearly missing a stroke.

He stepped behind the shed before the Fairlane got too close – he didn't want to be seen, or, God help him, recognized – but he tried to project a thought to the agitated driver: *Go to the Goodwill store before you eat. This is your last chance to find the book.*

He'd have known the book first by its binding, then by the inscription on the flyleaf – *Happy birthday, George – Love, Phyllis.* Too late now._No more birthdays now.

He realized abruptly that he would head out into the desert, and he started plodding away from the shed and the highway even as the thought came into his mind. Swinger had got that right. Get off the highway. There was no point lingering, no point going on skipping backward like a stone across a lake.

He felt light, as if a burden had fallen away, and the rocks and soft sand of the desert floor were no longer any kind of problem at all. He heard the Fairlane speed past, heading toward Arizona, but he didn't look back. He wondered whether he would run into Swinger again out here, somewhere on up ahead, and it seemed to him then that he could see the red suspenders and the black boots through the heat haze in the remote distance. He hoped so; he could use the company. Sometimes you couldn't choose.

Through and Through

ALREADY when he walked in through the side door, there were a few people sitting here and there, separately in the Saturday afternoon dimness. The air was cool, and smelled of floor-wax.

He almost peered at the shadowed faces, irrationally hoping one might be hers, come back these seven days later to try for a different result; but most of the faces were lowered, and of course she wouldn't be here. Two days ago, maybe – today, and ever after, no.

The funeral would be next week sometime, probably Monday. No complications about burial in consecrated soil anymore, thank God... or thank human mercy.

His shoes knocked echoingly on the glossy linoleum as he walked across the nave, pausing to bow toward the altar. In the old days he would have genuflected, and it would have been spontaneous; in recenter years the bow had become perfunctory, dutiful – today it was a twitch of self-distaste.

There were fewer people than he had first thought, he noted as he walked past the side altar and started down the wall aisle toward the confessional door, passing under the high, wooden Stations of the Cross and the awkwardly lettered banners of the Renew Committee. Maybe only three, all women; and a couple of little girls.

They never wanted to line up against the wall – a discreet couple of yards away from the door – until he actually entered the church; and then if there were six or so of them they'd be frowning at each other as they got up out of the pews and belatedly formed the line, silently but obviously disagreeing about the order in which they'd originally entered the church.

Last week there had been five, counting her. And afterward he had walked back up to the front of the church and stepped up onto the altar level and gone into the sacristy to put on the vestments for 5:30 Mass. Had he been worrying about what she had said? *What sins you shall retain, they are retained.* Probably he had been worrying about it.

As he opened the confessional door now, he nodded to the old woman who was first in line. The others appeared to be trying to hide behind her – he could see only a drape of skirt and a couple of shoes behind her. He didn't recognize the old woman.

He stepped into the little room and pulled the door closed behind him. They wouldn't begin to come in until he turned on the red light over the door, and he needed a drink.

The little room was brighter than the interior of the church, lit by a pebbled glass window high in the wall at his back. He opened the closet and shook out his surplice, a white robe that he pulled over his head. Then he undraped from a hanger the stole, a strip of cloth like a long, double-wide necktie, purple silk on one side and white on the other; and he draped it over his head and down the front of his surplice, with the purple side showing. The audience demands the costume, he thought as he bent down to snag a pint bottle of Wild Turkey from behind an old pair of shoes.

A couple of little girls out there, he thought. Chinese-restaurant-style confessions, those will be, one from column A and two from column B: *I quarreled with my brothers, I disobeyed my parents.* They look to be a little young yet for *impure thoughts.*

He unscrewed the plastic cap and took a mouthful of the warm bourbon, letting the vapors fill his head before he swallowed. And for their penances I'll tell them, *Say five Our Fathers and five Hail Marys.*

No use in being imaginative. Once he had told a young boy, *For your penance, I want you to tell your mother and father that you love them.* Later he'd learned that the boy had found this flatly impossible – apparently in the boy's family the declaration would have been taken as a symptom of insanity – and the boy had lived in silent fear of Hell for two weeks before his family had finally gone to Confession again, at which point the boy had taken the same old sins to another priest, one who would reliably give the conventional sort of penance.

Confession is good for the soul. I still believe that's true, he thought. It can make life easier to bear, after all, letting in the fresh air, sharing your secrets with another. But not when it's so tied in with the dread of Hell. That woman last week –

He took another sip of the bourbon to take the edge off the memory. And it hadn't been his fault – how could he have known how strangled she was with scruples and legalisms? She didn't need – hadn't needed – a sympathetic human being to talk to; what would have served her best would have been an 800 number – *If your sin has to do with the 6th Commandment, press 6 now.*

In his early years as a priest, he had seemed to feel heavier after hearing confessions, especially the marathon sessions before Easter, as if some residue of the absolved sins clung to him; and he had whimsically speculated that clouds of evicted sins polluted the air afterward, interfering with TV reception and making cars hard to start. Now he just felt tired afterward, as if he had spent the afternoon helping a lot of people to get their checking accounts unscrambled.

The woman last week hadn't wanted any *help,* not from him. She had sat her thin frame down in the chair across from his, awkwardly, tucking in her skirt and glancing around, clearly uneasy about the face-to-face style of Confession. She'd have been happier with the old booth arrangement, he thought, whispering through a screen so that priest and penitent saw each other only as dim silhouettes; though she had hardly looked more than thirty years old.

He took one more mouthful of the liquor now, and then screwed the cap back on and put the bottle away.

She had made the sign of the cross and then started right in, exhaling as she spoke: "Bless me, Father, I have sinned." Her voice was shaky. "My last Confession was … at least five years ago, before '96. I've meant to come – it's scary, though, a big speed bump to get over – last week I went to a wedding – " He noted that her left ring finger didn't have a ring on it; " – and there were family people there, people I hadn't seen since college. I took Communion. At the Mass."

He had nodded, and when she didn't go on he raised his eyebrows.

"I took Communion while in a state of mortal sin," she said.

"The Eucharist provides forgiveness of sins," he told her. He had preferred *Eucharist* to *Communion* ever since Whitley Strieber's book about space aliens had taken the latter term as its title.

"Father," she had said uncertainly, "not mortal sins. Which I'll get to a lot of, here, I hope. If you're not in a state of grace, Communion is like sugar to a diabetic – uh, damaging?" She spread her hands as if to catch a ball.

He had smiled at her, and he hoped now that his smile had not been patronizing. "God understands – " he began.

"But it's God, literally coming into us, right?" she interrupted. "If there's oily rags and newspapers around, you'll catch fire from the heat of Him, your soul gets scorched, right?" She laughed nervously. "And I've got a lot of oily rags in my soul. I don't like the idea that I've … " She shook her head and closed her mouth.

"Sin," he had said expansively. "What do we mean by it? Isn't the only *real* sin cruelty, to others – or to yourself?"

For a moment neither of them spoke, and he hoped this wouldn't take too long. How many more people were waiting out there?

"I came a long way to get here," she had said finally. "I didn't really think I'd get this far. I don't need to talk about 'What's sin?' with some *guy*. I've done some terrible things, and right now I think I can say them out loud; I think. I want absolution."

"Well," he said, "I'm not going to *absolve* you for something that isn't a *sin*."

Her mouth was open in evident disbelief. "As a favor to me," she said.

"No, it's ridiculous." He noticed her bony hands clutched together, and it occurred to him that she might be an addict – amphetamines, probably. "Don't trouble yourself over these – "

"'What sins you shall forgive, they are forgiven,'" she said, her voice getting brittle, "I remember that part. And 'What sins you shall retain, they are retained.' You're telling me you're retaining this one." Her smile made her cheekbones prominent. "I bet you'd retain them all, if you heard them. I bet none of them are sins anymore ... according to you."

"I'm not *retaining* anything! So far I haven't heard anything you've done wrong. Tell me – "

"No." She had stood up. "This was a mistake."

And she had walked out.

And on Thursday morning she had been found dead in a back pew of the church. Dead of an overdose of drugs – a speedball, he'd been told, cocaine and heroin. Her parents were long-time parishioners, and her funeral would be in this church. Luckily she had not left a note.

How long will it take, he wondered as he reached for the switch that would turn on the red light over the door outside, before people are ready to abandon the crude supernatural templates that obscure God's love? When will they see that God is in all of us, and that what we most need is to forgive ourselves?

The knob turned, and the door swung inward and a little girl in blue jeans and a green sweater stepped in, Reeboks scuffing the carpet. She appeared to be about eight years old, with short-cropped dark hair.

He wondered if she had shoved in ahead of the old woman he'd seen at the front of the line. The girl's face was narrow, with horizontal wrinkles in the lower eyelids already.

"Do sit down," he told her.

He had forgotten to put a stick of Doublemint gum in his mouth, but she didn't appear to notice any smell of liquor, and he'd remember to do it before the old woman came in.

She climbed into the chair, and her shoes didn't touch the carpet.

"Bless me, Father," she said, "I have sinned. My last Confession was too long ago to remember. These are my sins – I killed myself on Thursday." She looked at him mournfully. "I know that's very bad."

He was aware of cold air on his face – his forehead was suddenly dewed with sweat.

"That's not funny," he said, "a woman did – was found dead – "

"I want absolution," the little girl said. "I want the sacrament. I came a long way to get here. I didn't really think I'd get this far."

Abruptly he remembered that the door to the confessional opened outward.

He turned to look at it – it was closed now, and its frame didn't appear to have been tampered with any time lately – and when he turned back, it was a white-haired old woman who sat opposite him.

He jumped violently in his chair, inhaling in a whispered screech. High blood pressure made a ringing wail in his head, and his peripheral vision had narrowed to nearly nothing.

He blinked several times, and exhaled. "Who are you?" he asked in a rusty voice. His fingers were tingling, gripping the arms of his chair.

"And before that," quavered the old woman, "I took Communion while in a state of mortal sin." She had been looking down at her bony old hands, and now she looked up at him; and her eyes were empty holes in the wrinkled parchment of her face.

Through the holes he could see the fabric of the chair, bright in the afternoon light from the window at his back. She wasn't even casting a shadow.

It's a ghost, he told himself as he made himself breathe deeply. It's the ghost of that woman who was here a week ago. Priests have seen ghosts before.

He flexed his legs under the surplice. He didn't want to find that his legs had gone to sleep when he made a bolt for the door. He would say there'd been an electrical short, he smelled gas, felt faint, and if they found the Wild Turkey blame it on the Vietnamese priest.

But the old woman had reached out one papery hand as slow as drifting smoke, and now touched his knee; he shouldn't even have been able to feel the touch, through the fabric of the surplice and his slacks, but the impact punched another shrill wheeze out of him, and numbed his whole leg. His heart beat several times very fast, then seemed to stop; and he began panting in relief when his pulse began beating regularly again, though it was still fast.

"And before that," she said, in the same frail voice, "you took Communion in a state of mortal sin."

He remembered a Tennyson line: *The dead shall look me through and through.* It was probably true – he had not been to another priest for Confession in … months … and he took Communion many times a week, at every Mass he said.

She might kill him if she touched him again. Would it be deliberate, did she mean to hurt him?

He was dizzy, and he became aware that he could feel the late afternoon light on his face – but he was sure he hadn't turned his chair around in the spasm of her touching him. He blinked, but he couldn't see anything except a gray fog. Quickly he darted a hand to his right eye, and his dry fingers found only a hole in a numb, crackling surface.

"Bless me, Father," came his own voice from a few feet away, "I have sinned. My last Confession was a thousand years ago. I want absolution."

He jumped with all his will, but not physically – and then his hands were gripping the arms of his own chair, and the window was at his back and he could see again, and it was the little girl in the chair across from him now.

"Don't – do that again," he whispered. His heart was hammering again.

"I firmly resolve to sin no more," the little girl said, "and to avoid the near occasions of sin. Amen."

She can't do anything deliberately, he thought. She can't sin anymore, she's dead. She might kill me, but with no more moral responsibility than a sick dog would have.

She was waiting.

His sister baptized dogs and cats – just a lick of spit on a fingertip to make a cross on the furry forehead, a whispered *I baptize thee*... Why couldn't he just say the words here, give this lost revenant what it wanted? *Ego te absolvo a peccatis tuis*... but those were the old Latin phrases; these days it was *I absolve you from your sins in the name of the Father, and of the Son, and of the Holy Spirit.*

But this thing can't have contrition, he thought, it can't repent. Its living soul is with God – this is just a suffering cast-off shell.

But it is suffering, as dogs and cats do, and they don't have souls either.

Why was she appearing as a girl and an old woman? Why was she so widely avoiding the appearance she'd had when she'd come to Confession last week, the appearance she'd had when she'd died? Was it too traumatic?

And suddenly, with something like the intimacy of sore muscles, he knew that he was responsible for the form she took; when she walked in, she had been an uncollapsed wave of possible appearances, all the appearances she'd ever had; it was his guilt that had collapsed all the percentages of possibilities down to this small "one." A few moments ago he had even forced on her the appearance of an old woman, which was just a sheet of old skin because she would never actually live to that age.

Would a better priest, a better man, have seen the woman as she had appeared last week, when she'd been alive?

The world, before the first sentient man left the Garden of Eden and *looked* at it, had not yet been defined by attention – it had been a spectrum of worlds-in-potential that had not included humanity, an infinity of possible prehuman histories; but by the time Adam stepped out and turned his attention on it, he had sinned mortally, and so the history that came to the fore as the actual one was a history of undeserved suffering and death. When Adam's foot touched the soil, when his eyes took in the landscape, it stopped being many potentials and became one actual: a landscape that had been a savage killing-ground for millennia.

Light turns out to be particles if you measure for particles, he thought, waves if you measure for waves. Adam had helplessly measured for misery. What sort of world would a sinless first man have found pre-existent out there? Animals that had never starved, cats that had never killed?

I've measured for … evasion, he thought. Even last week, here.

"*Ego te* – " he began; then halted.

She might kill him if she touched him again. And where would he be then? A moment ago he had told himself that her soul was now with God – but what if it weren't? What if it were still sentient, but somewhere else?

What if Purgatory and Hell are real? It had been a long time since he had entertained any such notions; in fact it had been a long time since he'd believed in the existence of any sort of actual Heaven.

But this dead penitent sitting in front of him made all sorts of horrible ideas possible. Did he want to die right after using his priestly powers – *thou art a priest forever, according to the order of Melchizedek* – to perform the mockery of a sacrament? He had started to do it – *Ego te …*

And I'm not in a state of grace anyway, he thought, if all these damned *legalisms* actually *apply,* if all the awful old supernatural stories are *true!*

He wasn't aware of being scared, but he was shivering in the warm room, and his hands were tingling.

I'd probably go to – everlasting punishment! – and a snakeskin half-wit piece of me would join her in her lost ghosthood, to be another specter forever haunting confessionals, looking for impossible absolution. Visible, perhaps, only to other doomed priests.

"Can you *have* a firm purpose of amendment?" he asked her unhappily. "*Can* you … mend your ways, go and sin no more?"

The little girl held out her hand; not threateningly, but he flinched back from the offered touch.

"I came for the sacrament," she said.

He was suddenly sure that there was no one waiting outside the door – the others he had seen had only been *her,* fragmented as if in a kaleidoscope, and this conversation was taking place in some corner outside of normal time. If he were to open the door, *pull* it open, he'd see beyond the door frame only the gray fog he had seen when he had been in the shell of the old woman.

"There's nobody else," she said. 'Nobody else talks to me but you. Hollowed be thy name."

The dead shall look me through and through.

"Give me the sacrament," she said. "Deliver us from evil."

Or to it, he thought.

Her hand came up again, but hovered between them as if undecided between touching him and making the sign of the cross.

"Okay," he said.

The hand wavered sketchily in the air, and then subsided into her lap.

God help me, he thought. If I'm not dead already myself, and beyond all help.

He stood up slowly, his head bobbing; and the little girl just watched him solemnly. He stepped to the closet and slid from a high shelf one of his sick-call kits, a six-inch black leather box with hinges and a latch.

He returned to his chair and sat down, and he opened the box on his lap. Inside, tucked into fitted depressions in red velvet, were a silver crucifix, a silver holy-water sprinkler, a round silver box that held no consecrated hosts at the moment, a spare folded stole... and a little silver jar of oil.

It was olive oil, and it would probably be rancid by this time, but he recalled that the oil in this kit was real *Oleum Infirmorum*, blessed by the bishop.

In recent years he had come to the conclusion that the oil had no efficacy on its own – whether it was olive oil or motor oil, blessed or not – and was simply a comfort to sick people with heads full of Biblical imagery; but now he was cautiously glad this was precisely the prescribed kind.

"I've got a lot of oily rags in my soul already," the little girl said. She was frowning and shifting on the chair.

She looks me through and through, he thought. "I'm going to give you the sacrament," he said, forcing his voice to be steady.

He unscrewed the lid of the little silver jar, and leaned over it. "God of mercy," he said, "ease the suffering and comfort the weakness of your servant – uh – " He looked up at her with his eyebrows raised. He could feel drops of sweat on his forehead.

"Jane," the girl said. "This – isn't Confession."

"Jane... "

The breath caught in his throat as he abruptly remembered what would shortly be required of him here.

After several seconds he exhaled and went on, bleakly, "Jane, whom the Church anoints with this holy oil. We ask this through Christ our Lord."

"Amen," said Jane. "This is last rites."

"Yes," he said.

He would have to touch her. The sacrament of Extreme Unction – or Anointing of the Sick, as they called it now – would require that he touch her forehead.

Her light touch, through two layers of cloth, had nearly killed him a few moments ago. This would be virtually skin-to-skin, with only the insulation of the oil.

And was this just another mockery of a sacrament? The rules permitted this sacrament to be administered to a person who appeared to have been dead for as much as two hours, who might in fact very well *be* dead, since no one could be sure precisely when the soul left a body that had died.

But two days? – and anointing *this,* while the body was at a mortuary somewhere? Briefly he imagined explaining it to his bishop: *But she was still speaking!*

He dipped his right forefinger into the oil and lifted it out – but just sat staring at it while two drops formed and fell silently back into the jar.

He thought of his sister, baptizing cats and dogs; and he thought of Adam, who had imposed suffering and death on all soulless things.

And he dipped his finger again, and leaned forward. *"Per istam sanctam unctionem – "* he said, and he touched his finger to Jane's forehead.

Her skin was as cold as window-glass, and though he felt no impact and his heartbeat didn't accelerate wildly this time, his finger, and then his knuckles, were numb.

He drew the sign of the cross on her forehead with the oil and went on speaking, remembering now to do it in English, " – may the Lord in His love and mercy help you with the grace of the Holy Spirit."

Jane was motionless, looking up at him.

"Amen," she whispered.

Oil trickled down and collected under her eye sockets like tears. The numbness was gone from his hand, and he dipped his finger again.

With his left hand he took hold of her right hand – it was as cold as her forehead – and then made the sign of the cross on the back of her hand.

"May the Lord who frees you from sin save you and raise you up," he said.

"Amen," she said again. Her voice was remote now, as if she were speaking from the far end of a corridor.

He reached for her other hand, but it was gone; her face, alone, hung over the chair like a reflection of sunlight on a wall, and for an instant it was the face of the woman who had come in here a week ago.

He couldn't see her mouth move, but he heard the receding voice say, "And what's my penance?"

Five Our Fathers? Tell your parents you love them? You don't get a penance with Extreme Unction, he thought – but she seemed to need it. He was at a loss, and cast in his mind for some prayer out of the Bible.

Only after he had said it, and the face had seemed to smile and then disappeared, did he realize that what he said had not been from the Bible:

"Go gentle into that good night," he had told her. "Rest easy with the dying of the light."

Bastardized Dylan Thomas! But it seemed to have been adequate – he was alone in the room.

When his pulse and breathing had slowed to normal, he made the sign of the cross, spotting his surplice with oil, and he thought, was that all right?

There was only silence in his mind for an answer, but for once it was not an empty silence.

And so he sat motionless until the door opened – outward, giving him a glimpse, as he looked up, of the dim church beyond.

A young man stepped in hesitantly, sniffed the air, then shuffled to the chair that had so recently been Jane's.

"Bless me, Father," the young man said huskily as he sat down, "I have sinned."

And the priest listened, nodding, as the young man began talking, and he absently replaced the lid on the oil jar and put the sick-call kit aside.

We Traverse Afar

James P. Blaylock & Tim Powers

HARRISON SAT in the dim living room and listened to the train. All the sounds were clear – the shrill steam whistle over the bass chug of the engine, and even, faintly, the clatter of the wheels on the track.

It never rained anymore on Christmas Eve. The plastic rain gauge was probably still out on the shed roof; he used to lean over the balcony railing outside the master bedroom to check the level of the water in the thing. There had been something reassuring about the idea of rainwater rising in the gauge – nature measurably doing its work, the seasons going around, the drought held at bay....

But he couldn't recall any rain since last winter. He hadn't checked, because the master bedroom was closed up now. And anyway the widow next door, Mrs. Kemp, had hung some strings of Christmas lights over her back porch, and even if he *did* get through to the balcony, he wouldn't be able to help seeing the blinking colors, and probably even something like a Christmas wreath on her back door.

Too many cooks spoil the broth, he thought, a good wine needs no bush, a friend in need is one friend too many, leave me alone.

She'd even knocked on his door today, the widow had; with a paper plate of Christmas cookies! The plate was covered in red and green foil and the whole bundle was wrapped in a Santa Claus napkin. He had taken the plate, out of politeness; but the whole kit and caboodle, cookies and all, had gone straight into the dumpster.

To hell with rain anyway. He was sitting in the old leather chair by the cold fireplace, watching snow. In the glass globe in his hand a little painted man and woman sat in a sleigh that was being pulled by a little frozen horse.

He took a sip of vodka and turned the globe upside down and back again, and a contained flurry of snow swirled around the figures. He and his wife had bought the thing a long time ago. The couple in the sleigh had been on their cold ride for decades now. Better to travel than to arrive, he thought, peering through the glass at their tiny blue-eyed faces; they didn't look a day older than when they'd started out. And still together, too, after all these years.

The sound of the train engine changed, was more echoing and booming now – maybe it had gone into a tunnel.

He put the globe down on the magazine stand and had another sip of vodka. With his nose stuffed full of Vicks VapoRub, as it was tonight, his taste buds wouldn't have known the difference if he'd been drinking VSOP brandy or paint thinner, but he could feel the warm glow in his stomach.

It was an old LP record on the turntable, one from the days when the real hi-fi enthusiasts cared more about sound quality than any kind of actual music. This one was two whole sides of locomotive racket, booming out through his monaural Klipschorn speaker. He also had old disks of surf sounds, downtown traffic, ocean waves, birds shouting in tropical forests…

Better a train. Booming across those nighttime miles.

He was just getting well relaxed when he began to hear faint music behind the barreling train. It was a Christmas song, and before he could stop himself he recognized it – Bing Crosby singing "We Three Kings," one of her favorites.

He'd been ready for it. He pulled two balls of cotton out of the plastic bag beside the vodka bottle and twisted them into his ears.

That made it better – all he could hear now was a distant hiss that might have been rain against the windows.

Ghost rain, he thought. I should have put out a ghost gauge.

As if in response to his thought, the next sip of vodka had a taste – the full-orchestra, peaches-and-bourbon chord of Southern Comfort. He tilted his head forward and let the liquor run out of his mouth back into the glass, and then he stood up and crossed to the phonograph, lifted the arm off the record and laid it in its rest, off to the side.

When he pulled the cotton out of his ears, the house was silent. There was no creaking of floorboards, no sound of breathing or rustling. He was staring at the empty fireplace, pretty sure that if he looked around he would see that flickering rainbow glow from the dining room; the glow of lights, and the star on the top of the tree, and those weird little glass columns with bubbles wobbling up through the liquid inside. Somehow the stuff never boiled away. Some kind of perpetual motion, like those glass birds with the top hats, that bobbed back and forth, dipping their beaks into a glass of water, forever. At least with the Vicks he wouldn't smell pine sap.

The pages of the wall calendar had been rearranged sometime last night. He'd noticed it right away this morning when he'd come out of what used to be the guest bedroom, where he slept now on the single bed. The pink cloud of tuberous begonias above the thirty-one empty days of March was gone, replaced by the blooming poinsettia of the December page. Had he done it himself, shifted the calendar while walking in his sleep? He wasn't normally a sleep-walker. And sometime during the night, around midnight probably, he'd thought he'd heard a stirring in the closed-up bedroom across the hall, the door whispering open, what sounded like bedroom slippers shuffling on the living room carpet.

Before even making coffee he had folded the calendar back to March. She'd died on St. Patrick's Day evening, and in fact the green dress she'd laid out on the queen-size bed still lay there, gathering whatever kind of dust inhabited a closed-up room. Around the dress, on the bedspread, were still scattered the green-felt shamrocks she had intended to sew onto it. She'd never even had a chance to iron the dress, and, after the paramedics had taken her away on that long-ago evening, he'd had to unplug the iron himself, at the same time that he unplugged the bedside clock.

The following day, after moving out most of his clothes, he had shut the bedroom door for the last time. This business with the calendar made him wonder if maybe the clock was plugged in again, too, but he was not going to venture in there to find out.

Through the back door, from across the yard, he heard the familiar scrape of the widow's screen door opening, and then the sound of it slapping shut. Quickly he reached up and flipped off the lamp, then sat still in the darkened living room. Maybe she wasn't paying him another visit, but he wasn't taking any chances.

In a couple of minutes there came the clumping of her shoes on the front steps, and he hunkered down in the chair, glad that he'd turned off the train noise.

He watched her shadow in the porch light. He shouldn't leave it on all the time. It probably looked like an invitation, especially at this time of year. She knocked at the door, waited a moment and then knocked again. She couldn't take a hint if it stepped out of the bushes and bit her on the leg.

Abruptly he felt sheepish, hiding out like this, like a kid. But he was a *married man,* for God's sake. He'd taken a *vow.* And a vow wasn't worth taking if it wasn't *binding. She will do him good and not evil all the days of her life,* said Proverbs 31 about a good wife; *her lamp does not go out at night.*

Does not go out.

His thoughts trailed off into nothing when he realized that the woman outside was leaving, shuffling back down the steps. He caught himself wondering if she'd brought him something else to eat, maybe left a casserole outside the door. Once she'd brought around half a corned beef and a mess of potatoes and cabbage, and like the Christmas cookies, all of it had gone straight into the garbage. But the canned chili he'd microwaved earlier this evening wasn't sitting too well with him, and the thought of corned beef...

He could definitely hear something now from the closed-up bedroom – a low whirring noise like bees in a hive – the sewing machine? He couldn't recall if he had unplugged it too, that night. Still, it had no excuse....

He grabbed the cotton balls, twisting them up tight and jamming them into his ears again. Had the bedroom door moved? He groped wildly for the lamp, switched it on, and with one last backward glance he went out the front door, nearly slamming it behind him in his haste.

Shakily, he sat down in one of the white plastic chairs on the porch and buttoned up his cardigan sweater. If the widow returned, she'd find him, and there was damn-all he could do about it. He looked around in case she might have left him something, but apparently she hadn't. The chilly night air calmed him down a little bit, and he listened for a moment to the sound of crickets, wondering what he would do now. Sooner or later he'd have to go back inside. He hadn't even brought out the vodka bottle.

Tomorrow, Christmas day, would be worse.

What would he say to her if the bedroom door should *open*, and she were to step out? If he were actually to *confront* her.... A good marriage was made in heaven, as the scriptures said, and you didn't let a thing like that go. No matter what. Hang on with chains.

After a while he became aware that someone up the street was yelling about something, and he stood up in relief, grateful for an excuse to get off the porch, away from the house. He shuffled down the two concrete steps, breathing the cold air that was scented with jasmine even in December.

Some distance up the block, half a dozen people in robes were walking down the sidewalk toward his house, carrying one of those real estate signs that looked like a miniature hangman's gallows. No, only one of them was carrying it, and at the bottom end of it was a metal wheel that was skirling along the dry pavement.

Then he saw that it wasn't a real estate sign, but a cross. The guy carrying it was apparently supposed to be Jesus, and two of the men behind him wore slatted skirts like Roman soldiers, and they had rope whips that they were snapping in the chilly air.

"Get along, King of the Jews!" one of the soldiers called, obviously not for the first time, and not very angrily. Behind the soldiers three women in togas trotted along, shaking their heads and waving their hands. Harrison supposed they must be Mary or somebody. The wheel at the bottom of the cross definitely needed a squirt of oil.

Harrison took a deep breath, and then forced jocularity into his voice as he called, "You guys missed the Golgotha off-ramp. Only thing south of here is the YMCA."

A black couple was pushing a shopping cart up the sidewalk from the opposite direction, their shadows stark under the streetlight. They were slowing down to watch Jesus. All kinds of unoiled wheels were turning tonight.

The biblical procession stopped in front of his house, and Harrison walked down the path to the sidewalk. Jesus grinned at him, clearly glad for the chance to pause amid his travail and catch his breath.

One of the women handed Harrison a folded flier. "I'm Mary Magdalene," she told him. "This is about a meeting we're having at our church next week. We're on Seventeenth, just past the 5 Freeway."

The shopping cart had stopped too, and Harrison carried the flier over to the black man and woman. "Here," he said, holding out the piece of paper. "Mary Magdalene wants you to check out her church. Take a right at the light, it's just past the freeway."

The black man had a bushy beard but didn't seem to be older than thirty, and the woman was fairly fat, wearing a sweatsuit. The shopping cart was full of empty bottles and cans sitting on top of a trash bag half-full of clothes.

The black man grinned. "We're homeless, and we'd sure like to get the dollar-ninety-nine breakfast at Norm's. Could you help us out? We only need a little more."

"Ask Jesus," said Harrison nervously, waving at the robed people. "Hey Jesus, here's a chance to do some actual *thing* tonight, not just march around the streets. This here is a genuine homeless couple, give 'em a couple of bucks."

Jesus patted his robes with the hand that wasn't holding the cross. "I don't have anything on me," he said apologetically.

Harrison turned to the Roman soldiers. "You guys got any money?"

"Just change would do," put in the black man.

"Nah," said one of the soldiers, "I left my money in my pants."

"Girls?" said Harrison.

Mary Magdalene glanced at her companions, then turned back to Harrison and shook her head.

"Really?" said Harrison. "Out in this kind of neighborhood at night, and you don't even have quarters for phone calls?"

"We weren't going to go far," explained Jesus.

"Weren't going to go far." Harrison nodded, then looked back to Mary Magdalene. "Can your church help these people out? Food, shelter, that kind of thing?"

The black woman had walked over to Jesus and was admiring his cross. She liked the wheel.

"They'd have to be married," Mary Magdalene told Harrison. "In the church. If they're just… living together, we can't do anything for them."

That's great, thought Harrison, coming from Mary Magdalene. "So that's it, I guess, huh?"

Apparently it was. "Drop by the church!" said Jesus cheerfully, resuming his burden and starting forward again.

"Get along, King of the Jews!" called one of the soldiers, snapping his length of rope in the air. The procession moved on down the sidewalk, the wheel at the bottom of the cross squeaking.

The black man looked at Harrison. "Sir, could we borrow a couple of bucks? You live here? We'll pay you back."

Harrison was staring after the robed procession. "Oh," he said absently, "sure. Here." He dug a wad of bills out of his pants pocket and peeled two ones away from the five and held them out.

The man took the bills. "God bless you. Could we have the five too? It's Christmas Eve."

Harrison found that he was insulted by the *God bless you*. The implication was that these two were devout Christians, and would assuredly spend the money on wholesome food, or medicine, and not go buy dope or wine.

"No," he said sharply. "And I don't care what you buy with the two bucks." Once I've given it away, he thought, it shouldn't be my business. Gone is gone.

The black man scowled at him and muttered something obviously offensive under his breath as the two of them turned away, not toward Norm's and the dollar-ninety-nine breakfast, but down a side street toward the mini-mart.

Obscurely defeated, Harrison trudged back up to his porch and collapsed back into the chair.

He wished the train record was still playing inside – but even if it had been, it would still be a train that, realistically, had probably stopped rolling a long time ago. Listening to it over and over again wouldn't make it move again.

He opened the door and walked back into the dim living room. Just as he closed the door he heard thunder boom across the night sky, and then he heard the hiss of sudden rain on the pavement outside. In a moment it was tapping at the windows.

He wondered if the rain gauge was still on the roof, maybe measuring what was happening to Jesus and the black couple out there. And he was glad that he had had the roof redone a year ago. He was okay in here – no wet carpets in store for him.

The vodka bottle was still on the table, but he could see tiny reflected flickers of light in the glassy depths of it – red and green and yellow and blue; and, though he knew that the arm of the phonograph was lifted and in its holder, he heard again, clearly now, Bing Crosby singing "We Three Kings."

To hell with the vodka. He sat down in the leather chair and picked up the snow globe with trembling fingers. "What," he said softly, "too far? Too long? I thought it was supposed to be forever."

But rainy gusts boomed at the windows, and he realized that he had stood up. He pried at the base of the snow globe, and managed to free the plug.

Water and white plastic flecks bubbled and trickled out of it, onto the floor. In only a minute the globe had emptied out, and the two figures in the sleigh were exposed to the air of tonight, stopped. Without the refraction of the surrounding water the man and the woman looked smaller, and lifeless.

"Field and fountain, moor and mountain," he whispered. "Journey's done – finally. Sorry."

He was alone in the dark living room. No lights gleamed in the vodka bottle, and there was no sound but his own breath and heartbeat.

Tomorrow he would open the door to anyone who might knock.

Where They Are Hid

WHEN HE STEPPED out of the doorway and sniffed the warm air, he had a feeling that he'd finally finished the reluctant, years-long, trial-and-error journey – and he was sure of it when, after squinting around for a couple of moments, he saw the woman pushing the baby carriage along the sidewalk. And though now that it was all over he felt like staring in horror, or crying, or just running away, he forced himself to do nothing more than pat the pockets of his coat and smile casually as he strolled up to her. He said good afternoon and peered into the carriage.

He remarked on what a nice-looking son she had, and the mother gave him a smile, but then let it relax back into her habitual bored pout when it became clear that the man really had stopped only to admire the baby. The man pulled a pair of glasses out of his coat pocket, and when a wad of bills tumbled to the sidewalk the young mother darted around to the front of the carriage, recovered the money, and handed nearly all of it back to him.

He had been leaning over the carriage, doing something with the baby's bottle, and when the mother handed him the bills he thanked her with as good a show of surprise and sincerity as he could muster.

The woman nodded and began pushing the carriage on down the sidewalk. Neither she, nor, probably, the baby, had noticed that the stranger had switched bottles. Certainly neither of them was aware of the paper he'd tucked under the blanket.

When the man turned away, his face stiff with grief and fear, he let his left hand fall out from under his coat, and he was gripping the snatched baby bottle so tightly that his knuckles were white.

Just from habit – for there was certainly no need to look sharp for the visitor he was expecting – the secret ruler of the world glanced at himself in the full-length closet door mirror, and then he leaned forward and pressed a lever on his desktop intercom.

The lever broke right off. "Damn it," he muttered, glancing at his watch and pushing his chair back to stand up. The casters emitted a loud squeal, and his secretary was already looking up when he yanked the connecting door open.

"No calls or visitors for the next fifteen minutes," he said distinctly.

The girl's eyebrows went up. "But Mr. Stanwell, I thought you were having lunch with the Trotsky Youth rep."

"That's at eleven," said Stanwell irritably. "It's only a quarter after ten now."

"So you want… what was it? A sno-cone and ribs, did you say? And – "

"I said *no calls or visitors. For the next fifteen minutes.* For God's sake. Now repeat that back to me."

She managed to, despite the stutter that seemed to be fashionable or epidemic or something these days, and he went back into his office and crossed to the window.

"Good news about something," he whispered, looking out across the Santa Ana business district and trying to notice the trucks zooming efficiently past on Main Street rather than the work crew that was somehow still finding something to fool with under the ripped-up pavement of Civic Center Drive. "The labor unions deciding to rejoin us at last, employment up," he was whispering with

his eyes shut now, "the colors getting brighter again, the hallucinations stop – bring me good news about *something*."

When the familiar *thump* jarred him and rattled the window he
opened his eyes and turned around.

There was a man standing on the other side of the desk now,
and though the newcomer was dressed in blue jeans and a flannel
shirt with a heavy coat over his arm, and kept alternately looking at
and sucking on a cut thumb, he was otherwise an identical twin to
Stanwell.

"Glad to see you," said Stanwell. "We okay? What happened to
the thumb?"

The other man waved impatiently. "Little cut," he said. "I'd
explain what I did, but you'd probably be tempted to fix it so it
wouldn't happen."

Stanwell frowned. "You know I'm always careful to – "

"Sure. Look, I'm not really in the mood to stay back here very
long, you know? I'm damn busy, and of course I've been through
this conversation once before."

Stanwell looked hurt, but asked, "Anything you'd like me to
change? Anything I should buy, anybody to – "

"Nope," said his double. "Just hang in there. We're doing fine."

Stanwell was frowning as he turned to the liquor cabinet and
reached down a bottle of Stolichnaya. "I gather," he said a little
stiffly, "that something goes right, and you're afraid that if I know
about it in advance I'll fumble the ball." He tonged ice cubes into
two glasses and poured vodka over them. "Well, if genuine sponta-
neity is absolutely necessary, I understand. But I'd like at least *some*
answers." He turned and held one glass out toward the visitor. "For
example, in what direction do Poland and Mexico – "

"No, thank you, we've given up drink. And I've got to go. Just
wanted to show you we're okay."

"What, already?" asked Stanwell, disconcerted. "But usually we
stay – "

"Not this time, old buddy," said the double, who was obviously not enjoying the conversation. He shut his eyes – then opened them and hesitantly held out his right hand. "I wish," he said quietly as the mystified Stanwell took it, "that we could have got to know each other."

Abruptly the visitor disappeared, and Stanwell stumbled forward, his ears ringing and his wrist almost sprained from the sudden, close implosion of air. He flexed his fingers ruefully.

"You okay, Mr. Stanwell?" came his secretary's call from beyond the closed door.

"Yes," he shouted. "Don't interrupt." Some soundproof door, he thought bitterly.

It was his turn now to reassure the next man back, but he sat down first and took a long sip of the vodka. What can I tell him? he wondered helplessly. Well of course I'll *tell* him whatever it was that I *heard* a year ago; but the next-up man then sure looked more confident than I feel now.

He glanced at the neat stack of typed pages on the bookshelf, and he wished he could still read his unfinished autobiography and derive inspiration and that sense of high purpose from it; but during the last year it had seemed to him that the margins were wider than he remembered, and that the text had become a little murky and ambiguous, and that all the moving or funny or tragic anecdotes had had the pith leached out of them.

Though he modestly intended that the book should be published after his death, he had put together a selection of accompanying photographs, and had even commissioned a painting for the cover. He swivelled his chair around now so that he faced the big canvas that occupied most of one wall.

It he still liked. It was an impressionist view of a tree, with an infant – looking almost embarrassingly Christ-childlike – perched in the high branches. Years ago Stanwell had tried to locate the very tree in which he'd been mysteriously found in 1950, but he learned that they'd built the Pasadena Freeway right over the field in which the tree had stood. He'd considered going back and making them build the damn freeway along a different route, in case subsequent generations might want to make a shrine or something around the tree, but he'd decided that such a move would be a needlessly egotistical strain on the fabric – and besides, the real tree probably hadn't looked half so imposing as this painted one.

He drained the drink and stood up. Hell, he thought, take the long view. What if we haven't made a lot of progress *this* year? The man ahead had seemed busy, if rude, and things have been getting steadily better ever since I engineered Roosevelt's death to occur in '44 instead of '45, so that it was Henry Wallace, not Harry Truman, who inherited the presidency. Stanwell smiled out the window at the multitudes below. Hardly any of you know who I am, he thought, and not one of you knows my real function, but I prevented the bomb and Korea and Vietnam and Nixon for you. I don't look for thanks – how could you thank me for deflecting calamities you never heard of? – I do it only so that we may all have a better world to live in. Mine is a...where did I once read this phrase?...a high and lonely destiny.

Feeling confident enough now to go and give encouragement to the next man back, he stepped into the middle of the room, frowned for a moment in concentration, and then disappeared.

The implosion of air cracked the window and snatched the top few pages of his autobiography off the stack; they whirled to the floor, and one of them hid the impression his shoes had left in the carpet.

The telephone was still ringing when Keith Bondier blinked back into awareness of his surroundings.

Should have known better than to try and answer it, he thought groggily as he rolled over on the kitchen floor. You knew today was the day you can *count* on the fainting fits – every July first, at exactly fifteen minutes after ten, and then another one a while later. Usually, though, the second fit happens at least half an hour after the first one. I really thought I could get to the phone and then back to bed before it hit.

His kneecaps were resonating with pain and his shoulder throbbed, but his head only stung a little above one ear, so it couldn't have been a bad fall.

The phone was still ringing, though, so he struggled wincingly to his feet and fumbled the receiver off the hook. *"Ah.* Yeah?"

"Keith? You okay?"

"Yeah yeah, fine. Hi Margie. What's up?"

"Shopping. Errands. You want to come along?"

He smiled, his aches forgotten. "Sure, and I just got my disability check, so I can buy us lunch."

"Oh, I'll pay my half."

"No, Marge, you always have to drive."

"Keith, as soon as they get you on the right medication you'll be able to get a license – then I'll make you drive all the time. Today we'll go Dutch."

"Nah, I'll get it," he said hastily. "Let me, while I've got a fresh check." He figured that paying for her lunch would make it a real *date,* rather than just two friends out wandering around. "When can you get here?"

"Hm? Oh, five minutes. I'm ready to go."

"Great. See you soon."

After he hung up the phone he sat down and rubbed his knees as he looked around his apartment. The place looks neat enough, he thought. Only a few clothes on the floor. If I straighten it up, she'd be able to tell, and it'd put her on guard. Right. Got to strive to make it look spontaneous. I'd better eat some toothpaste, though, for the old breath's sake.

Halfway to the bathroom he stopped, a pained expression on his face, for once again he had caught a tart-sweet whiff of garbage. He was sure it was just another olfactory hallucination, that visitors couldn't smell it, but it was hardly the sort of thing to get him in the mood to try and seduce Margie; and while the smell was – just barely! – tolerable, he couldn't say the same for the sort of auditory and visual hallucinations that occasionally followed. He fervently hoped this wasn't going to be one of his bad days.

But just as he was squeezing a dab of toothpaste onto his finger-tip he heard a hoarse voice cry, "You better put all that trash back in them barrels, lady!" – and though it sounded as though the man who'd yelled was standing right beside him, the cry had an unconfined sound, as if it had occurred outdoors.

The sudden voice had startled Bondier, and the curl of toothpaste had wound up on the mirror. He swore under his breath and steeled himself against any further intrusions, and he managed to get a blob of toothpaste into his mouth in spite of an old woman's voice snarling, "Screw yaself, I'm on public propitty," as he lifted his hand.

He resolutely chewed the toothpaste, then spat it out and rinsed his mouth. It occurred to him that he ought to shave, and during the task he was subjected to no further phantom noises except a few bangs and clatters, which he ignored.

The doorbell rang just as he'd sat down and got a cigarette lit, which pleased him, for he thought he looked less like an invalid when he was smoking. "Come on in, Marge, it's not locked."

The door opened and Margie bustled inside. She was a bit older than Bondier, but her pale skin, wool skirt, eye-magnifying glasses and brown hair – pulled functionally back in a bun – made her seem younger, or at least made the question of her age somehow irrelevant. Her head and hands and feet were just perceptibly bigger than scale, and sometimes when he was in a bad mood he thought she looked like one of those human-body drawings that exaggerated the bits that had greater nerve sensitivity.

"Ready to go?" she asked, brightly cheerful as always.

Bondier could hardly hear her over the new hallucinatory noise, a measured series of sharp metallic crunchings, as if someone was methodically stomping a line of flimsy toy cars. "Sure," he said, trying not to raise his voice. "But you just got here – sit down. Can I get you a cup of coffee?"

"Lady, you can't flatten 'em here, my tenants gotta park here," rasped the man's voice again, and Bondier had missed Margie's answer.

"What?"

"I said no thanks, let's go before the rain starts." Marge cocked her head and blinked at him. "You sure you're all right?"

"Well," said Bondier, unable to think of any other way to make her alight, "I did have one of my blackouts a few minutes ago. A couple of 'em, actually."

He heard a car start up, sounding like it was right in the room with them, and he was wearily glad that Margie didn't share his hallucinations, for the following gust of engine fumes would have driven her out of the apartment if she'd been able to smell them. He stubbed out his cigarette in a coffee cup.

"Oh, you poor thing," Marge said with sudden concern, shutting the door and crossing to join him on the couch. "Did you fall?"

"Stupid old bitch," the man's voice growled.

"Just a … sort of tumble," said Bondier. He draped an arm around her shoulder. "I'm still a little dizzy, though." Start, rain, he thought. Start hard.

Trying not to seem either hesitant or hurried, he leaned over to kiss her.

A sharp but silent flash in the room made him jerk around involuntarily – and then it took all his control not to yell in surprise, for his kitchen was gone, and his living room now opened onto a brightly sunlit parking lot, and, standing only a few yards away from him, facing away toward the cars, was a fat old man in overalls who was meditatively scratching his rear end.

Oh, God, it's bigger and vivider than my *apartment*, than *I* am, thought Bondier shrilly; but it'll go away. I'm getting worse, but it *will go away* – if I ignore it, don't acknowledge it, really act as if it's not – intolerably! – there.

He turned back to Marge, squinting against the impossible glare and hoping his voice wouldn't quaver when he apologized for having jumped, but she was leaning back against the couch-arm, with her eyes closed, and really didn't seem to have noticed. Her lips were open and working, and at first he thought she was somewhat grotesquely inviting a kiss, but then he saw that her arms were extended to form a ring, as though she was in the *process* of kissing someone, someone invisible.

And a moment later he actually shrieked, for he had looked down and seen that there was a hole that extended across her belly and part of the couch, and through the hole he could clearly see a trash can full of old milk cartons and sour cream tubs and crumpled bags from some takeout restaurant he'd never heard of called McDonald's.

He was on his feet, gagging and near panic.

The front end of his apartment, he noted numbly, not only still showed a gray day behind the blinds, but also wasn't even a bit lighted by the – yes, it was all still there – bright sunlight on the other side of the room.

"I'm sorry, Marge," he said in a constricted voice as he stared hard at the room's normal half. "I think I took more of a knock than I realized. Let's get some fresh air, okay?"

There was no answer, so he forced himself to turn around.

On the couch – between Bondier and the fat man in overalls, who was still scratching his rear end – Marge was now reclining on her back, making soft sounds of protest but still working her mouth and caressing empty air. As Bondier watched, her blouse rippled and the top button slowly undid itself.

"*Marge,*" he said loudly, fear putting a whining tone in his voice.

She didn't hear him.

"*Marge!*" he shouted, suddenly so dizzy that he grabbed the arm of a chair in case he had another blackout.

The old man stopped scratching and turned around to stare unseeingly in Bondier's direction. "Who's that?" he called.

"*Goddamn it, Marge, can't you hear me?*" screamed Bondier.

"Hey, keep it down, there," said the old man. "Where are you, anyway?"

The old man started forward, and Bondier's nerve broke; he whirled around, snatched open his front door and bolted down the walkway toward the street. A cat scampered out of his path and ran straight up a wooden fence.

He desperately wished there was someone he could talk to, someone who was close enough to him to listen without making judgements about his sanity. He had a few friends, but none of them would welcome this kind of confidence.

Family, he thought, that's what I wish I had right now, people who would have known me since I was a baby. A brother to share this with, a mother on whose lap to tearfully dump it all. Of course I *do* have a mother – somewhere, if she hasn't died by now.

He smiled bitterly at the thought. He'd never known his mother, hadn't even seen her since the court took him away from her when he was still a baby, but she didn't seem to have been the sort of woman who could be bothered with comforting an upset son. She almost certainly *had* thrown his twin brother off that overpass onto the Pasadena Freeway in 1954, as several witnesses had attested; and if the little corpse hadn't evidently been carried right away by one of the passing vehicles, she'd have had to put up with the inconvenience of a murder trial ... and she hadn't made even a token protest when the authorities subsequently relieved her of the remaining member of the pair.

Sure, he told himself, trying desperately to be adult and jocularly independent about it. Look *her* up. *That'd* make you feel better. Jesus.

He'd slowed to a walk, and now stopped and turned to look at his apartment, two blocks back. It looked the same as it always did, a pair of windows in the long rust-streaked building, and Marge's battered old Volkswagen sat as placidly as ever by the curb. A young man had ducked behind a tree across the street, probably – knowing this neighborhood – to take a piss.

It occurred to him that the cars in the hallucinated parking lot had all been models he'd never seen. They'd been littler, and rounder.

He took several deep breaths. It must have been an aftereffect of the two blackouts, he thought. This was the worst yet, but it seems to be over. I ought to head back.

But he decided to clear his head with some brisk walking and fresh air first, and let the chilly breeze brush even the memory of the garbage-reek out of his hair. He walked randomly for ten minutes, up this alley and down that street, and his heartbeat was nearly back to normal, his mouth beginning to lose the dry taste of unreasoning fear, when he turned onto Main Street, aiming to get a beer at Trader Joe's, and to hell with the doctor's warnings about drinking while on medication. Some medication it had turned out to be.

He heard brakes and a sudden metallic crunch a couple of blocks behind him, and when he turned he saw that a delivery van had backed into a parked car – several cardboard boxes toppled out and split open, and cigarette cartons spilled into the gutter. He started back, hoping to be first among the mob that would quickly be gathering to snatch them up, but then he saw the thing striding massively down the sidewalk toward him.

Keeping his face very stiff so as not to let his aides know that something was wrong, Stanwell walked steadily from the cab to the door of the Corday Hotel.

The hardest part was to keep from alternately narrowing and unnarrowing his eyes as the hallucination of a bright, sunny day flashed on and off every few seconds. It was easier when he'd got inside Andre's, the ground-floor restaurant, and been shown to a table, for though the room kept changing from an elegant restaurant to a shabby laundromat and back again, as abruptly as if the restaurant scene was a photograph someone kept shoving in his face and then yanking away, he could lean back and shut his eyes. At least the feel of his chair, and the tablecloth under his hands, were steady.

"You're certain you're all right, sir?"

Stanwell nodded without opening his eyes. "Gribbin be here soon?"

"That's what his man said on the phone, sir. Of course you know how the subways are. But if you feel at all bad, it'd be easy to – "

"I'm fine, damn it," Stanwell snapped, his eyes still shut. "Tired, is all."

He thought, if only that son-of-a-bitch, year-older version of me could have said whether or not these damned hallucinations have let up by his time! Or if only I could circumvent him, break the now-barrier: travel farther into the future than the somehow-constant now-line, which moves forward only at the agonizingly slow rate of a day per day.

He sighed, opened his eyes long enough for the restaurant to appear, and grabbed his water glass.

I suppose, he thought as he took a sip and replaced the glass by touch, that if an ordinary person, condemned, as each of them is, to be a steadily moving point on the time chart, unable to edge even one second further ahead or back than the instant of now – if one of them could know of my capabilities, he'd probably think I had incalculable freedom…the fool.

I guess I can see why there is the now-barrier – it's the freshly woven edge of the fabric, beyond which is only emptiness and God's moving shuttle – or uncollapsed probability waves – but what's the problem with the *other* direction? Why in hell can't I jump forward again from any point further back than 1953?

Thank God, he thought with a shiver, I didn't have to jump any further back than 1943 to learn that. *That* was a horrible decade for me, unable to jump and concluding that the talent had been lost; having to get jobs and apartments, and simply *live* my way ploddingly up the years, until mid-1953 finally rolled around again, and I found the talent had been restored, and I could jump up to *now*, which had been … what, 1975 then.

And why in hell should it be the case that I can only do it if I'm in – of all places – downtown Santa Ana, California? It's as if there's some kind of psychic power-station locally.

"Ah, I see Gribbin coming up the steps now, sir," said one of his aides, and Stanwell ventured to open his eyes.

The hallucinatory tug-of-war seemed to have been settled in favor of the restaurant, he noted with relief, and he beckoned to the drink steward. Being from New York, Stanwell reasoned, Gribbin might like to take the opportunity to try some tequila – just as whenever I'm back east I always make it a point to get hold of some real Scotch.

A few moments after Stanwell had placed the drinks order, Gribbin's driver walked up to the table and pulled out a chair, and then after a pause pushed it in again.

"Where's Mr. Gribbin?" Stanwell asked him.

The man didn't answer.

"Excuse me, I asked you where Mr. Gribbin is."

The man on Stanwell's right leaned forward and shook hands with the empty air over the ashtray. "And I'm Bob Atkins, Mr. Gribbin," he said respectfully

The drink steward returned and set down two glasses of tequila, one in front of Stanwell and one at the empty place across the table. "I trust you'll enjoy that, sir," said the steward to the empty chair.

The thing was no taller than Bondier, but it was so broad – from its shopping-cart shoulders to its fringed, elephantine feet – that it seemed to loom over him as it advanced up the street, filling the sidewalk and spinning heedless pedestrians out of its way. Its mouth was a wide square hole, studded with bits of jagged metal, and its eyes were two big tin pie-plates, with riddlings of tiny holes at their centers like the holes boys punch into jar lids to let captive insects breathe; but the eyes were spinning back and forth on the front of the rubbish head, and a harsh roaring was echoing out of the mouth.

It was rushing at him fast, and the pure, idiot ferocity that glared like tropical sunlight off of the blunt face made Bondier cry out in shock and cringe back against the wall.

It slid to a halt, dust and smoke bursting from its substance and whirling away in spirals, and then it turned its terrible head toward him, and for the first time he realized that it was composed of trash. Bags and cans and old bits of cloth heaved as it flexed itself, and then a long, shapeless limb had lashed out and a paw made of coat hangers and branches had grabbed Bondier under the chin and was crushing him against the wall.

Bondier managed to force out a choked scream, but the people on the sidewalk were oblivious of both the monster and him; even as he sobbed and tore uselessly at the garbage cable that had him pinned, several pedestrians at once collided with the trash-creature's back, then expressionlessly righted themselves and resumed their walking.

The thing's steady roaring became recognizable as many voices only when all of them began to speak in unison; suddenly it was a senilely shrill babble that came rasping out of the big hole in the face, and Bondier was able to catch words: "... *see who pays the piper now, Stanwell, you can dish it out, all right, but now we'll see ... throat out, rip his balls off, right here in front of God'n'everybody ... but wait a minute, any of you remember, we saw him, just a min- ute ago, at that restaurant, that Andre's fency-shmency ... back the street ... yeah ... this ain't him, this is got no gray hair – young, too young, this boy.*"

For a moment the wires and branches pressed a little less tightly against Bondier's larynx, and he got his legs braced for a breakaway and mad sprint, but before he could choose his moment the inhuman grip tightened again, so tight this time that his breath whistled in his throat and his vision started to darken.

"It's the twin, then, we knew *there was a twin… maybe if we kill the twin, Stanwell will die – and then we can have our real lives!"*

And then, without releasing his throat, it had crowded up to the wall and was embracing him, hugging him to its greasy, crumbling chest, and when he opened his mouth to scream again an oil-soaked rag wormed in between his jaws; cigarette butts and old straws had found his nostrils and were burrowing up into his head, and cords and lengths of cloth looped around his arms and legs and began pulling them upward and inward. Pressed rib-crackingly hard against the wall, he was simultaneously being folded up into a fetal position and smothered.

More bits of trash were forcing their way into his nose and mouth – he coughed gaggingly, but only wound up letting them get further in; they were well down his throat by now, with more packing themselves in every second. Then there was a sharp pain in his side, and instantly afterward a feeling of heat and running wetness, and he realized that some jagged component of the thing had stabbed him, and that the garbagey member was about to begin probing the interior of his abdomen.

It galvanized him. He gave one last, mighty convulsion – but it wasn't a physical one, and he felt the whole world jump with him.

In an instant the thing was gone, every bit of it, and he had fallen forward hard onto his hands and knees, and he was retching and coughing up all kinds of litter onto the sidewalk. After a few moments he was able to breathe, and when he stopped whooping he sat up and pulled up his shirt – the cut in his side wasn't bleeding too badly, and didn't look nearly as deep as it had felt. He folded his handkerchief into a pad and unlooped his belt to rebuckle it across his stomach, pressing the handkerchief against the cut, and then he tucked in his shirt. Finally he stood up, shakily, grinning in embarrassment at the people near him, but they weren't looking at him, just as they hadn't seemed to be able to see the trash-thing.

He hurried away, and all he permitted himself to think about on the way back to his apartment was how he was going to crawl into bed and pull the covers over his head... and then see the doctor tomorrow morning and request, demand, some vastly more potent medication. He assured himself that the trash monster had just been one more hallucination... and that probably the bruise on his throat and the cut in his side were imaginary too.

He was even beginning to relax as he rounded the last corner and saw his apartment – and Marge's car, still! Bless her – ahead. But then he saw his front door yanked open, and a young man came running out, scaring a cat out of his path, and Bondier realized he wasn't clear of it yet, for the obviously terrified young man sprinting up the sidewalk on the other side of the street was himself.

Okay, he told himself tensely, you're still in it, it's the same hallucination. It's even got a certain consistency – that's probably the twin that that monster referred to. See? It's just *one* of your fits, not even several. You're probably still on the couch, actually. Don't start crying.

But the air felt too cold, and the street was too normally wide, and the building was at once too detailed and too insignificant-looking for him to believe that this was a hallucination. He cowered behind a tree and watched while the young man paused and looked back.

Then he remembered the cat that had run out of his path... and with the irrational certainty of real nightmares he was sure he knew what the frightened young man was thinking at this moment: *Too bad I don't have a family, ought to go back, no, bit of a walk first, clear my head, and then maybe swing by Trader Joe's for a beer and who's that guy taking a piss behind the tree across the street there?*

When the other Bondier had rounded the corner, Bondier stepped out from behind the tree. A crazy thought had come to him, so crazy that it was in itself pretty good evidence that he was in some kind of dream state.

That last convulsion of mine, he thought, when the trash-creature was about to choke me or rip out my entrails – which way did I jump? The thing wasn't even around afterward. Could I have… *jumped back?*

In which corner of the compass is *ago?*

He glanced at his watch. Five minutes to eleven. He wondered if that other Bondier's watch read about twenty of. He walked slowly back to the apartment and pushed open the door. Marge was still on the couch, and he was relieved to see that the kitchen was restored, but the very first thing he glanced at was the clock over the oven.

It read 10:41.

If it was right, he had gained fifteen minutes on the world.

"All *along,*" Marge said, evidently emphasizing some point she'd made in the minute or two when neither of him had been there. She was wrapped up in the tapestry he covered the threadbare couch with, and though her glasses were off she was staring at the chair he usually sat in. He crossed to it, stepping over her discarded skirt and blouse and underwear, and sat down.

Now she was staring right at him, and it was suddenly much harder to suppose that this scene was automatic, and would continue whether he stayed or not.

"Hi, Marge," he said helplessly as he unbuttoned his blood-blotted shirt. "The universe or me – one of us is real sick."

"Oh *don't* tell me that," she groaned, tossing her head. He noticed that without glasses her eyes were smaller and seemed to have too much white skin around them. "You don't mean it," she went on, "you're just… throwing that to me, the way you'd throw a dog a bone to make it stop bothering you."

He tossed the bloody shirt onto the floor, stood up and ducked into the narrow bathroom, and reappeared with a glass bottle of Bactine. He splashed some onto his reddening handkerchief-bandage and put the bottle down. "Listen, Marge," he said, leaning forward and forcing his voice to come out in a reasonable tone, "can you hear me?"

She didn't answer.

"Well," he went on, picking up a comparatively clean shirt from the floor, "I saw a thing today, walking around like a human, but it was entirely... made out of *trash*, I swear, it – was just *made out of trash*." He laughed hollowly as he buttoned the fresh shirt. "And this trash-thing could talk. It said I was – some kind of twin – of some guy they're afraid of. I should have said it talks in lots of voices, shouldn't I? I can't tell this right. But these voices said that this twin is right now having lunch at Andre's. That's the posh place in the Corday." He sat down again so that when she talked it would be toward him.

"You knew I wasn't ready for this kind of thing," said Marge unhappily. "Just friends, we agreed."

"Jesus, Marge, I'll tell you the truth, it's hard for me to feel... *to blame* about whatever's been going on here, you know? But listen, Marge, I *did* have a twin. I never told you about this, but I did. My mother pitched him off a pedestrian overpass onto the Pasadena Freeway in '54, when he and I were both a year old. She only wanted to keep *me,* though they took me away from her too. But – this just occurred to me, and you're gonna think I'm really nuts – what if my one-year-old brother's reaction to total terror was the same as what I right now suspect mine is? To jump backward in time? Then maybe he *isn't* dead. Maybe in mid-fall he jumped back, maybe all the way to a time before the freeway was built, and wound up in a field somewhere, and was found alive. He'd never know he had a twin brother."

Marge had been muttering for the last several seconds, and when he paused he heard her saying, " ... as a free lunch, and there has to be *commitment,* and I frankly – (sniff) – don't think you're capable of that."

"You're probably right, Marge, though I'll bet I wind up committed." The joke, muffled by the stained carpet and drapes, sounded dead even to him. "You know what I get lately when I'm walking down the street? Claustrophobia. I feel like I'm in a diorama, you know, like the statues of Neanderthals in the museum, I'm afraid I'll notice that the sun's a light bulb, and my buddies are just painted statues, and the sky's got corners."

In spite of his efforts his voice had got whimpery, and he took a few deep breaths.

Suddenly Marge looked up, and he gathered that he'd been supposed to get to his feet. He stayed where he was.

"No, don't touch me," Marge cried, shoving herself backward across the couch and getting one bare foot caught in a hole in the fabric.

"I'm just sitting here, Marge," he said, bleakly sure that no one in the universe could hear him.

"You do?" she quavered now, looking up toward the ceiling light. "Really, Keith? It isn't just a ... sop to my pride? You *do* love me?"

"*I* don't know, Marge," said Bondier unhappily, still in his chair. "I don't know if I'm even – "

"Oh, Keith, I love you too," she whispered, and let the tapestry fall from her white shoulders.

He felt as though cold water had been splashed in his face. The breath caught in his throat, and all at once he was ashamed of himself; of course it had all been hallucinations – this was *Margerie,* not some figure from a nightmare, and he *did* love her.

He unbent himself out of the chair and fitted himself beside her on the couch, kissing her as he had always meant to, running his trembling, bloodstained hands over her bare breasts ... but she was stiff, and though her lips were obviously responding, they weren't responding to *him,* and when she made a cupping gesture in empty air and smiled seductively past him at the ceiling he broke free of the off-center embrace and stood up, panting with renewed fear.

She rocked over onto her back, and Bondier found himself almost able to gauge the actions of her invisible partner by her motions. What if he should begin to see a cloudy figure there – and what if it were to look up at him?

Again he ran out of the apartment, and again the pavements and buildings were too clear for him to believe that they weren't real. He began walking, and the only destination he could think of was the restaurant where, maybe, his twin was. He didn't want to think, so he walked faster instead, and when he sped up he discovered that he'd been correct when he'd thought the passersby couldn't see him. Okay, that makes sense, he told himself desperately – keep the fear at arm's length, boy. Of *course* they can't see you, you're out of your slot, you're fifteen minutes away from where you're supposed to be at this moment.

But even before I time-jumped, he thought, Margie couldn't see or hear me. She was kissing the nonexistent me even *before*.

There were young women in the crowds on Main Street, office workers out for lunch, and he found himself looking at them speculatively. They couldn't see him, he could do anything to them he wanted to, knock one of them down and take her clothes off right in the gutter. No one would know – not even her.

He paused and grinned, not accepting the idea but not necessarily discarding it either – until he remembered that the many-voiced garbage-giant might still be able to see him, and he couldn't know which window or rooftop or trash can it might be peering at him from, preparing to rush at him again.

The thought started him moving again, and when he tried to imagine what Marge might be up to by this time, all alone back in his shabby apartment, he began to hurry toward the Hotel Corday.

Moving through the blind, mechanical crowd required a specialized pace that seemed similar to both broken-field running and bullfighting cape-work; and just as Bondier was beginning to get accustomed to the lateral hops and quick backtracking and the occasional necessity of a close whirl around a straight-oncoming pedestrian, a flash of light blinded him.

The light stayed on, and he winced and braced himself for the first collision, determined at least not to fall under the inexorable feet – but nothing touched him, and the air was warmer suddenly, and smelled fresher, and after a few seconds he squintingly looked up.

It was a bright summer day with a few clouds sailing past unbelievably high overhead, and though the sidewalk wasn't as crowded now, a number of people – all of whom seemed more three-dimensional than the people he'd been dodging moments ago – were staring at him in surprise.

"Where'd you drop from, son?" one man wonderingly inquired, and Bondier had just opened his mouth to stammer a reply when the sunlight went out again and a fat lady rammed him broadside and propelled him against the wall of the Corday Hotel.

He glanced around wildly, wondering for the first time if this whole *world* might be the hallucination, and the sunlit world the real one. In comparison, this one seemed so… dark and gray and depthless.

A bright blue dot flared in the sky, then slowly became a line like a luminous jet trail. The first crack, he thought.

He edged his way to the entrance of Andre's and shoved against the glass door, and then pulled, but it didn't open, didn't even rattle against a bolt – it was as if he'd grabbed a section of brickwork.

What is this, he thought, they can't be *closed,* it isn't even noon yet, and I can see people inside.

He saw a portly, toothpick-chewing man striding up the hall toward the entrance, and he took a step back in case the glass should break when the man hit the immovable door, but to Bondier's surprise the door swung open easily at the man's push. Bondier sprang forward and caught the edge of the door as the man joined the street throng – but the door swung shut, no faster or slower than normal, despite Bondier's straining, heel-dragging effort to hold it open, and finally he had to let go in order to save his fingers.

I'm not a member of this world at all anymore, he thought. Maybe I was never more than half-connected, but now all these things are as impervious to me as objects in a newspaper photograph would be to a fly crawling over the paper. A tossed bottle-cap might knock me down – or punch right through me. Christ, is this world's oxygen still willing to combine with the hemoglobin in my blood, or whatever it is it's supposed to do?

He glanced desperately at the sky. The bright blue line was longer now, and branched at one end. Hurry, he thought.

Another patron, a woman, left the restaurant, and this time Bondier scuttled in around her and rolled inside before the irresistible door closed.

Every table in the elegant dining room was occupied, but the talking and the clatter of cutlery was muffled. There were no smells – and as Bondier walked in and looked around for someone who looked like himself, he noted that the carpeting under his feet seemed to be frozen, or shellacked; and then he realized that it simply wasn't yielding under him. I'd probably break a tooth if I tried to eat a forkful of mashed potatoes, he thought.

He heard a crash out on Main Street, and he knew it was the delivery truck bumping the car and spilling the cigarette cartons, right on schedule. He glanced toward the noise.

When he turned back to the dining room he saw him, the man he knew must be his twin, sitting with a couple of other men at a table by the window. The man was older, his hair gray at the temples, but the eyes, nose and chin were the same ones Bondier saw every morning in the mirror. The twin was talking angrily – and, it seemed to Bondier, a little fearfully – to a man who'd just walked up to the table; but the new arrival, and the others at the table too, were ignoring him and talking cheerfully among themselves.

I do believe, thought Bondier, that my brother is also beginning to notice a bit of dislocation. Bondier had just opened his mouth to call out a greeting when his twin abruptly went limp and collapsed face down on the tablecloth.

Alarmed, Bondier hurried forward. The other men at the table were now quiet, and were looking attentively at a point over the inert twin's head, and then at an empty chair on the other side of the table, and then over the twin's head again, and Bondier guessed that, according to the universe's script, a dialogue was going on.

Bondier hoisted up his unconscious brother and let him slump back in the chair. He was breathing, at least.

"Uh, that was last Tuesday, sir," put in the man by the window.

"Who asked you, clown," said Bondier absently. He took one of the slack wrists. The pulse was steady and strong.

It's just like one of my blackout fits, he reflected. In fact it's probably the same malady, something that runs in the family. I wonder if *his* doctors have been able to diagnose it. He looks like he could afford private practice ones. Well, if that's what it is he ought to be coming out of it in a minute or two.

Bondier glanced at his watch. Exactly eleven. Right about now, he thought, a block or two south of here, that trash-thing is jumping on the fifteen-minutes-younger me, and I'm disappearing.

"That's correct, sir," said the window-seat man.

"Shut up," Bondier told him. As a matter of fact, he thought, my time-jump and his blackout were, as far as I can tell, simultaneous. I wonder if my time-jump – only a few seconds ago by every watch but mine – could be the *cause* of this blackout.

And has that all along been the cause of mine? That *he's* been jumping? If so, why the hell does he every year make two jumps on the morning of July first?

Like someone trying to deduce the reason behind a puzzling chess move, Bondier mentally put himself in his twin's place –

and he was beginning to get a glimmer of an answer to his question, when Stanwell inhaled sharply, stiffened, opened his eyes and glanced around.

"I seem to have passed out," he said uncertainly to the man by the window, who happened to be looking at him.

"They can't hear you," said Bondier quietly, crouched beside Stanwell's chair.

Stanwell jumped, then turned on Bondier a glare with more than a little fear in it. "And just who the hell are – " he began, then his eyes widened and he reached down and gripped Bondier's shoulder. "My God," he said softly, "is this a … a trick? Is your hair dyed? But it's thicker, too … and no facelift could have restored my youth so perfectly … My God, boy, you've broken the barrier, you jumped forward past your local now! Tell me how you did it – and then we can *all* get together, and dispense with this business of the once-a-year backward relay of reassurance messages."

"It was getting tiresome," hazarded Bondier, pretty sure of his guess now, "every July first."

Stanwell's face had lost its look of reined-in panic, and he laughed jovially. "You don't know how tiresome, my boy," he said. "I wish you'd been in my office earlier today and seen the me – the us, I should say – from next year. Un*pardon*ably rude, abrupt, wouldn't tell me anything… hah! But now we can cross the barrier and go have some fun with him, pretend we won't tell him how – but wait a minute! Have you tried – you might not have – have you tried to jump *forward* again from earlier than 1953? *I* can't do it, though I don't know why. Maybe…"

Stanwell's voice drifted off and he glanced around the restaurant uneasily. "This is lasting a little long," he said. "Maybe you've already noticed instances of it back when you're from, times when people can't see or hear you … sometimes if you *shout* they can, but then if you can get them to answer, it's just stuttering, as if you're forcing a machine… But this has been several minutes now, it's bound to click in again soon. Why don't you stand back by the hall there, so no one will see you just appear out of nowhere, and then I'll introduce you as my younger brother."

"I don't think we'll show up for a while yet," said Bondier gently. He stood up and stepped around to the empty chair that was Gribbin's, and sat down in it. "This guy's just plain gone," he observed, patting the arms of the chair. "Has that ever happened before? One of the actors just doesn't show up, but everyone else carries on as if he were present and following the script?"

"Well, no," Stanwell admitted. "I think we ought to jump ahead and make sure everything's – "

"I need some filling in," said Bondier. "You've been fooling with history?"

"Well, certainly," said Stanwell. "How young are you, anyway? That's my – our – purpose. That's why God put us in that tree."

Bondier blinked at him. "Tree? Wait, wait a minute, I've got it – in a place now occupied by the Pasadena Freeway, right?"

"Of course. You knew that. We knew that when we were seven." Another guess confirmed. "Just wanted to be sure."

There was a conclusion implicit in all this, and he knew it was going to be terrifying, and he knew too that he'd suffer it whether he learned its nature or not – but he found that he couldn't back away from it and, even for the little time he might have left, never know. "Have you killed many people?"

Stanwell stared at him. "When *are* you from? You look like about 1970, and we were jumping pretty frequently by the late sixties; it only took a couple of jumps to learn how to do it without having to be scared to death in order to provoke it. We'd done plenty by your time, hadn't we? Or hadn't we started *facing* it yet? I hadn't thought we were so cowardly. Yes, we've shortened some world-lines, and probably eliminated some altogether, but always for the world's good. Christ, you must remember the original version more clearly than I do – Vietnam, Nixon – "

"Do these people *stay* erased? Don't you worry that maybe you've stretched the fabric so tight with your alterations that... I don't know... it starts to crack and split a little, here and there, faster than you can scramble with your needle and thread?"

"That's nonsense, of course they stay erased, what are you – "

"Have you... have you ever seen a thing made of animated trash that walks around and talks with a lot of voices?"

"I think he's got a point, sir," piped up the man beside Stanwell. Both twins looked at him, but the man was still oblivious of them.

Stanwell had turned pale. "How can you know about that thing? You look like you're from absolutely no later than '72 or so, and I only first saw it last year – and I've *never* heard it," he shuddered, *"speak."*

"Maybe you *can't* erase people," said Bondier, smiling nervously as he shifted back and forth on the unyielding seat cushion. "Maybe you can eliminate the bodies they would have got, cut their life-lines out of the four-dimensional hypercube, but their minds hang around anyway... faded and imbecilic let's say, and malevolent as nasty children, but present... and if they get together, enough of them, maybe they can animate lightweight stuff and come looking for the guy who evicted them from the story." He shook his head and reached for Gribbin's glass of tequila, but it stuck to the table as if bolted there. "I don't think you've rerouted history. I think the real world, the original version, is still going on, independent of this. You've just engineered a... an interesting short circuit.

"I guess it's pretty clear what I've got to do," he said, and as Stanwell opened his mouth to say something further, Bondier closed his eyes and, finally, let himself realize that his identity – the whole neurally-coded accumulation of memories, prejudices, fears and ambitions that was himself – was about to wink out of existence along with the fake world that had collaborated in their creation.

His twin brother was speaking, but Bondier had opened his eyes and looked down at his lap, and instead of his hands he saw a wire basket full of dirty T-shirts and jeans – he was even now falling out of the world, and he convulsed in icy vertigo at the realization.

And the whole world imploded.

Bondier looked back over his shoulder and though he was still squinting in the sunlight he could see the young mother and the baby carriage moving steadily away. I wonder, he thought, what she's planning to buy with the five dollar bill she palmed from the roll I let fall? A drink to steady her nerves afterward? A new dress? How far does a fiver go in '54, anyway?

But you'll never get to spend it, Mom. This time they'll find the little corpse.

Reaching into his flannel shirt, he touched his side and felt the scar he would now never acquire. It hadn't healed quickly; for the entire first year of this clumsy, backward-jumping journey it had been inflamed and infected ... and even now, after years of searching and time-jumping and searching some more, it still sometimes woke him up with a sudden twinge.

He walked away, looking around at the buildings and the bulbous, incongruously shiny cars. What have I got, he wondered, ten minutes? It'll take her about that long to wheel that thing to the freeway overpass, and by then my poor brother will have consumed enough of that codeine-laced milk to have rendered himself unconscious, and unable to feel any fear when the moment comes.

He remembered something his brother had said – Have you tried to jump forward again from earlier than 1953? I can't do it ...

Of course he couldn't do it, Bondier thought now. Before 1953 we weren't born yet – he couldn't jump back up from before then, because I was his overdrive time-jumping engine, and before 1953 I didn't exist.

I could still stop her.

Sure, he thought with a fragile grin, I could let him live and then have my own try at rewriting history, use his mind as my overdrive engine for the time-jumps, let him *be the invalid with the blackouts this time, as I was in his version. But my version would certainly run down and stop too.*

He hoped the police would find the epitaph he had written on a piece of paper and tucked into his infant brother's blanket. It was from A.E. Housman:

> But I will go where they are hid
> That never were begot,
> To my inheritance amid
> The nation that is not.

I wonder, he thought, what Keith Bondier's life is like in the real world. I hope I don't get involved with Margie. I hope I still like Beethoven and Hemingway and Monet and Housman. I hope the real world isn't as bad off as my poor doomed brother thought it was. At least it'll be the real one.

He looked back toward the freeway again, but he couldn't see them anymore. So long, Mom and brother, he thought. Though I'll see you one more time, brother. It'll only take me a couple of jumps to get up to that July first where you're waiting for that progress report. The last one – when, according to you, I'll be "unpardonably rude and abrupt" and not tell you anything. I suppose I'll seem that way. What could I say, though?

In his tight-clutching hand the baby bottle broke, spattering the dusty pavement with milk. Bondier absently dropped the pieces, and after a few moments he noticed that his thumb was bleeding. He sucked on it.

And then, having no reason to delay here any longer, he disappeared, and this time there was no sound to mark his passage, nor any slightest ripple in the dust.

The Better Boy

James P. Blaylock & Tim Powers

KNOCK KNOCK.

Bernard Wilkins twisted the scratched restaurant butter-knife in his pudgy hand to catch the eastern sun.

There was a subtle magic in the morning. He felt it most at breakfast – the smells of bacon and coffee, the sound of birds outside, the arrangement of clouds in the deep summer sky, and the day laid out before him like a roadmap unfolded on a dashboard.

This morning he could surely allow himself to forget about the worms and the ether bunnies.

It was Saturday, and he was going to take it easy today, go home and do the crossword puzzle, maybe get the ball game on the radio late in the afternoon while he put in a couple of hours in the garage. The Angels were a half game out and were playing Oakland at two o'clock. In last night's game Downing had slammed a home run into the outfield scoreboard, knocking out the scoreboard's electrical system, and the crowd had gone flat-out crazy, cheering for six solid minutes, stomping and clapping and hooting until the stands were vibrating so badly that they had to stop the game to let everybody calm down.

In his living room Wilkins had been stomping right along with the rest of them, till he was nearly worn out with it.

He grinned now to think about it. Baseball – there was magic in baseball, too … even in your living room you could imagine it, beer and hot dogs, those frozen malts, the smell of cut grass, the summer evenings.

He could remember the smell of baseball leather from his childhood, grass-stained hardballs and new gloves. Chiefly it was the dill pickles and black licorice and Cokes in paper cups that he remembered from back then, when he had played little league ball. They had sold the stuff out of a plywood shack behind the major league diamond.

It was just after eight o'clock in the morning, and Norm's coffee shop was getting crowded with people knocking back coffee and orange juice.

There was nothing like a good meal. Time stopped while you were eating. Troubles abdicated. It was like a holiday. Wilkins sopped up the last of the egg yolk with a scrap of toast, salted it, and put it into his mouth, chewing contentedly. Annie, the waitress, laid his check on the counter, winked at him, and then went off to deal with a wild-eyed woman who wore a half dozen tattered sweaters all at once and was carefully emptying the ketchup bottle onto soda crackers she'd pick out of a basket, afterward dropping them one by one into her ice water, mixing up a sort of poverty-style gazpacho.

Wilkins sighed, wiped his mouth, left a twenty percent tip, heaved himself off the stool and headed for the cash register near the door.

"A good meal," he said to himself comfortably, as if it were an occult phrase. He paid up, then rolled a toothpick out of the dispenser and poked it between his teeth. He pushed open the glass door with a lordly sweep, and strode outside onto the sidewalk.

The morning was fine and warm. He walked to the parking lot edge of the pavement, letting the sun wash over him as he hitched up his pants and tucked his thumbs through his belt loops. What he needed was a pair of suspenders. Belts weren't worth much to a fat man. He rolled the toothpick back and forth in his mouth, working it expertly with his tongue.

. . .

He was wearing his inventor's pants. That's what he had come to call them. He'd had them how many years? Fifteen, anyway. Last winter he had tried to order another pair through a catalogue company back in Wisconsin, but hadn't had any luck. They were khaki work pants with eight separate pockets and oversized, reinforced belt loops. He wore a heavy key chain on one of the loops, with a retractable ring holding a dozen assorted keys – all the more reason for the suspenders.

The cotton fabric of the trousers was web-thin in places. His wife had patched the knees six different times and had resewn the inseam twice. She wasn't happy about the idea of him wearing the pants out in public. Some day, Molly was certain of it, he would sit down on the counter stool at Norm's and the entire rear end would rip right out of them.

Well, that was something Wilkins would face when the time came. He was certain, in his heart, that there would always be a way to patch the pants one more time, which meant infinitely. A stitch in time. Everything was patchable.

"Son of a bitch!" came a shout behind him. He jumped and turned around.

It was the raggedy woman who had been mixing ketchup and crackers into her ice water. She had apparently abandoned her makeshift breakfast.

"What if I *am* a whore?" she demanded of some long-gone debating partner. "Did he ever give *me* a dollar?"

Moved somehow by the sunny morning, Wilkins impulsively tugged a dollar bill out of his trousers. "Here," he said, holding it out to her.

She flounced past him unseeing, and shouted, at no one visibly present, a word that it grieved him to hear. He waved the dollar after her halfheartedly, but she was walking purposefully toward a cluster of disadvantaged-looking people crouched around the dumpster behind the restaurant's service door.

He wondered for a moment about everything being, in fact, patchable.

But perhaps she had some friends among them. Magic after all was like the bottles on the shelves of a dubious-neighborhood liquor store – it was available in different proofs and labels, and at different prices, for anyone who cared to walk in.

And sometimes it helped them. Perhaps obscurely.

He wasn't keen on revealing any of this business about magic to anyone who wouldn't understand; but, in his own case, when he was out in the garage working, he never felt quite right wearing anything else except his inventor's pants.

Somewhere he had read that Fred Astaire had worn a favorite pair of dancing shoes for years after they had worn out, going so far as to pad the interior with newspaper in between re-solings.

Well, Bernard Wilkins had his inventor's trousers, didn't he? And by damn he didn't care what the world thought about them. He scratched at a spot of egg yolk on a pocket and sucked at his teeth, clamping the toothpick against his lip.

Wilkins is the name, he thought with self-indulgent pomposity – invention's the game.

What he was inventing now was a way to eliminate garden pests. There was a subsonic device already on the market to discourage gophers, sure, and another patented machine to chase off mosquitoes.

Neither of them worked worth a damn, really.

The thing that *really* worked on gophers was a wooden propeller nailed to a stick that was driven into the ground. The propeller whirled in the wind, sending vibrations down the stick into the dirt. He had built three of them, big ones, and as a result he had no gopher trouble.

The tomato worms were working him over hard, though, scouring the tomato vines clean of leaves and tomatoes in the night. He sometimes found the creatures in the morning, heavy and long, glowing bright green with pirated chlorophyll and wearing a face that was far too mammalian, almost human.

The sight of one of them bursting under a tramping shoe was too horrible for any sane person to want to do it twice.

Usually what he did was gingerly pick them off the stems and throw them over the fence into his neighbor's yard, but they crawled back through again in the night, further decimating the leaves of his plants. He had replanted three times this season.

What he was working on was a scientific means to get rid of the things. He thought about the nets in his garage, and the boxes of crystal-growing kits he had bought.

Behind him, a car motor revved. A dusty old Ford Torino shot toward him from the back of the parking lot, burning rubber from the rear tires in a cloud of white smoke, the windshield an opaque glare of reflected sunlight. In sudden panic Wilkins scuffed his shoes on the asphalt, trying to reverse his direction, to hop back out of the way before he was run down. The front tire nearly ran over his foot as he yelled and pounded on the hood, and right then the hooked post from the broken-off passenger-side mirror caught him by the keychain and yanked his legs out from under him.

He fell heavily to the pavement and slid.

For one instant it was a contest between his inventor's pants and the car – then the waistband gave way and the inseam ripped out, and he was watching his popped-off shoes bounce away across the parking lot and his pants disappear as the car made a fast right onto Main.

License number! He scrabbled to his feet, lunging substantially naked toward the parking lot exit. There the car went, zigging away through traffic, cutting off a pickup truck at the corner. He caught just the first letter of the license, a G, or maybe a Q. From the mirror support, flapping and dancing and billowing out at the end of the snagged keychain, his inventor's pants flailed themselves to ribbons against the street, looking for all the world as if the pant legs were running furiously, trying to keep up with the car. In a moment the car was gone, and his pants with it.

The sight of the departing pants sent him jogging for his own car. Appallingly, the summer breeze was ruffling the hair on his bare legs, and he looked back at the restaurant in horror, wondering if he had been seen.

Sure enough, a line of faces stared at him from inside Norm's, a crowd of people leaning over the tables along the parking lot window. Nearly every recognizable human emotion seemed to play across the faces: surprise, worry, hilarity, joy, disgust, fear – everything but envy. He could hear the whoop of someone's laughter, muffled by the window glass.

One of his pennyloafers lay in the weeds of a flowerbed, and he paused long enough to grab it, then hurried on again in his stocking feet and baggy undershorts, realizing that the seat of his shorts had mostly been abraded away against the asphalt when he had gone down.

Son of a bitch, he thought, unconsciously echoing the raggedy woman's evaluation.

His car was locked, and instinctively he reached for his key chain, which of course was to hell and gone down Seventeenth Street by now. "Shit!" he said, hearing someone stepping up behind him. He angled around toward the front of the car, so as to be at least half-hidden from the crowd in Norm's,

Most of the faces were laughing now. People were pointing. He was all right. He hadn't been hurt after all. They could laugh like zoo apes and their consciences would be clear. Look at him run! A fat man in joke shorts! Look at that butt!

It was an old man who had come up behind him. He stood there now in the parking lot, shaking his head seriously.

"It was hit and run," the old man said. "I saw the whole thing. I was right there in the window, and I'm prepared to go to court. Bastard didn't even look."

He stood on the other side of the car, between Wilkins and the window full of staring people. Someone hooted from a car driving past on Sixteenth, and Wilkins flinched, dropping down to his hands and knees and groping for the hide-a-key under the front bumper. He pawed the dirty underside of the bumper frantically, but couldn't find the little magnetic box. Maybe it was on the rear bumper. He damned well wasn't going to go crawling around after it, providing an easy laugh…

A wolf-whistle rang out from somewhere above, from an open window across Sixteenth. He stood up hurriedly.

"Did you get the license?" the old man said.

"What? No, I didn't." Wilkins took a deep breath to calm himself.

The goddamn magnetic hide-a-key. It had probably dropped off down the highway somewhere. Wouldn't you know it! Betrayed by the very thing…

His heart still raced, but it didn't pound so hard. He concentrated on simmering down, clutching his chest with his hand. "Easy, boy," he muttered to himself, his eyes nearly shut. That was better. He could take stock now.

It was a miracle he wasn't hurt. If he were a skinny man the physical forces of the encounter would probably have torn him in half. As it was, his knee was scraped pretty good, but nothing worse than ten million such scrapes he had suffered as a kid. His palms were raw, and the skin on his rear-end stung pretty well. He felt stiff, too.

He flexed his leg muscles and rotated his arms. The wolf-whistle sounded again, but he ignored it.

Miraculously, he had come through nearly unharmed. No broken bones. Nothing a tube of Bengay wouldn't fix, maybe some Bactine on the scrapes.

He realized then that he still had the toothpick in his mouth. Unsteadily, he poked at his teeth with it, hoping that it would help restore the world to normalcy. It was soft and splintered, though, and no good for anything, so he threw it away into the juniper plants.

"You should have got his license. That's the first thing. But I should talk. I didn't get it either." The old man looked back toward the window, insulted on Wilkins's behalf, scowling at the crowd, which had dwindled now. "Damned bunch of assholes ... " A few people still stood and gaped, waiting to get another look at Wilkins, hoping for a few more details to flesh out the story they would be telling everyone they met for the next six weeks. Six months, more likely. It was probably the only story they had, the morons. They'd make it last forever. "Got your car keys, didn't they?"

Wilkins nodded. Suddenly he was shaking. His hands danced against the hood of his car and he sat back heavily on the high concrete curb of a planter.

"Here now," the old man said, visibly worried. "Wait. I got a blanket in the car. What the hell am I thinking?" He hurried away to an old, beaten Chevrolet wagon, opening the cargo door and hauling out a stadium blanket in a clear plastic case. He pulled the blanket out and draped it over Wilkins's shoulders.

Wilkins sat on the curb with his head sagging forward now. For a moment there he had felt faint. His heart had started to even out, though. He wanted to lie down, but he couldn't, not there on the parking lot.

"Shock," the old man said to him. "Accompanies every injury, no matter what. You live around here?"

Wilkins nodded. "Down on French Street. Few blocks."

"I'll give you a ride. Your car won't go nowhere. Might as well leave it here. You can get another key and come back down after it. They get your wallet, too?"

His wallet gone! Of course they had got his wallet. He hadn't thought of that. He wasn't thinking clearly at all. Well, that was just fine. What was in there? At least thirty-odd dollars and his bank card and gas card and Visa – the whole magilla was gone.

The old man shook his head. "These punks," he said. "This is Babylon we're living in, stuff like this happens to a man."

Wilkins nodded and let the old man lead him to the Chevy wagon.

Wilkins climbed into the passenger seat, and the man got in and fired up the engine. He backed out terrifically slowly, straight past the window where a couple of people still gaped out at them. One of the people pointed and grinned stupidly, and the old man, winding down the window, leaned out and flipped the person off vigorously with both hands.

"Scum-sucking pig!" he shouted, then headed out down the alley toward Sixteenth, shaking his head darkly, one wheel bouncing down off the curb as he swerved out onto the street, angling up Sixteenth toward French.

"Name's Bob Dodge," the man said, reaching across to shake hands.

Wilkins felt very nearly like crying. This man redeems us all, he said to himself as he blinked at the Good Samaritan behind the wheel. "Bernard Wilkins," he said, shaking the man's hand. "I guess I'm lucky. No harm done. Could have been worse." He was feeling better. Just to be out of there helped. He had stopped shaking.

"Damn right you're lucky. If I was you I'd take it easy, though. Sometimes you throw something out of kilter, you don't even know it till later. Whiplash works that way."

Something out of kilter! Wilkins rejected the thought. "I feel… intact enough. Little bit sandpapered, that's all. If he'd hit me…" He sighed deeply; he didn't seem to be able to get enough air. "Take a right here. That's it – the blue house there with the shingles." The car pulled into the driveway, and Wilkins turned to the old man and put out his hand again. "Thanks," he said. "You want to step in for a moment, and I'll give you the blanket back. I could probably rustle up a cup of java."

"Naw. I guess I'll be on my way. I left a pal of mine back in the booth. Don't want to stiff him on the check. I'll see you down to Norm's one of these days. Just leave the blanket in the back of your car."

"I will."

Wilkins opened the car door, got out, and stood on the driveway, realizing for the first time that the blanket he was wearing had the California Angels logo on it, the big A with a halo. He watched Bob Dodge drive off. An Angels fan! He might have known it. Had he been there when Downing wrecked the big scoreboard? Wilkins hoped so.

Some destructions didn't matter, like the scoreboard, and those clear plastic backboards that the basketball players were routinely exploding a few years ago, with their energetic slam dunks. There were repairmen for those things, and the repairmen probably made more money in a week than Wilkins pulled down from Social Security in a year. He thought of his pants, beating against the street at forty miles an hour. Where were they now? Reduced to atoms? Lying in a ditch?

Hell.

He went in through the front door, and there was Molly, drinking coffee and reading the newspaper. Her pleasant look turned at once to uncomprehending alarm.

"What – ?" she started to say.

"Lost the pants up at Norm's," he said as breezily as he could. He grinned at her. This was what she had prophesied. It had come to pass. "A guy drove me home. No big deal!" He hurried past her, grinning and nodding, holding tight to the blanket so that she wouldn't see where his knee was scraped. He didn't want any fuss. "I'll tell you in a bit!" he called back, overriding her anxious questions. "Later! I've got to... damn it – " He was sweating, and his heart was thudding furiously again in his chest. "Leave me alone! Just leave me alone for awhile, will you?"

. . .

There had to be something that could be salvaged. In his second-best pair of fancy-dinners pants, he plodded past the washer and drier and down the back steps.

His backyard was deep, nearly a hundred feet from the back patio to the fence, the old boards of which were almost hidden under the branches and tendrils and green leaves of the tomato plants. Sometimes he worried about having planted them that far out. Closer to the house would have been safer. But the topsoil way out there was deep and good. Avocado leaves fell year round, rotting down into a dark, twiggy mulch. When he had spaded the ground up for the first time, he had found six inches of leafy humus on the surface, and the tomatoes that grew from that rich soil could be very nearly as big as grapefruit.

Still, it was awfully far out, way past the three big windmilling gopher repellers. He couldn't keep an eye on things out there. As vigilant as he was, the worms seemed to take out the tomatoes, one by one. He had put out a pony-pack of Early Girls first, back in February. It had still been too cold, and the plants hadn't taken off. A worm got five of the six one night during the first week in March, and he had gone back to the nursery in order to get more Early Girls. He had ended up buying six small Beefsteak plants too, from a flat, and another six Better Boys in four-inch pots, thinking that out of eighteen plants, plus the one the worms had missed, he ought to come up with something.

What he had now, in mid-June, were nine good plants. Most of the Early Girls had come to nothing, the worms having savaged them pretty badly. And the Beefsteaks were putting out fruit that was deformed, bulbous, and off-tasting.

The Better Boys were coming along, though. He knelt in the dirt, patiently untangling and staking up vines, pinching off new leaves near the flower clusters, cultivating the soil around the base of the plants and mounding it up into little dikes to hold water around the roots. Soon he would need another bundle of six-foot stakes.

There was a dark, round shadow way back in there among the Better Boys, nearly against the fence pickets; he could make out the yellow-orange flush against the white paint. For a moment he stared at it, adjusting his eyes to the tangled shadows. It must be a cluster of tomatoes.

He reached his arm through the vines, feeling around, shoving his face in among them and breathing in the bitter scent of the leaves. He found the fence picket and groped around blindly until he felt them –

No. It.

There was only one tomato, one of the Better Boys, deep in the vines.

It was enormous, and it was only half-ripe. Slowly he spread his hand out, tracing with his thumb and pinky finger along the equator of the tomato.

"Leaping Jesus," he said out loud.

The damned thing must have an eight-inch diameter, ten-inch, maybe. He shoved his head farther in, squinting into the tangled depths. He could see it better now. It hung there heavily, from a stem as big around as his thumb.

Knock, Knock, he thought.

Who's there?

Ether.

Ether who?

Ether bunnies.

No ball game today, he thought. No crossword puzzle.

He backed out of the vines and strode purposefully toward the garage. He hadn't planned on using the ether nets this year, but this was a thing that needed saving. He could imagine the worms eyeing the vast Better Boy from their – what, nests? Lairs? – and making plans for the evening. Tying metaphorical napkins around their necks and hauling out the silverware.

He pulled open the warped garage door and looked at the big freezer in the corner and at the draped, fine-mesh nets on the wall. The crystals might or might not be mature, but he would have to use them tonight.

He had read the works of Professor Dayton C. Miller, who had been a colleague of Edward Williams Morley, and, like Miller, Wilkins had become convinced that Einstein had been wrong – light was not in any sense particles, but consisted of waves traveling through a medium that the nineteenth-century physicists had called ether, the luminiferous ether.

"Luminiferous ether." He rolled the phrase across his tongue, listening to the magic in it.

Ordinary matter like planets and people and baseballs traveled through the ether without being affected by it. The ether passed through them like water through a swimming-pool net. But anything that *bent* light, anything like a magnifying glass, or a prism, or even a Coke bottle, *participated* with the ether a little, and so experienced a certain drag.

Molly had a collection of glass and crystal animals – people had offered her serious money for them, over the years – and Wilkins had noticed that in certain seasons some of them moved off of their dust-free spots on the shelf. The ones that seemed to have moved farthest were a set of comical rabbits that they had picked up in Atlantic City in – it must have been – 1954. He had come to the conclusion that the effect occurred because of the angle and lengths of the rabbits' ears.

A correctly shaped crystal, he reasoned, would simply be stopped by the eternally motionless ether, and would be yanked off of the moving Earth like ... like his pants had been ripped off of his body when the car-mirror post had hooked them.

And so he had bought a lot of crystal-growing kits at a local hobby store, and had "seeded" the Tupperware growing environments with spatially customized, rabbit-shaped forms that he'd fashioned from copper wire. It had taken him months to get the ears right.

The resulting crystalline silicon-dioxide shapes would not exhibit their ether-anchored properties while they were still in the refractive water – frozen water, at the moment – and he had not planned to put them to the test until next year.

But tonight he would need an anchor. There was the Better Boy to be saved. The year, with all of its defeats and humiliations, would not have been for nothing. He grinned to think about the Better Boy, hanging out there in the shadows, impossibly big and round. A slice of that on a hamburger...

Knock knock.

Who's there?

Samoa.

Samoa who?

Samoa ether bunnies.

He whistled a little tune, admiring the sunlight slanting in through the dusty window. The Early Girls and the misshapen Beefsteaks would have to be sacrificed. He would drape the nets under them. Let the worms feast on them in outer space if they had the spittle for it, as Thomas More had said.

Molly's Spanish aunt had once sent them a lacy, hand-embroidered bedspread. Apparently a whole convent-full of nuns had spent the bulk of their lifetimes putting the thing together. *Frank Sinatra* couldn't have afforded to buy the thing at the sort of retail price it deserved. Wilkins had taken great pains in laying the gorgeous cloth over their modest bed, and had luxuriated in lying under it while reading something appropriate – Shakespeare's sonnets, as he recalled.

That same night their cat had jumped onto the bed and almost instantly had vomited out a live tapeworm that must have been a yard long. The worm had convulsed on the bedspread, several times standing right up on its head, and in horror Wilkins had balled the bedspread up around the creature, thrown it onto the floor and stomped on it repeatedly, and then flung the bundle out into the yard. Eventually Wilkins and his wife had gone to sleep. That night it had rained for eight hours straight, and by morning the bedspread was something he'd been ashamed even to have visible in his trash.

When the obscuring ice melted, the rabbit-shaped crystals would be the floats, the equivalent of the glass balls that Polynesian fishermen apparently used to hold up the perimeters of their nets. The crystals would grab the fabric of the celestial ether like good tires grabbing pavement, and the lacy nets – full of tomato worms, their teeth in the flesh of the luckless Early Girls and Beefsteaks – would go flying off into space.

Let them come crawling back *then*, Wilkins thought gravely. He searched his mind for doubt but found none. There was nothing at all wrong with his science. It only wanted application. Tonight, he would give it that.

Still wearing his go-out-to-dinner pants, Wilkins expertly tied monkey-fist knots around the blocks of ice, then put each back into the freezer. Several times Molly had come out to the garage to plead with him to quit and come inside. He had to think about his health, she'd said. Remonstrating, he called it. "Don't *remonstrate* with me!" he shouted at her finally, and she went away in a huff. Caught up in his work, he simmered down almost at once, and soon he was able to take the long view. Hell, she couldn't be expected to see the sense in these nets and blocks of ice. They must seem like so much lunacy to her. He wondered whether he ought to wake her up around midnight and call her outside when the nets lifted off…

Luckily he had made dozens of the rabbit-forms. There would be plenty for the nets. And he would have to buy more crystal kits tomorrow.

Knock knock.

Who's there?
Consumption.
Consumption who?
Consumption be done about all these ether bunnies?
He laughed out loud.

By dinnertime he had fastened yellow and red twist ties around the edges of the nets. It would be an easy thing to attach the ether bunnies to the twist ties when the time was just right. He had spread the nets under all the tomato plants around the one that bore the prodigious Better Boy, pulling back and breaking off encumbering vines from adjacent plants. He hated to destroy the surrounding plants, but his eggs were all going into one basket here. If you were going to do a job, you did a job. Wasn't that what Casey Stengel always said? Halfway measures wouldn't stop a tomato worm. Wilkins had found that out the hard way.

Molly cooked him his favorite dinner – pork chops baked in cream of mushroom soup, with mashed potatoes and a vegetable medley on the side. There was a sprig of parsley on the plate, as a garnish, just like in a good restaurant. He picked it up and laid it on the tablecloth. Then, slathering margarine onto a slice of white bread and sopping up gravy with it, he chewed contentedly, surveying their kitchen, their domain. Outside, the world was alive with impersonal horrors. The evening news was full of them. Old Bob Dodge was right. This was Babylon. But with the summer breeze blowing in through the open window and the smell of dinner in the air, Wilkins didn't give a damn for Babylon.

He studied the plate-rack on the wall, remembering where he and Molly had picked up each of the souvenir plates. There was the Spokane plate, from the World's Fair in '74. And there was the Grand Canyon plate and the Mesa Verde one next to that, chipped just a little on the edge. What the hell did a chip matter? A little bit of Super Glue if it was a bad one…

There was a magic in all of it – the plates on the wall, the little stack of bread slices on the saucer, the carrots and peas mixing it up with the mashed potatoes. There was something in the space around such things, like the force-field dome over a lunar city in a story. Whatever it was, this magic, it held Babylon at bay.

He remembered the cat and the Spanish bedspread suddenly, and put his fork down. But hell – the ether bunnies, the saving of the enormous tomato – tonight things would go a different way.

He picked up his fork again and stabbed a piece of carrot, careful to catch a couple of peas at the same time, dredging it all in the mushroom gravy.

He would have to remember to put the stadium blanket into the trunk. Bob Dodge.... Even the man's name had a ring to it. If God were to lean out of the sky, as the Bible said He had done in times past, and say "Find me one good man, or else I'll pull this whole damned shooting match to pieces," Wilkins would point to Bob Dodge, and then they could all relax and go back to eating pork chops.

"More mashed potatoes?" Molly asked him, breaking in on his reverie.

"Please. And gravy."

She went over to the stove and picked up the pan, spooning him out a big mound of potatoes, dropping it onto his plate, and then pushing a deep depression in the middle of the mound. She got it just right. Wilkins smiled at her, watching her pour gravy into the hole.

"Salt?"

"Doesn't need it," he said. "It's perfect."

Molly canted her head and looked at him: "A penny?"

He grinned self-consciously. "For my thoughts? They're not worth a penny – or they're worth too much to stick a number on. I was just thinking about all this. About us." He gestured around him, at the souvenir plates on the wall and the plates full of food on the table.

"Oh, I see," she said, feigning skepticism.

"We could have done worse."

She nodded as if she meant it. He nearly told her about the ether bunnies, about why he had bought the old freezer and the nets, about Einstein and Miller – but instead he found himself finally telling her about Norm's, about having nearly got run down in the parking lot. Earlier that day, when he had borrowed her keys and gone down to retrieve the car, she hadn't asked any questions. He had thought she was miffed, but now he knew that wasn't it. She'd just been giving him room to breathe.

"Sorry I shouted at you when I got home," he said when he had finished describing the ordeal. "I was pretty shook up."

"I guess you would be. I wish you would have told me, though. Someone should have called the police."

"Wouldn't have done any good. I didn't even get the guy's license number. Happened too fast."

"One of those people in Norm's must have got it."

Wilkins shrugged. Right then he didn't give a flying damn about the guy in the Torino. In a sense there had not been any guy in the Torino, just a … a force of nature, like gravity or cold or the way things go to hell if you don't look out. He hacked little gaps in his mashed potatoes, letting the gravy leak down the edges like molten lava out of a volcano, careful not to let it all run out. He shoveled a forkful into his mouth and then picked up a pork chop, holding it by the bone, and nibbled off the meat that was left. "No harm done, "he said. "A few bucks …"

"What you ought to have done after you'd got home and put on another pair of pants was drive up Seventeenth Street. Your pants are probably lying by the roadside somewhere, in a heap."

"First thing in the morning," he said, putting it off even though there was still a couple hours worth of daylight left.

But then abruptly he knew she was right. Of course that's what he should have done. He had been too addled. A man didn't like to think of that sort of embarrassment, not so soon. Now, safe in the kitchen, eating a good meal, the world was distant enough to permit his taking a philosophical attitude. He could talk about it now, admit everything to Molly. There was no shame in it. Hell, it was funny. If he had been watching out the window at Norm's, he would have laughed at himself, too. There was no harm done. Except that his inventor's pants were gone.

Suddenly full, he pushed his plate away and stood up.

"Sit and talk?" Molly asked.

"Not tonight. I've got a few things to do yet, before dark."

"I'll make you a cup of coffee, then, and bring it out to the garage."

He smiled at her and winked, then bent over and kissed her on the cheek. "Use the Melitta filter. And make it in that big, one-quart German stein, will you? I want it to last. Nothing tastes better than coffee with milk and sugar in it an hour after the whole thing has got cold. The milk forms a sort of halo on the surface after a while. A concession from the Brownian motion."

She nodded doubtfully at him, and he winked again before heading out the back door. "I'm just going down to Builders Emporium," he said at the last moment. "Before they close. Leave the coffee on the bench, if you don't mind."

Immediately he set out around toward the front, climbing into his car and heading toward Seventeenth Street, five blocks up.

He drove east slowly, ignoring the half a dozen cars angrily changing lanes to pass him. Someone shouted something, and Wilkins hollered "That's right!" out the window, although he had no idea what it was the man had said.

The roadside was littered with rubbish – cans and bottles and disposable diapers. He had never noticed it all before, never really looked. It was a depressing sight. The search suddenly struck him as hopeless. His pants were probably caught on a tree limb somewhere up in the Santa Ana mountains. The police could put their best men on the search and nothing would come of it.

He bumped slowly over the railroad tracks, deliberately missing the green light just this side of the freeway underpass, so that he had to stop and wait out the long red light. Bells began to ring, and an Amtrak passenger train thundered past right behind him, shaking his car and filling the rear window with the sight of hurtling steel. Abruptly be felt cut off, dislocated, as if he had lost his moorings, and he decided to make a U-turn at the next corner and go home. This was no good, this futile searching.

But it was just then that he saw the pants, bunched up like a dead dog in the dim, concrete shadows beneath the overpass. He drove quickly forward when the light changed, the sound of the train receding into the distance, and he pulled into the next driveway and stopped in the parking lot of a tune-up shop closed for the night.

Getting out, he hitched up his dinner pants and strode back down the sidewalk as the traffic rushed past on the street, the drivers oblivious to him and his mission.

The pants were a living wreck, hopelessly flayed after having polished three blocks of asphalt. The wallet and keys were long gone.

He shook the pants out. One of the legs was hanging, pretty literally, by threads. The seat was virtually gone. What remained was streaked with dried gutter water. For a moment he was tempted to fling them away, mainly out of anger.

He didn't, though.

Would a sailor toss out a sail torn to pieces by a storm? No he wouldn't. He would wearily take out the needle and thread, is what he would do, and begin patching it up. Who cared what it looked like when it was done? If it caught the wind, and held it.... A new broom sweeps clean, he told himself stoically, but an old broom knows every corner.

He took the pants with him back to the car. And when he got home, five minutes later, there was the cup of coffee still steaming on the bench. He put the pants on the corner of the bench top, blew across the top of the coffee, and swallowed a big slug of it, sighing out loud.

The moon was high and full. That would mean he could see, and wouldn't have to mess with unrolling the hundred-foot extension cord and hanging the trouble-light in the avocado tree. And he was fairly sure that moonlight brought out the tomato worms, too. The hypothesis wasn't scientifically sound, maybe, but that didn't mean it wasn't right. He had studied the creatures pretty thoroughly, and had come to know their habits.

He set down the styrofoam ice chest containing the ice-encased ether bunnies, studied the nets for a moment, and then opened a little cloth-covered notebook, taking out the pencil clipped inside the spine. He had to gauge it very damned carefully. If he tied on the ice-encased bunnies too soon or too late, it would all come to nothing, an empty net ascending into the stratosphere. There was a variation in air temperature across the backyard – very slight, but significant. And down among the vines there was a photosynthetic cooling that was very nearly tempered by residual heat leaking out of the sun-warmed soil. He had worked through the calculations three times on paper and then once again with a pocket calculator.

And of course there was no way of knowing the precise moment that the worms would attempt to cross the nets. That was a variable that he could only approximate. Still, that didn't make the fine-tuning any less necessary. All the steps in the process were vital.

He wondered, as he carefully wired the ether bunnies onto the nets, if maybe there wasn't energy in moonlight, too – a sort of heat echo, something even his instruments couldn't pick up. The worms could sense it, whatever it was – a subtle but irresistible force, possibly involving tidal effects. Well, fat lot of good it would do him to start worrying about that now. It clearly wasn't the sort of thing you could work out on a pocket calculator.

He struggled heavily to his feet, straightening up at last, the ice chest empty. He groaned at the familiar stiffness and shooting pains in his lower back. Molly could cook, he had to give her that. One of these days he would take off a few pounds. He wondered suddenly if maybe there weren't a couple of cold pork chops left over in the fridge, but then he decided that Molly would want to cook them up for his breakfast in the morning. That would be good – eggs and chops and sourdough toast.

She had come out to the garage only once that evening, to remonstrate with him again, but he had made it clear that he was up to his neck in what he was doing, and that he wasn't going to give himself any rest. She had looked curiously around the garage and then had gone back inside, and after several hours she had shut the light off upstairs in order to go to sleep.

So the house was dark now, except for a couple of sconces burning in the living room. He could see the front porch light, too, shining through the window beyond them.

The sky was full of stars, the Milky Way stretching like a river through trackless space. He felt a sudden sorrow for the tomato worms, who knew nothing of the ether. They went plodding along, inexorably, sniffing out tomato plants, night after night, compelled by Nature, by the fleeing moon. They were his brothers, after a fashion. It was a hard world for a tomato worm, and Wilkins was sorry that he had to kill them.

He fetched a lawn chair and sat down in it, very glad to take a load off his feet. He studied the plants. There was no wind, not even an occasional breeze. The heavy-bodied tomato worms would make the branches dip and sway as they came along, cutting through the still night. Wilkins would have to remain vigilant. There would be no sleep for him. He was certain that he could trust the ether bunnies to do their work, to trap the worms and propel them away into the depths of space, but it was a thing that he had to see, as an astronomer had to wait out a solar eclipse.

He was suddenly hungry again. That's what had come of thinking about the pork chops. He was reminded of the tomato, nearly invisible down in the depths of the vines. How many people could that Better Boy feed, Wilkins wondered, and all at once it struck him that he himself was hardly worthy to eat such a tomato as this. He would find Bob Dodge, maybe, and give it to him. "Here," he would say, surprising the old man in his booth at Norm's. "Eat it well." And he would hand Dodge the tomato, and Dodge would understand, and would take it from him.

He got up out of his chair and peered into the vines. The ice was still solid. The night air hadn't started it melting yet. But the worms hadn't come yet either. It was too soon. He found a little cluster of Early Girls, tiny things that didn't amount to anything and weren't quite ripe yet. Carefully, he pulled a few of them loose and then went back to his chair, sucking the insides out of one of the tomatoes as if it were a Concord grape. He threw the peel away, tasting the still-bitter fruit.

"Green," he said out loud, surprised at the sound of his own voice and wishing he had some salt. And then, to himself, he said, "It's nourishing, though. Vitamin C." He felt a little like a hunter, eating his kill in the depths of a forest, or a fisherman at sea, lunching off his catch.

He could hear them coming. Faintly on the still air he could hear the rustle of leaves bending against vines, even, he'd swear, the munch-munch of tiny jaws grinding vegetation into nasty green pulp in the speckled moonlight. It was a steady susurration – there must have been hundreds of them out there. Clearly the full moon and the incredible prize had drawn the creatures out in an unprecedented way. Perhaps every tomato worm in Orange County was here tonight to sate itself.

And the ice wasn't melting fast enough. He had miscalculated.

He forced himself up out of the lawn chair and plodded across the grass to the plants. He couldn't see the worms – their markings were perfect camouflage, letting them blend into the shifting patches of moonlight and shadow – but he could hear them moving in among the Early Girls.

Crouched against the vines, he blew softly on the ice blocks at the outside corners of the net. If only he could hurry them along. When they warmed up just a couple of degrees, the night air would really go to work on them. They'd melt quickly once they started. Abruptly he thought of heading into the garage for a propane torch, but he couldn't leave the tomato alone with the worms now, not even for a moment. He kept blowing. Little rivulets of water were running down the edges of the ice. Cheered at the sight of this, he blew harder.

Dimly, he realized that he had fallen to his knees.

Maybe he had hyperventilated, or else had been bent over so long that blood had rushed to his head. He felt heavy, though, and he pulled at the collar of his shirt to loosen it across his chest. He heard them again, close to him now.

"The worms!" he said out loud, and he reached out and took hold of the nearest piece of string-bound ice in both hands to melt it. He didn't let go of it even when he overbalanced and thudded heavily to the ground on his shoulder, but the ice still wasn't melting fast enough, and his hands were getting numb and beginning to ache.

The sound of the feasting worms was a hissing in his ears that mingled with the sound of rushing blood, like two rivers of noise flowing together, into one deep stream. The air seemed to have turned cold, chilling the sweat running down his forehead. His heart was pounding in his chest, like a pickaxe chopping hard into dirt.

He struggled up onto his hands and knees and lunged his way toward the Better Boy. He could see them.

One of the worms was halfway up the narrow trunk, and two more were noodling in along the vines from the side. A cramp in his chest helped him to lean in closer, although he gasped at the pain and clutched at his shirt pocket. Now he could not see anything human or even mammalian in the faces of the worms, any more than he had been able to see the driver of the hit-and-run Torino behind the sun-glare on the windshield.

He made his hand stretch out and take hold of one of the worms. It held on to the vine until he really tugged, and then after tearing loose it curled in a muscular way in his palm before he could fling it away. In his fright and revulsion he grabbed the next one too hard, and it burst in his fist – somehow, horribly, still squirming against his fingers even after its insides had jetted out and greased Wilkins's thumb.

He spared a glance toward the nearest chunk of ice, but he couldn't see it; perhaps they were melting at last.

Just a little longer, he told himself, his breath coming quick and shallow. His hands were numb, but he seized everything that might have been a worm and threw it behind him. He was panting loud enough to drown out the racket of the feasting worms, and the sweat stung in his eyes, but he didn't let himself stop.

His left arm exploded in pain when he took hold of another one of the creatures, and he half believed the thing had somehow struck back at him, and then at that moment his chest was crushed between the earth and the sky.

He tried to stand, but toppled over backward.

Against the enormous weight he managed to lift his head – and he was smiling when he let it fall back onto the grass, for he was sure he had seen the edges of the nets fluttering upward as the ether bunnies, freed at last from the ice, struggled to take hold of the fabric of space – struggled inadequately, he had to concede, against the weight of the nets and the plants and the worms and the sky, but bravely nevertheless, keeping on tugging until it was obvious that their best efforts weren't enough, and then keeping on tugging even after that.

. . .

He didn't lose consciousness. He was simply unable to move. But the chill had gone away and the warm air had taken its place, and he was content to lie on the grass and stare up at the stars and listen to his heart.

He knew that it had probably been a heart attack that had happened to him – but he had heard of people mistaking for a heart attack what had merely been a seizure from too much caffeine. It might have been the big mug of coffee. He'd have to cut down on that stuff. Thinking of the coffee made him think of Molly asleep upstairs. He was glad that she didn't know he was down here, lying all alone on the dewy grass.

In and out with the summer night air. Breathing was the thing. He focused on it. Nothing else mattered to him. If you could still breathe you were all right, and he felt like he could do it forever.

When the top leaves of his neighbor's olive tree lit gold with the dawn sun he found that he could move. He sat up slowly, carefully, but nothing bad happened. The morning breeze was pleasantly cool, and crows were calling to each other across the rooftops.

He parted the vines and looked into the shadowy depths of the tomato plants.

The Better Boy was gone. All that was left of it was a long shred of orange skin dangling like a deflated balloon from its now foolish-looking stout stem. The ether bunnies, perhaps warped out of the effective shape by the night of strain, lay inert along the edges of the nets, which were soiled with garden dirt now and with a couple of crushed worms and a scattering of avocado leaves.

He was all alone in the yard – Molly wouldn't wake up for an hour yet – so he let himself cry as he sat there on the grass. The sobs shook him like hiccups, and tears ran down his face as the sweat had done hours earlier, and the tears made dark spots on the lap of his dinner pants.

Then he got up onto his feet and, still moving carefully because he felt so frail and weak, walked around to the front of the house.

The newspaper lay on the driveway. He nearly picked it up, thinking to take a look at the sports page. He had been so busy yesterday evening that he had missed the tail end of the ballgame. Perhaps the Angels had slugged their way into first place. They had been on a streak, and Wilkins wanted to think that their luck had held.

He turned and went into the silent house. He didn't want to make coffee, so he just walked slowly from room to room, noticing things, paying attention to trifles, from the bright morning sun shining straight in horizontally through the windows to the familiar titles of books on shelves.

He felt a remote surprise at seeing his inventor's pants on the top of the dirty clothes in the hamper in the bathroom, and he picked them up.

No wonder it had been late when Molly had finally turned out the bedroom light. She had sewn up or patched every one of the outrageous tears and lesions in the old pants, and now clearly intended to wash them. Impulsively he wanted to put them on right then and there ... but he wouldn't. He would let Molly have her way with them, let her return the pants in her own good time. He would wear them again tomorrow, or the day after.

There was still a subtle magic in the morning.

Knock knock.

Who's there?

Samoa.

He let the pants fall back onto the pile, and then he walked slowly, carefully, into the kitchen and opened the refrigerator door. He would make breakfast for her.

Night Moves

WHEN a warm midnight wind sails in over the mountains from the desert and puffs window shades inward, and then hesitates for a second so that the shades flap back and knock against the window frames, southern Californians wake up and know that the Santa Ana wind has come, and that tomorrow their potted plants will be strewn up and down the alleys and sidewalks; but it promises blue skies and clean air, and they prop themselves up in bed for a few moments and listen to the palm fronds rattling and creaking out in the darkness.

Litter flies west, papers and leaves and long veils of dust from lots where the tractors wait for morning, and tonight a dry scrap cartwheeled and skated through Santa Margarita's nighttime streets; it clung briefly to high branches, skipped over the roofs of parked cars, and at one point did a slow jiggle-dance down the whole length of the north window sill at Guillermo's Todo Noche Cantina. The only person who noticed it was the old man everybody called Cyclops, who had been drinking coffee at the counter for hours in exchange for a warm, lighted place to pass the night, and until the thing tumbled away at the west end of the windowsill he stared at it, turning his head to give his good eye a clear look at it.

It looked, he thought, like one of those little desiccated devilfish they sell at swap-meets; they cut three slits in the fish's body before they dry it, so after it dries it looks as if it has a primate body and stunted limbs and a disproportionately large head with huge, empty eye sockets. When you walk out of the swap-meet area in the late afternoon, out of the shadow of the big drive-in movie screen, you sometimes step on the stiff little bodies among the litter of cotton candy and cigarette butts and bits of tortilla.

Cyclops had noticed that it danced west, and when he listened he could hear the warm wind whispering through the parallel streets outside like a slow breath through the channels of a harmonica, seeming to be just a puff short of evoking an audible chord. Realizing that this was no longer a night he needed shelter from, Cyclops laid two quarters on the counter, got to his feet and lumbered to the door.

Outside, he tilted back his devastated hat and sniffed the night. It was the old desert wind, all right, hinting of mesquite and sage, and he could feel the city shifting in its sleep – but tonight there was a taint on the wind, one that the old man smelled in his mind rather than in his nose, and he knew that something else had come into the city tonight too, something that stirred a different sort of thing than leaves and dust.

The night felt flexed, stressed, like a sheet of glass being bent. Alertly Cyclops shambled halfway across Main Street and then stopped and stared south.

After eleven o'clock the traffic lights stopped cycling and switched to a steady metronomic flashing, all the north-south lights flashing yellow for caution while the east-west ones, facing the smaller cross-streets, flashed red for stop. Standing halfway across the crosswalk Cyclops could see more than a mile's worth of randomly flashing yellow lights receding away south down Main, and about once every minute the flashes synchronized into one relayed pulse that rushed up the long street and past him over his head, toward the traffic circle at Bailey, half a mile north of where he stood.

He'd stood there often late at night, coming to conclusions about things by watching the patterns of disorder and synchronization in

the long street-tunnel of flashing yellow lights, and he quickly realized that tonight they were flashing in step more frequently than
normal, and only in pulses that swept north, as if delineating a landing pattern for something.

Cyclops nodded grimly. The night was warped, all right – as
much curvature as he'd ever seen. The Great Gray-Legged Scissors
Men would be out tonight in force.

He squared his shoulders, then strode away purposefully up
Main, the once-per-minute relay-pulse of yellow light sweeping
past him overhead like luminous birds.

Benny Kemp carried his drink out to the dark porch and sat down
on the bench that his father had built there more than fifty years
earlier. Someone had once tried to saw it away from the wall, but
the solid oak had proved too hard, and the attempt had apparently
been abandoned before any serious damage had been done. Running his hand over the wood now in the absolute darkness, Kemp
couldn't even find the ragged groove.

He took a sip of his wine, breathing shallowly and pretending
that the air carried the scent of night-blooming jasmine and dewy
lawns instead of the smell of age-soured wood and rodent nests,
and that it moved. In his imagination he watched moths bumble
against the long-gone porch light.

He never turned on the real light; he knew that his cherished
fantasy wouldn't survive the sight of the solid wall that crowded
right up against the porch rail. There was a doorway where the
porch steps had once been, but it led into the entry hall of the apartment building his father's house had been converted into, and all
that was out there was a pay phone, cheap panelling peeling off the
new walls, and, generally, a shopping cart or two. The entry hall
and office had been added right onto the front of the old house –
completely enclosing the porch and making an eccentric room of it
– but he seldom entered or left the building through the new sec-

tion, preferring the relatively unchanged back stairs.

He leaned back now and let the wine help him pretend. He'd never told any of the long string of renters and landlords that this was the house he had grown up in – he was afraid that sharing that information would diminish his relationship with the old building, and make it impossible for him to sit here quietly like this and, late at night, slide imperceptibly into the past.

The moths thumped and fluttered softly against the light, and, inhaling through the wine fumes, Kemp caught a whiff of jasmine, and then a warm breeze touched his cheek and a moment later he heard a faint pattering as jacaranda flowers, shaken from the tree out front, fell like a sower's cast of dead butterflies to the sidewalk and the street.

He opened his eyes and saw the tree's branches shift slowly against the dark sky, and coins of bright moonlight appeared, moved and disappeared in the tree's restless shadow. Kemp stood up, as carefully as a man with a tray of fragile, antique glass in his hands. He moved to the porch steps, went gingerly down them and then stole down the walkway to the sidewalk.

To his right he could see the railroad yard and, beyond it, the agitated glow that was the freeway. Too… hard, Kemp thought, too solidified, too much certainty and not enough possibility. He looked left, toward the traffic circle. It was quieter in that direction and aside from the moon the only source of illumination was the flashing yellow of the traffic lights. The wind seemed warmer in that direction, too. Trembling, he hurried toward the circle; and though he thought he glimpsed a couple of the tall, lean people in gray leotards – or maybe it was just one, darting rapidly from this shadowed area to that – tonight, for once, he was not going to let them frighten him.

The wind was tunnelled stronger under the Hatton Park bridge, and a plastic bag in a shopping cart bellied full like the sail of a ship, and pulled the cart forward until it stopped against the sneakered foot of an old woman who slept next to it. Mary Francis woke up and looked around. The trash-can fires had all burned out – it had to be closer to morning than to dusk.

She sniffed the intrusive desert wind, and her pulse quickened, for there were smells on it that she hadn't known in forty years, not since the days when this area was more orange groves than streets.

She fumbled in her topmost coat for one of her mirrors, and after she'd pulled out the irregular bit of silvered glass and stared into it for a few moments she exhaled a harsh sigh of wonder.

She had known this would happen if she worked hard enough at her collecting – and it seemed she finally had. Still staring into the mirror, she stood up and pushed her shopping cart out from under the bridge. In the moonlight all the scraps of cloth in her cart should have looked gray, but instead they glowed with their true color, the special sea-green that was the only hue of rag she would deign to pick up in her daily circuit of the trash cans and dumpsters – the never-forgotten color of the dress she'd worn at her debut in 1923. In recent years it had occurred to her that if she could find even a scrap of that dress, and then hang onto it, it might regenerate itself... slowly, yes, you couldn't be in a hurry, but if you were willing to wait... and she suspected that if the cloth were with her, it might regenerate her, too... banish the collapsed old wrinkled-bedsheet face and restore her real face, and figure, not only re-create the dress but also the Mary Francis that had worn it...

And look, now on this magic night it had happened. The face in the mirror was blurry, but it was clearly the face of the girl she'd never really stopped being. Oval face, big dark eyes, pale, smooth skin... that unaffected, trusting innocence.

She turned east, and the focus became clearer – but it was the what's-this-I-found-in-the-back-of-yer-old-garage face. Quickly she turned west, and was awed by the beauty of her own smile of relief when the girl-face returned, more clearly now.

She was facing the traffic circle. Keeping her eyes fixed on the ever-more-in-focus image in the mirror, she began pushing her shopping cart westward, and she didn't even notice the agile, face-less gray figures that dropped from trees and jackknifed up out of the sewer vents and went loping silently along toward the circle.

The traffic circle at Main and Bailey was the oldest part of town. Restaurants wanting to show a bit of local color always had to hang a couple of old black-and-white photographs of the circle with Pierce-Arrows and Model-T Fords driving around it and men in bowler hats and high collars sitting on the benches or leaning on the coping of the fountain. People in the restaurants would always look at the old photographs and try to figure out which way was north.

The flattened leathery thing that Cyclops had thought was a dried devilfish sailed on over the roof of the YMCA, frisbeed over the motorcycle cops who were waiting for someone to betray drunken-ness by having trouble driving around the circle, and then like a dried leaf it smacked into the pool of the old fountain. It drifted to the tiled pillar in the center and wound up canted slightly out of the water against the tiles, its big empty eyes seeming to watch the rooftops.

"Are you okay?"

"Yes," he croaked, concealing his irritation at her tone, which had seemed to imply that he must be either crazy or having a fit to jump out of bed that way; but if he had objected she'd reply, in hurt surprise, "All I said was, 'are you okay?',", which would put him two points down and give her the right to sigh in a put-upon way and make a show of having trouble getting back to sleep. "Just a dream," he said shortly.

"Fine," she said, and then added, just a little too soon, "I only *asked."*

He suppressed a grin. She'd been too eager, and done a riposte when there had only been a feint. He gave her a wondering look and said, "Gee, relax, hon. Maybe you were in the middle of a dream too, huh?" He chuckled with a fair imitation of fondness. "We *both* seem to be acting like *lunatics*." One-all, his advantage.

"What was the dream about?" she asked.

Oh no you don't, he thought. "I don't remember." He walked to the window and looked down at Main Street. The palm trees were bending and he could hear the low roaring of the wind.

Debbie rolled over and began breathing regularly, and Roger knew that until she really did go to sleep any noise he made would provoke the rendition of a startled awakening, so he resolved to stand by the window until he was certain she wasn't shamming. Of course she'd know what he was thinking and try to draw him into an error with convincing breathing-hitches and even – a tactical concession – undignified snortings.

He would wait her out. He stared down at the street and thought about his dream.

It was a dream he used to have fairly frequently when he was a child, though he hadn't had it since coming to California. Jesus, he thought, and I came to California in '57, when I was six years old. What does it mean, that I'm having it again after almost thirty years? And – I remember now – that dream always heralded the arrival of Evelyn, my as-they-like-to-call-it imaginary playmate.

The dream tonight had been so exactly the same as before that when he woke up he'd thought at first that he was in one of the many bedrooms he'd had back east, in the year – 1956, it must have been – when his parents had been moving around so much. The dream always started with a train, seen from a distance, moving down a moonlit track across a field, with buildings a remote unevenness on the dark horizon. Then, and it was never *quite* scary in the dream, the whistle wailed and the smokestack emitted a blob of white smoke; the smoke didn't dissipate – it billowed but kept its volume like a splash of milk in a jug of clear oil, and when the train had disappeared in the distance the blob of smoke slowly formed into a white, blank-eyed face. And then, slow as a cloud, the face would drift into town and move up and down the dark streets, and at every bedroom window it would pause and silently peer in … until it came to Roger's window. When it came to his, it smiled and at last dissolved away, and then there was the sense of company in his mind.

He remembered, now, the last time he'd had the dream; it had been the night before his parents abandoned him. He had awakened early the next morning, and when his mother had walked into the kitchen to put on the coffee pot he'd already fixed himself a bowl of Cheerios.

"Up already, Rog?" his mother asked him. "What have we told you about getting into the fridge without asking?"

"Sorry," he'd said, and for at least a year afterward he had been certain that they'd abandoned him because he'd broken the rule about the refrigerator. "Evelyn's back," he remarked then, to change the subject.

His mother had frozen, holding the can of ground coffee, and her face had seemed to get leaner. "What – " she began harshly; then, in a desperately reasonable tone, "What do you mean, honey? She can't be. I know she found us again after we moved from Keyport to Redbank, and all those other times since, but we're in *New York* now, almost all the way to Buffalo, she can't have followed us all that way. You're just … *pretending,* this time, right?"

"Nah," he'd replied carelessly. "But she says it was a long trip. How long since we moved away from Atlantic City?"

His mother had sat down across the table from him, still holding the coffee can. "Five months," she whispered.

"Yeah, she flew over a river, the … she says Del Ware? And then she had to go around Phil-a-delph-ia, 'cause there was too many people there, and they – them all thinking, and wishing for things

– started to bend the air, like too many people on a trampoline, and it would have bent all the way around and made a bubble, and she wouldn't a been able to get out of it, back to real places. And then, she says, she went around Scranton and Elmira, and now here she is."

The six-year-old Roger had looked up from his cereal then, and he realized for the first time that his mother was afraid of Evelyn. And now, standing at his bedroom window in Santa Margarita while Debbie pretended to be asleep in the bed behind him, it suddenly and belatedly occurred to him that it might have been Evelyn's remarkable tracking abilities that had made his parents move so frequently during that year.

But why, he wondered, would they both so fear a child's imaginary playmate? It wasn't as if Evelyn could be seen, or move things, or say where lost watches and rings had got to... much less hurt anyone, like the "imaginary playmate" in the story by John Collier. The only one she got even remotely forceful with was me, censoring my dreams whenever I dreamed about things she didn't like. And hell, when I first started talking about her, my Mom was just amused... used to ask me how Evelyn was, and even cut a piece of cake for her on my fifth birthday. It wasn't until I started telling Mom things that Evelyn had told me – like that Evelyn was three years older than me, to the month – that Mom stopped finding the idea of an imaginary playmate charming.

Roger thought about the current unpaid bill from the private investigator. If he can find you before I become too broke to pay for his services, he thought, I'll get a chance to *ask* you what bothered you about Evelyn, *Mom* – after I get through asking you and Dad about the ethics of sending a six-year-old boy into a drug store with a quarter to buy candy with, and then driving away, forever, while he's inside. And it might be soon – if the investigator's deductions from studying money-order records and Social Security payments are correct, and you and Dad really do live within blocks of here.

Someone was shouting furiously, down the street... and walking this way, by the sound of it. A male voice, Roger noted – probably old Cyclops. What the hell is it that makes so many street bums shout? Old women at bus stops who make heads turn two blocks away with the volume and pure rage of their almost totally incoherent outbursts, men that walk out into traffic so that screeching brakes punctuate their wrathfully delivered catalogue of the various things they are not going to stand for anymore... and people who, like Cyclops here tonight, simply walk up and down the empty nighttime streets shouting warnings and challenges to imaginary enemies: it must be some kind of urban malady, new to civilization as far as I know. Maybe it's contagious, and sometime it'll be me and Debbie down there shaking our fists at empty stretches of sidewalk and screaming, *Oh yeah, you sons of bitches?*

He glanced back at Debbie. Her sooner than me, he thought. If her parents didn't live in Balboa and own a boat and a cabin up at Big Bear, and lots all over hell, would I be intending to marry such a mean, skitzy specimen? No way. And if I do succeed in finding my parents, and if they prove to be as affluent as my memories of their cars and houses indicate they were, I'll send this animated bird's-nest of neuroses and obsessions back to her parents. My gain and their loss.

He shivered. The room wasn't cold, but he'd felt a draft of... of success passing by; a breath of impending squalor stirring the dust under the bedroom door, and he thought the bills on the desk were softly rustled by a stale shift of air that somehow carried the smell of gray hair and temporary jobs, and trash bags full of empty cans of creamed corn and Spam and corned beef hash.

I can't let go of her, he thought, until I'm *certain* about my parents – until I've not only found them, but found out how much they're worth, and then shamed or even blackmailed them into giving me a lot of money, and making me their heir. Only then will I be able to ditch poor loony Debbie... as any saner or less-ambitious man would have done right after that first time she ran back to her parents.

It had been about four months earlier. As soon as he'd realized she had left him, he had known where she must have gone. He had taken the bus down to her parents' house the next day. He'd been prepared to claim that he loved their overweight, manic-depressive monster of a daughter, and to explain that the two of them had been living together only because they couldn't get married yet; he'd braced himself for a lot of parental disapproval, even for violence ... but he had not been prepared for what awaited him.

Debbie's mother had opened the door when he knocked, but when, nervously defiant, he introduced himself, she only smiled. "Oh, you're Roger! I'm so pleased to meet you, Debbie's told us so *much* about you! Do come in and say hello, I know a visit from you will cheer her up ... " He wanted to explain that he'd come to take her back with him, but her mother was still speaking as she led him inside, out of the sunlight and into the living room, where curtains had been drawn across all the windows and no lights were on. There was a chair standing in the middle of the floor. "Yes, our Debbie likes to go out and make new friends," the mother was saying cheerfully, "but," she added with a wave toward the chair, "as you can see, she always comes home again."

Peering in the dimness, Roger had finally noticed that Debbie was sitting motionless in the chair, staring blankly ... and then that she was *tied* into the chair, with belts around her waist, wrists and ankles. Without conscious thought he had left the house, and he walked quite a way up Main before remembering that he would have to get a bus if he wanted to get home before dark.

Later he had gone back again to that house, and caught Debbie in a more accessible segment of whatever her doomed mood-cycle was, and he talked her into returning to the apartment they'd been sharing: in his more fatuous moments he told himself that he'd gone back for her in order to save her from that environment and her evidently demented mother, but late on frightened nights like this one he could admit, to himself at least, that his concern for her was the concern a man feels for his last uncancelled credit card.

Debbie now emitted a prolonged sound that was halfway between a snore and a sentence, and he knew she must really be asleep. I'll wait till old Cyclops has gone by, Roger thought, and then crawl carefully back into bed. I wonder if Evelyn will still censor my dreams. What was it she used to object to? The dreams she didn't like were all prompted by something I experienced, so she was probably just my subconscious mind suppressing memories which, in some unacknowledged way, I found traumatic. I still remember the time my parents took me to the Crystal Lake amusement park in New Jersey – they were jovial during the first half of the drive, but when we got off the turnpike they seemed to unexpectedly recognize the area, and they got very tense – and, after that, Evelyn wouldn't let me dream about that neighborhood. And once I saw a cowboy movie in which, at one point, a cavalry soldier was shot and fell off his horse but had one foot caught in the stirrup and got dragged along, bouncing like a rag doll over the prairie – Evelyn always squelched any dream that began to include that bit. And after I got my tonsils taken out, she wouldn't let me dream about the smell of the ether; I was free to dream about the hospital and the sore throat and the ice cream, but not that smell.

"Climb back down into your holes, you bastards!" shouted Cyclops on the sidewalk below. Debbie shifted and muttered, and Roger mentally damned the noisy old bum. *"Dare to come near me,"* Cyclops added, *"and I'll smash your gray faces for you! Break your scissor legs!"*

Interested in spite of himself, Roger glanced down at the street – and then peered more closely. Cyclops, as usual, was lurching along the sidewalk and shaking his fists at dire adversaries, but tonight, for once, he seemed to be yelling at people who were actually there. A half-dozen dark figures were bounding about on the shadowed lawns and turning fantastic cartwheels in the dimness between streetlights. Roger's first guess was that they must be young theater majors from some local college, out larking and wino-hassling after some rehearsal or cast-party, for the figures all seemed to be dressed in gray leotards and wearing gray nylon stockings pulled down over their faces. Then he saw one of them spring from a grasshopper-crouch ... and rise all the way up to the third floor of an office building, and cling to the sill of a dark window there for a moment, before spider-jumping back down to the pavement.

The yellow-flashing traffic lights were strangely coordinated, flinging relayed pulses past at the height of his window, and he felt Evelyn's presence very strongly. *Come out, Roger,* she called to him from out in the warm-as-breath night. *Decide what you want, so I can give it to you.*

"Can you find my Mom and Dad?" he whispered.

Debbie instantly sat up in bed behind him. "What?" she said. "Are you crazy?"

Yes, came Evelyn's answer from outside. *Look. Here they are. I'll bring them out for you.*

Roger stepped away from the window and began pulling on his pants.

"Roger!" said Debbie sharply, real concern beginning to show through her reflexive malice. "You're walking in your sleep. Get back in bed."

"I'm awake," he said, stepping into his shoes without bothering about socks. "I'm going out. You go back to sleep."

Aware that she was being left out of something, Debbie bounded out of bed. "I'm coming with you."

"No, damn it," he said almost pleadingly as he buttoned alternate buttons on his shirt. "What do you want to come for?"

"Because you don't want me to," she said, her voice muffled under the dress she was pulling on over her head. She stepped into shoes on her way to the door and had it open before he'd even finished tucking in his shirt. "At least I'm waiting for you."

They left the apartment by the front door and hurried down the stairs to the pavement. Leaves and flattened paper cups whirled through the air like nocturnal birds, and Cyclops was already a block ahead of Roger and Debbie. Looking past the old man, Roger could see that the stop lights north of the traffic circle were sending synchronized yellow pulses south; the pulses from south and north Main met at the circle like tracer bullets from two directions being fired at a common target.

His feet were suddenly warmer, and, glancing down, he noticed that he had socks on; also, every button of his shirt was fastened, and his shoes looked polished.

He began running toward the bending palms that ringed the circle. Debbie, running right behind him, called out in a voice made timid by fright or wonder, "Where are we going?"

"I could be wrong," he shouted without looking back, "but I think that, tonight at least, it's the place where dreams come true."

Jack Singer straightened the knot of his tie and then stood back from the mirror and admired his reflection. A well-tailored suit certainly did things for a man – not only did he look lean and fit, with somehow no trace of projecting belly, but even his face seemed tanned and alert, his hair fuller and darker. He patted his breast pocket and felt the slim billfold there, and without having to look he knew it contained a Diner's Club card, and a Visa – one with that asterisk that means you're good for more than the average guy – and a gold American Express card, and a few crisp hundred dollar bills for tips.

He stepped away from the mirror and took a sip of brandy from the glass on the bureau. Good stuff, that five-star Courvoisier. "You about ready, dear?" he called toward his wife's dressing room.

"In a minute," she said. "The diamond fell out of one of my fingernails, and I've got it Super Gluing."

He nodded, and though his smile didn't falter, his fine-drawn eyebrows contracted into a frown. Diamonds in her *what?* Her *fingernails?* He'd never heard of such a thing... but he knew better than to ask her about it, for it was clearly just one more part of this weirdly wonderful evening.

For just a moment, after they had awakened an hour ago, he had thought it was the middle of the night, and their apartment seemed to be... a shabby one they had lived in once. But then the hot Santa Ana wind had puffed in at the window and he had remembered that it was early evening, and that his wife and he were due to attend the dinner being given in their honor at the... what was the name of the hotel? ... just the finest hotel in the state... the *Splendide,* that was it.

He glanced out the window. "The limo is here, darling," he called.

"Coming." His wife appeared from her dressing room. Fine clothes had done wonders for her, too – she looked twenty pounds slimmer, and would be described as voluptuous now instead of just plain damn fat.

The chauffeur knocked quietly at the door, and Singer held out his arm for his wife to take.

They dutifully had a drink apiece in the limousine as it carried them smoothly west on Bailey, and though they couldn't recall gulping them the glasses were empty by the time the chauffeur made the sweeping turn around three-quarters of the traffic circle and then with never a jiggle turned south onto Main and drew in to the curb in front of the *Hotel Splendide.* A man in an almost insanely ornate red coat and gold-crusted hat opened the door for them.

Singer got out and then helped his wife out, and he noticed that the sidewalk, which had the *Splendide* insignia inset into the cement every yard or so, was so brightly lit by spotlights on the lawn and the dozen huge chandeliers in the lobby that he and his wife cast no shadows.

"They are awaiting you in the Napoleon Lounge, M'sieur," said the doorman, bowing obsequiously, "drinks and hors d'oeuvres there, and then you are to dine in the Grand Ballroom." Out of sight somewhere, an orchestra was richly performing a medley of favorites from the 1940s.

Singer produced a hundred-dollar bill and let it disappear into the man's gloved hand. "Thank you, Armand."

They strolled across the carpeted floor, surreptitiously admiring their reflections in the tall mirrors that alternated with marble panels on all the walls, and when they walked through the gilded arch into the Napoleon Lounge the other guests all greeted their appearance with delighted cries.

And they were all elegant – the lovely young woman in the striking sea-green dress, the piratically handsome old fellow with the eyepatch, the young couple who had been filling two plates over at one of the hors d'oeuvre tables… and especially the woman who was walking toward them with her hands out in welcome, a smile on her porcelain-pale face …

"Good evening," the woman said, "we're all so glad to see you. I'm your hostess this evening – my name is Evelyn."

Roger, looking up from the plate he'd been filling with caviar and thin slices of some black bread that was thick with caraway seeds, saw the newcomers flinch, just perceptibly, when Evelyn introduced herself, and instantly he knew that this couple must be his parents. They quickly recovered their poise and allowed Evelyn to lead them in, and Roger studied them out of the corner of his eye as, trying not to betray the trembling of his hands and the hard thudding of his heart, he forked a devilled egg and a tiny ear of pickled baby corn onto his plate. They do look prosperous, he thought with cautious satisfaction.

Evelyn was leading the couple straight toward the table beside which Roger and Debbie stood. "Jack and Irma," she said to Roger's parents, "this is Debbie and Roger." Again his parents flinched, and Irma stared hard and expressionlessly at Roger for a couple of seconds before extending her hand. She opened her mouth as if to say something, but Evelyn spoke first.

"Ah, here come the stewards," she said. "The cocktails are all first-rate here, of course, and on the table there is a list of the particular specialties of the house. And now you must excuse me – I think our Mr. Kemp has a question." She smiled and spun away toward a middle-aged man who was eyeing the stewards with something like alarm. As much to postpone confronting his parents as from thirst, Roger squinted at the sheet of apparently genuine vellum on which, in fancy calligraphy, the specialty drinks were described, but they were all frothy things like Pink Squirrels and White Russians and Eggnog, and he decided to follow his usual custom in dressy bars and ask for Chivas Regal Royal Salute 25-Year-Old… in a snifter. That always impressed people.

The steward who approached their table, a tall, thin fellow in dark gray, bowed and said, "Can I bring you anything from the bar?"

"I'll have one of your Pink Squirrels, but made with *whiskey* instead of *bourbon*," said Debbie in her best misconception-squared style.

Roger looked up to give the steward a *humor-her* wink, but he stepped back quickly with a smothered exclamation, for the man's face, just for a fraction of a second, had seemed to be a featureless gray angularity, like a plastic trash bag stretched taut across the front of a skull.

A moment later it was just an indistinct face, but Roger said, "Uh, right, and a Scotch for me, excuse me," and took a couple of steps toward the center of the room.

The dignified man with the eyepatch was staring at him, and Roger realized that it was Cyclops, not looking nearly as ridiculous in antique Navy dress blues as one might have expected. Cyclops, who wasn't holding a drink, crossed to him and said quietly, "You saw that one, didn't you? For a second you saw it wasn't a waiter, but one of the Great Gray-Legged Scissors Men."

Oh Jesus, thought Roger unhappily. Where in hell is my Scotch? "One of the *what?*"

"Oh, sorry, right – I just call 'em that 'cause they look like that guy in the old kids' rhyme, remember? The Great Red-Legged Scissors Man, who dashes up with a huge pair of scissors and cuts the thumbs off kids that suck their thumbs? How's it end? – 'I knew he'd come … to naughty little suck-a-thumb.'"

"They're …" began Roger, so wildly disoriented that it was hard to take a deep breath or refrain from giggling, "They're going to cut off our thumbs, are they?"

Cyclops looked disgusted. "No. Are you drunk? I *said* I just call 'em that 'cause they look like the guy in the picture that went with that poem. Except these here guys are all gray. No, *these* guys appear out o' nowhere when somebody who can boost dreams comes along, the way raindrops appear out o' nowhere when a low-pressure area comes along. Maybe the gray guys are the deep roots of our own minds, curled back up so they poke out o' the ground near us and seem separate, like the worm that got himself pregnant; or maybe they're ghosts that you can only see in the spirit light that shines from one of these imagination-amplifier people." He nodded toward Evelyn, "She's the one doing it here tonight. The trouble is, such people warp the night, and the more minds she's overdriving the sharper the angle of the curve, like blowing in one of those kid's-toy loops that holds a flat surface of soap-film, you know? You blow harder and harder, and the film bellies out rounder and rounder, and then – pop! – it's a bubble, broke loose and drifting away."

"Right," Roger said, nodding repeatedly and looking around for, if nothing else, a drink someone had abandoned. "Right – a bubble floating away, gotcha. Scissors men. You don't see a *drink* anywhere, do – "

"It's gonna happen tonight," said Cyclops harshly. "Damn soon. Did you notice the traffic signals? You know why they're all flashing at the same second so often now? 'Cause we're only still intersecting with a few of 'em, what seems like many is just lots o' reflections of only a couple. When they're perfectly in step that'll mean there's only one left, and the connection between this bubble and the real world is just a thin, thin tunnel."

"OK, but…"

"I'm leaving now," Cyclops interrupted. "If you got any sense, you'll come too. In five minutes it may be too late."

"Uhh…" Roger looked thoughtfully down at the elegant Yves St. Laurent suit he'd found himself wearing when he had approached the hotel, and he looked back at the low-cut, sequined gown that Debbie was – just as inexplicably – wearing. Now he held his hand out, palm up, fingers slightly curled, and he concentrated – and then suddenly he was holding a snifter that had an inch of amber fluid swirling in the bottom of it. He smiled up at the stern old man. "Imagination-amplifier, hey?" he said slowly. "I'll stay for just a little while, thanks. Hell, five minutes – that's plenty of time."

Cyclops smiled with pity and contempt, then turned and strode out of the room. Roger stared over at Evelyn. Who *was* she, *what* was she? Clearly something more than a child's imaginary playmate, or – what had he guessed her to be, earlier? – just a function of his subconscious mind. Of course, maybe he was better off not knowing, not asking inconvenient questions.

He carried his drink back to where Debbie and his parents were standing. "Well!" he said heartily. "Mom, Dad – it's good to see you again after all these years."

He was shocked by the physical change these words produced in the couple – his father shrank, and was suddenly balding and gray, and the gaps between the buttons of his ill-fitting suit were pulled wide by an abrupt protrusion of belly, and his mother became ludicrously fat, her expression of well-bred amusement turning to one of petulant unhappiness – and belatedly it occurred to Roger that their apparent affluence might be as ephemeral as his own suit and snifter of Scotch.

"You ... *are* Roger, aren't you?" the old woman whispered. "And," she added, turning in horror toward their hostess, "that is Evelyn."

"Yes," Roger said, a little surprised to realize that his adventurous delight in this evening had, all at once, evaporated, leaving him feeling old and bitter. "She only found her way back to me tonight. The trip took her more than twenty-five years ... but, you remember, she always avoided very populated areas."

"Until tonight," his father pointed out quietly.

"Until tonight," Roger agreed.

His father's smile was sickly. "Look," the old man said, "we've got lots to discuss, I'll admit – lots to, uh, beg forgiveness for, even – but can we get *out* of here right now? Without attracting the attention of ... our hostess?"

Roger looked around. Evelyn was chatting gaily with the group on the other side of the room, and every time she glanced up the chandeliers brightened and the trays of hors d'oeuvres came into clearer focus, but the stewards were getting leaner and taller, and their features were fading like images cast by a projector with a dimming bulb, and peripherally Roger saw one of them out in the lobby leap right up to the ceiling and cling there like a big fly.

"Yeah," said Roger, suddenly frightened and taking Cyclops' warning seriously. He let his drink evaporate, glass and all. "If anybody asks, say we're just going out for some fresh air – and go on about what a great time you're having." He took Debbie's arm. "Come on," he said.

"No, I'm staying. You know what they put in this drink, after I *told* them not to?"

"We're only going for a stroll, just to take a look at the front of the building – but sure, stay if you want."

"No, I'm coming." She put her drink down, and Roger noticed that the glass broke up silently into an unfocussed blur when she let go of it.

The four of them made their way to the lobby unhindered – Evelyn even saw them go, but looked more exasperated than angry – and Roger led them around the faceless, ceiling-crouching thing and across the carpeted floor, through the front doors, and down the marble steps to the sidewalk.

"South on Main, come on," he said, trying not to panic in spite of how synchronized the traffic signals were, "away from the circle."

As they trudged along, Roger felt a sudden slickness against his feet, and he realized that his socks had disappeared. He didn't have to glance to the side to know that Debbie was back in the old sack dress she'd pulled on over her head right after leaping out of bed. Behind him the ticktack of his mother's heels and the knock of his father's shoes became a flapping – bedroom slippers, it sounded like. Good, Roger thought – I guess we weren't too late.

He looked up, and the whole sky was turning slowly, like a vast, glitter-strewn wheel, and he couldn't decide whether to take that as a good sign or a bad one. Funny how the night moves, he thought nervously. I don't think this is what Bob Seger meant.

And then his feet were comfortable again, and even though they'd been walking in a straight line he saw the traffic circle ahead, and, from around the corner to the right, the glow of the *Splendide*'s main entrance.

The others noticed it too, and slowed. "We were walking south on Main," Debbie said, "… away from the traffic circle."

"And now, without having changed course," said Roger wearily, "we're headed east on Bailey, toward it. We waited too long."

Jack Singer was smiling broadly. "Screw this," he said, and his voice was cheerful, if a bit shrill. "I'll see you all later." He turned and fled back the way they'd come, his newly restored suit and shoes disappearing within a few yards, leaving him an overweight man in pajamas and slippers, puffing and flapping like a clown as he ran.

Roger's mother took a hesitant step after him, but Roger took her arm. "Don't bother, Mom – I'm pretty sure the quickest way to catch up with him is to just keep going straight ahead."

Debbie was patting the fabric of her sequined gown. "I hope I get to keep this," she said.

The traffic lights were in perfect step now. Roger considered leading the two women around the circle and straight out Bailey, eastward, but he was fatalistically sure that Bailey Boulevard, as they proceeded along it, would within half a block or so become Main Street, and they'd be facing the circle again. Neither his mother nor Debbie objected when he turned right at Main, toward the *Splendide*.

The entrance was more brightly illuminated than ever, but it was a harsh glare like that cast by arc lights, and the cars pulling up and driving away moved in sudden hops, like spiders, or like cars in a film from which a lot of the frames have been cut. The music was a weary, prolonged moaning of brass and strings. Jack Singer, once again in his suit, slouched up from the far side of the hotel and joined them on the steps.

Roger thought of making some cutting remark – something like, "Not so easy to ditch me this time, huh, Pop?" – but both his parents looked so unhappy, and he himself was so frightened, that he didn't have the heart for it.

"Oh, God," wailed his mother, "will we ever get back home?"

Roger was facing the hotel, but he turned around when he heard splashing behind him. It was the fountain – the traffic circle was now right in front of the hotel, and the pavement below the steps wasn't the Main Street sidewalk any longer, was now just a concrete walkway between the grass of the circle and the steps of the hotel.

Dark buildings, as nondescript as painted stage props, crowded up around the other sides of the circle, and Roger could see only one traffic light. It was flashing slower, and its yellow color had a faint orange tint.

"Do come in," called Evelyn from the open lobby doors. "It's just time to sit down for dinner." Her face was paler, and she seemed to be trembling.

Roger glanced at his mother. "Maybe," he said. Then he turned toward the circle and concentrated; it was harder than making a snifter of Scotch appear, but in a moment he had projected, blotting out the dim traffic circle, a downtown street he remembered seeing on the way to the Crystal Lake amusement park in New Jersey. It was one of the things Evelyn had never permitted him to dream about.

He was surprised at how clearly he was able to project it – until he saw that the sky behind the shabby New Jersey office buildings was overcast and gray instead of the brilliant blue he remembered, and he realized that someone else, perhaps unintentionally, perhaps even against their will, was helping to fill out the picture, using their own recollections of it.

Behind him Evelyn gasped – and the one visible traffic signal began to flash a little faster, and to lose some of the orange tint.

Okay, Roger thought tensely, the cord isn't quite cut yet. What else was there? Oh yeah...

He made the New Jersey street disappear and instantly replaced it with a prairie, across which a horse and rider galloped. At first the rider was a cavalry soldier, as in the movie scene Roger remembered, but again someone else's projection changed the scene – the rider was smaller now, and not dressed in blue... it was hard to see clearly, and again Roger got the impression that this altering of what he was projecting was unintentional... and when the rider fell off the horse it was hard to tell which foot had caught in the stirrup...

The pavement below him had widened, and now he could see another traffic light. The two were still in step, but were at least flashing in their normal pace and color.

He replaced the vision of the galloping horse and the suffering figure behind it with a rendition of the hospital room in which he'd awakened after the removal of his tonsils... and this time the picture was altered instantly and totally, though the lingering-in-the-back-of-his-throat smell of ether grew stronger. He saw a windowless room with newspapers spread neatly all over the floor, and there was a sort of table, with...

The night shuddered, and suddenly he could see down Main Street – and, way down south, he saw one yellow light blinking out of synch. "This way out," he said, stepping to the sidewalk and walking south. "Walk through the visions – I'm building us a bridge."

Again the downtown New Jersey street appeared, and without his volition a young couple – hardly more than teenagers – entered the picture. They both looked determined and scared as they walked along the sidewalk looking at the address numbers on the buildings.

Roger kept leading his group southward, and when the New Jersey picture faded he saw that the out-of-step signal was closer. Debbie was walking carefully right beside him. Thank God, he thought, that she hasn't chosen this occasion to be difficult – but where are my parents?

He couldn't turn to look behind him, for the next projection was appearing, cleaving a path out of Evelyn's imploding fake world. Obviously Evelyn's aversion to these memories was strong, for her own projection simply recoiled from these the way a live oyster contracts away from lemon juice squeezed onto it.

The cowboy movie memory was now altered out of recognition, though it was the most effective yet at re-randomizing the traffic lights; now it was a girl instead of a cavalry soldier, and somehow she still had *both* feet in the stirrups, and though there was blood she didn't seem to be being dragged over any prairie... in fact she was lying on a table in a windowless room with newspapers all over the floor, and the ether reek was everywhere like the smell of rotten pears, and her young boyfriend was pacing the sidewalk out in front of the shabby office and at last the overcast sky had begun dropping rain so that he needn't struggle to hold back his tears any longer...

"Woulda been a girl, I think," came the multiply remembered voice of a man...

Shock and sudden comprehension slowed Roger's steps, and involuntarily he turned and looked back at Evelyn as bitterness and loss closed his throat and brought tears to his eyes. The man knew his business, he thought. "Goodbye, Evelyn," he whispered.

Goodbye, Roger, spoke a voice – a receding voice – in his head.

The projected scene ahead was even clearer now, but beyond it lay the real pre-dawn Santa Margarita streets. "Come on," said Roger, stepping forward again. "We're almost out of it."

Debbie was right beside him, but he didn't hear his parents, so he paused and turned.

They were stopped several yards back, staring at the pavement.

"Come on," Roger said harshly. "It's the way out."

"We can't go through it," his father said.

"Again," added his mother faintly.

"We weren't *married* yet, then, in – '48..." his father began; but Roger had taken Debbie's hand and resumed their forward progress.

They moved slowly through the windowless room, every full stride covering a few inches of newspaper-strewn floor, and then there was the fluttering thump of something landing in a paper-lined wastebasket and they were out in the streets and the air was cold and Roger didn't have socks on and the traffic signals, ready for all the early-morning commuters, were switching through their long-green, short-yellow, long-red cycles, and the one-eyed old

hobo standing in the street nodded curtly at them and then motioned them to step aside, for an ancient woman was puffing along
the sidewalk behind them, pushing a shopping cart full of green
scraps of cloth, and behind her trotted a lean little old fellow whom
Roger remembered having seen many times walking the streets of
Santa Margarita, lingering by empty lots when the workmen had
gone home and the concrete outlines of long-gone houses could
still be seen among the mud and litter and tractor tracks. There was
no one else on the street. The sky was already pale blue, though the
sun wasn't up yet.

Debbie glanced down at herself and pursed her lips angrily to
see that her fine gown had disappeared again. "Are you through
with your games?" she snapped. "Can we go home now?"

"You go ahead," Roger told her. "I want to walk some."

"No, come back with me."

He shook his head and walked away, slapping his pants pockets
for change and trying to remember where he'd seen the all-night
Mexican diner with the sign about the menudo breakfast.

"When you do come back," Debbie called furiously, "I won't be
there! And don't bother going to my parents' house, 'cause I won't
be there either!"

Good for you, he thought.

And as the first rays of the sun touched the tall palms around the
traffic circle a scrap of something, unnoticed by anyone, sank to the
bottom of the fountain pool, at peace at last.

TIM POWERS was born in Buffalo, New York, on Leap Year Day in 1952, but has lived in southern California since 1959. He graduated from California State University at Fullerton with a BA in English in 1976; the same year saw the publication of his first two novels, *The Skies Discrowned* and *Epitaph in Rust* (both from Laser Books).

Powers's subsequent novels are *The Drawing of the Dark* (Del Rey, 1979), *The Anubis Gates* (Ace, 1983, winner of the Philip K. Dick Memorial Award and the Prix Apollo), *Dinner at Deviant's Palace* (Ace, 1987), *The Stress of Her Regard* (Ace, 1989), *Last Call* (Morrow, 1992, winner of the World Fantasy Award), *Expiration Date* (Tor, 1996), *Earthquake Weather* (Tor, 1997), and *Declare* (Morrow, 2001).

Powers has taught at the Clarion Science Fiction Writers' Workshop at Michigan State University six times, and has three times co-taught the Writers of the Future Workshop with Algis Budrys.

Powers lives with his wife Serena in San Bernardino, California.